WILDCAT HILLS

Center Point
Large Print

Also by Wayne D. Dundee and available from Center Point Large Print:

Dismal River
Rainrock Reckoning
The Forever Mountain
The Coldest Trail
The Gun Wolves
Massacre Canyon

WILDCAT HILLS

A Lone McGantry Western

WAYNE D. DUNDEE

CENTER POINT LARGE PRINT
THORNDIKE, MAINE

This Center Point Large Print edition
is published in the year 2024 by arrangement with
Wolfpack Publishing.

Copyright © 2023 by Wayne D. Dundee.

All rights reserved.

This book is a work of fiction. Any references to historical events, real people or real places are used fictitiously. Other names, characters, places and events are products of the author's imagination, and any resemblance to actual events, places or persons, living or dead, is entirely coincidental.

The text of this Large Print edition is unabridged.
In other aspects, this book may vary
from the original edition.
Printed in the United States of America
on permanent paper sourced using
environmentally responsible foresting methods.
Set in 16-point Times New Roman type.

ISBN: 979-8-89164-242-3

The Library of Congress has cataloged this record
under Library of Congress Control Number: 2024935507

CHAPTER ONE

The pop of gunfire from not too far off caused Lone McGantry to draw back on the reins and bring Ironsides, his big gray stallion, to a halt. Sound sometimes had a funny way of traveling over these rolling, mostly treeless hills of western Nebraska's high plains. But Lone's ears, as well as other senses, were finely honed to the setting. A single shot might have been somewhat difficult to pinpoint, but what he was hearing in this instance was coming in clusters, sporadic exchanges being issued by a mix of pistols and rifles, and he was convinced they were being triggered due ahead.

The question now was: What business was it of his? Or, more to the point, should he *make it* any of his business?

As befitting his name, Lone's way was to mostly avoid meddling in matters not directly affecting him. On the other hand, that nasty old trait called Curiosity had been known more than once in times past to tug hard enough at the prominent nose planted in the middle of his squarish, weathered face to end up with him poking it in where it would have been better off staying out of. And now, right on cue, Curiosity started tugging again.

At the same time, Ironsides emitted a low snort. Lone wasn't sure if it was meant as a warning not to get involved, or a sign of impatience to go ahead and get on with what the big gray figured was inevitable.

"Tell you what," Lone muttered, half in response to the horse and half to himself, "we'll ride to the top of that hill up ahead. If the shootin's takin' place right on the other side—like I figure, and therefore smack in our intended path which would rightly make it our concern—then we'll have to take a closer look. If it's somewhere off another way, we'll just continue on and ignore it."

A handful of minutes later they reached the top of the hill. A fringe of tall grass, yellowed and stiff after another dry summer, ran along its crest. The sound of the gunfire was louder and closer now, leaving little doubt it was coming from just the other side. Lone dismounted and whispered for Ironsides to stay put. Then, removing his flat-crowned Stetson, he moved in a half-crouch to the crest and parted the tall grass for a cautious look-see.

What he gazed down on was a scene straight off the cover of some lurid dime novel.

There was a carriage, halted in the middle of the trail, confronted by three heavily armed men with bandannas tied over their faces to mask their identities. At this juncture, the masked men, apparently having failed at stopping the carriage and getting what they wanted without a fight, were backed off about twenty yards from the stalled rig. They'd taken to cover on either side of the trail, two of them in a clump of rocks on the south side, the third in a stand of scrawny cottonwood trees on the north. The pair in the rocks were using rifles, the owlhoot in the trees a six-shooter.

The horse that had been pulling the carriage lay dead in its traces. Whether shooting it to ensure stopping the rig had been the opening salvo of the hold-up men or the animal had taken a bullet in the ensuing gun battle, Lone had no way of knowing. Either way, the sprawled carcass was now serving as a barricade from behind which the two men who'd evidently been the carriage's passengers were shooting back at their would-be robbers.

Yeah, Lone couldn't help thinking again, it would have made a rip-roaring cover scene to be sure. Promising a heady sample of the thrills to be found in the accompanying pages and thereby sure to whet the appetite of readers with a taste for such adventurous melodrama.

Trouble was, this was no mere artist's rendition meant to capture a few passages of fiction. This was the real thing. Life-or-death real for the two men under fire from the road agents.

Lone's mouth pulled into a grimace and he

swore under his breath. A lot more than just the tug of Curiosity came into play now. The lines between right and wrong were pretty clearly drawn down at the bottom of the long slope he poised on the crest of. And it left him no choice but to get involved, to get down there and try to take a hand in the outcome.

Wheeling around, he trotted back to Ironsides and sprang to the saddle. His mind churned with thoughts on what might be his best course of action. He toyed with the notion of simply pulling his Winchester Yellowboy from its saddle scabbard and returning with it to the top of the hill from where he could open fire down on the masked men. He'd no doubt be able to pick off at least one, leaving the others, finding themselves caught in a crossfire, likely to be sent packing. That might be the easiest, surest way to break up this current situation. But it would only leave the escaping skunks free to pull more robberies, or worse, somewhere else.

Not that Lone felt any duty to try and save the world, but neither did he believe in doing a job half-assed. If he was going to get involved in stopping the trio of robbers, then he damn well meant to stop them all the way.

Having no time to waste chewing his options too fine, Lone settled on a plan and heeled Ironsides into motion. With the gunfire cracking steadily enough to drown out the sound of pounding hooves, Lone set the big gray at a hard gallop in a westerly direction across the breadth of the hill, just back from the top. When he reckoned he had gone far enough, he again reined up and dismounted. This time he brought the Yellowboy with him and once more made his way to the crest of the hill.

Peering down from this new vantage point, Lone saw he had calculated correctly. He was about twenty yards past where the owlhoots had taken to cover on either side of the trail. He was looking down, at a forty-five-degree angle, on the pistol shooter in the stand of trees. Behind him, on the back side of the trees and thus hidden from the sight of the shooters at the carriage, three horses were tied. From his current high position, the foliage of the cottonwood trees prevented Lone from being able to see the men over in the rocks. But once he'd worked his way down lower it would be a different story. And in the meantime, between their focus being locked on the carriage and the trees also blocking their peripheral view, neither could the riflemen spot him.

With a fresh round jacked into the Yellowboy's chamber and the hammer cocked, Lone started slowly down the slope in a half crouch. As he was making this descent, Lone noted that the cadence of the shooting—particularly that coming from the carriage—seemed to be slowing.

Then, abruptly, it lagged altogether. Lone dropped lower in the tall grass and froze, concerned for a moment that his movement might have somehow been the distraction. Thankfully, a long, tense clocktick passed with no indication of this actually being the case.

The quiet was broken by a harsh voice from the rocks calling to those pinned down at the carriage. "What's a-matter, boys? All of a sudden you don't seem so eager to be throwin' lead. Could it be you're runnin' low on bullets for those little pea shooter hideaways you're makin' noise with?"

A response came promptly. "If you think that's the case, why don't you show your mangy head and find out for sure? And if you're so scornful of our 'pea shooters,' the sight of which sent the three of you scattering like rabbits, as I recall, then it ought not make much difference anyway."

Lone grinned, appreciating the spunk being displayed by the men at the carriage. He couldn't see them very well, hunkered down behind the horse carcass like they were. From what he could tell, though, by the gray-streaked heads of hair he caught sight of, they were a couple gents packing some age. And the dark business style jackets, string ties, and white shirts he also glimpsed indicted men of some prominence. Which was no doubt what had made them targets for the trio of jackals thinking them a source for a bit of quick, easy cash.

Lone's grin took on a bitter twist. But it was turning out to be not quite as easy as the jackals figured. And, if he had his way, it was about to get a hell of a lot harder still.

"You can huff and bluff all you want," called the owlhoot from the rocks, apparently the leader of the pack, "but you two Fancy Dan geezers ain't foolin' nobody. Yeah, you surprised us by whippin' out those stingy guns. Okay. That earns you a red whisker of respect, but I still don't believe you're packin' enough spare cartridges for those poppers to keep this up much longer. Nevertheless, I'll make you a one-time offer that will give you the chance to walk away without your wrinkled old asses gettin' shot full of holes."

Again the response came promptly. "You want to waste more breath making that offer, or do you want the answer right now? Either way it's the same. We don't make deals with snakes, neither the kind that slither across the ground nor the kind that walks on two legs."

This produced a fresh, furious barrage of gunfire from the owlhoots, turning the air blue with roiling clouds of powder smoke sliced by sizzling lead that hammered the carriage and thumped dully into the wall of dead horse flesh. No matter how much ammunition the men at the carriage might or might not have had, they were for the moment kept too pinned down to attempt even a single shot of return fire. If the owlhoots had had any battle smarts, they might have used the opportunity to try and close on their opposition. But they didn't. All they knew was rage and brute force, so they just stayed in place and kept burning powder for a full minute and more.

Lone, however, *did* take the opportunity to close on his target. Trained in the ways of stealth from years as an army scout and from overall wilderness survival, Lone reckoned he could have easily crept up on the handgunner in the trees, no matter what. But the prolonged noise of the shooting sure didn't hurt. By the time it subsided again, he was only a few feet behind his man. His intent was to throttle the unsuspecting varmint until he was out cold, then get the drop on the others over in the rocks. If they were smart enough to give up, he'd deliver the whole bunch to Marshal Dalrymple in North Platte. If they were stupid enough or stubborn enough to try and resist, well, Lone was prepared to play it that way, too.

The former scout was poised, gripping his Yellowboy in both hands—his left just behind the trigger guard, his right out near the end of the barrel—ready to reach forward and swoop the rifle down in front of the owlhoot's face and then jerk it back under his chin, hard against his throat, holding it there until the victim was choked into unconsciousness.

Lone was seconds away from executing this move, when one of the damn horses betrayed him!

CHAPTER TWO

Although the three tethered mounts had been holding relatively still all during the exchanges of gunfire (evidently used to being in the proximity of such), for some inexplicable and unexpected reason one of them decided to be unnerved by the presence of Lone slipping past and moving into the trees behind the masked pistolero. The way this hammerhead demonstrated its displeasure was to jerk suddenly back on the tie rope while sounding a shrill whinny accompanied by a bit of petulant foot stomping. Had it done this while the guns were going off, it almost certainly would have gone unnoticed. But coming right at the start of the abrupt silence following the cessation of the latest barrage, it *was* noticeable. For sure to the man Lone was getting ready to jump. Meaning that when the man all of a sudden turned to see what was troubling the hayburner, he found himself practically nose to nose with Lone.

The hombre proved to be no slouch when it came to fast reflexes. In turning his body to look around at the horse, he also swung around his gun hand. At the sight of Lone looming before him, he instantly started to raise the Remington revolver in his fist and aim it at Lone's middle from a distance of less than a foot.

But neither was Lone lacking in the reflex department. With his Yellowboy already raised to chest level, getting ready to swoop it up and over the pistolero's head, he shifted instead to slamming it down hard on the wrist of the man's gun hand. The wrist bone broke with a loud *crack!* a fraction of a second ahead of the Remington discharging an even louder roar. The blow from the rifle's forestock came in time, however, to knock away the six-gun's muzzle and send the slug it spat a hair's breadth past Lone's hip and down into the dirt.

A scream of pain started to gurgle in the pistolero's throat. But before it could escape, Lone jerked the Yellowboy—still gripped in two hands—upward in a vicious, slashing uppercut that slammed under the point of the man's chin. His feet were lifted off the ground, his head snapped back like it was on a hinge, and he fell away as if he'd been blown over by a strong wind. The Remington went flying from his grip and his body landed outside the trees and partly on the edge of the trail.

Lone had succeeded in cold-cocking his man—only not quite as planned.

And naturally the remaining two robbers over in the rocks, alerted by the errant pistol shot and then the sight of the man who'd fired it toppling out onto the side of the trail, took notice. They wasted no time demonstrating this by quickly swinging their rifles around and sending a hail of bullets in Lone's direction. He managed to dive low in behind some tree trunks, though, allowing the shots to harmlessly smack into wood and chip away shards of bark above and around him.

But in their anger and haste to retaliate for the sight of their fallen friend, the remaining pair were foolishly careless in keeping to cover. This came at a sudden and harsh cost.

First Lone, quickly rolling and squirming in behind yet another tree trunk, leaned out and around with the Yellowboy now gripped for shooting. His sights immediately fell on a burly individual under a wide-brimmed Boss of the Plains hat and half a heartbeat later Lone stroked the Yellowboy's trigger. The rifle spat flame and lead and a thumb-sized hole appeared just ahead of the man's left ear. His head jerked sharply away, spraying gore out the opposite side, and he sagged into a lifeless heap, his own rifle falling and clattering down onto the rocks.

Lone immediately levered a fresh round and sought to lock his aim on the single remaining robber. Before he found his target, however, a pair of rapid-fire shots sounded from the direction of the carriage and by the time Lone's sights landed on the man he was doubling over from the impact of those rounds and tipping forward to fall flat on his face. His rifle also slipped from lifeless fingers and clattered onto blood-stained rocks.

Just that fast it was all over.

But in case not everybody saw it that way, Lone didn't get in a hurry to reveal himself. He rose to his feet, remaining within the trees.

Things stayed still and quiet only briefly before a familiar voice called out from the carriage. "You there, stranger . . . Friend . . . Are you okay?"

Lone grinned wryly. "A sight better than these three polecats who clearly were *not* your friends. So are we in agreement there's no call for any more shootin'?"

"Absolutely! The only thing called for now is a round of sincere gratitude to be expressed by my companion and I for your timely intervention!"

Lone stepped out from the trees and saw that the two men from the carriage were already striding toward him. He paused a moment to check the owlhoot he'd slammed with his rifle and found him dead from a broken neck. That hadn't been the intent, but neither was it cause for any great remorse.

Lone proceeded to meet the men headed his way. In full view, they showed themselves to be not very different from the appraisal he'd been able to make earlier. Both were average in height and build, both dressed in well-tailored, good quality business suits (though a bit rumpled and dusty under the circumstances). One had a mustache and well barbered hair liberally shot with streaks of white; he seemed to walk with a faint limp. The other stood straighter and a trace taller, was cleanly shaven but with iron gray hair spilling long and thick over his shirt collar.

As he drew closer to them, Lone's gaze lingered on the man with the limp and he couldn't help thinking he knew him from somewhere.

This was confirmed a moment later when the man abruptly declared, "Lone McGantry, by all the ironies!"

Lone recognized the voice as that which had been trading words with the would-be robbers, but it still didn't—And then, suddenly, recognition hit him. "Major North! What in blazes are you doin' out this way?"

Frank North smiled. "You can drop the 'major,' son. Just like the army did when they mustered me out. Heck, I was never no *real* officer anyway, and everybody knew it."

"You'll always be Major to me, sir."

The men had come together now, at a midpoint between the stalled carriage and where the robbers had bit the dust. North's smile widened as he craned his neck to look up at the tall, broad-shouldered man before him, at the same time extending his hand to take Lone's in a firm grip "If you insist, then. You're too blasted big to argue with. And after what you just did to save our hides, being contrary with you is the last thing I wish to do."

"Pitched in where I could," Lone allowed. "But it wasn't all my doin'—those shots that punched down that last hombre came from your direction."

"Don't look at me," said the man standing next to North. Then, his mouth twisting ruefully, he added, "I threw my share of lead during that skirmish, mostly just making noise. But the marksman—him and the 'pea shooter' that oaf in the rocks was so quick to ridicule—was strictly Frank here."

Gesturing to the speaker, North said, "Lone, let me introduce you to another Frank. *Doctor* Frank Powell."

Lone shook Powell's hand and they exchanged "pleased to meet yous." Frowning, Lone added, "Seems I've heard your name, Doctor. But I'm blamed if I can place where."

North said, "That's easy. He's a friend of Bill Cody's. Hell, come to think of it, who in these parts *doesn't* claim to be a friend of Cody's? Well"—cutting a quick glance in the direction of the dead men down the trail—"except maybe for those three scoundrels."

"Speakin' of those three," said Lone, "how did you get crossways of 'em anyway?"

"We had little choice. They caught us by surprise," North explained, "surging around our carriage from behind, wearing masks and brandishing guns. They immediately shot our poor horse to ensure we were brought to a halt, and then demanded we hand over all our money and valuables. They clearly took us for a couple of dandies not willing to put up any resistance."

Powell took over, saying, "But Frank quickly changed their minds about that when he reached inside his jacket, supposedly to withdraw his wallet, and instead brought out that Colt Lightning he carries in a shoulder holster."

As a veteran of numerous battles during the Indian Wars, primarily as interpreter/leader of the legendary Pawnee Scouts—the service which earned him his appointment as major—even an aged Frank North would never be an easy target for the likes of the three would-be robbers.

"I should have cut down one of the skunks right there," North said, scowling, "but his horse jerked at the last second and my shot missed."

"Yeah, I had some bad luck thanks to one of their horses, too," Lone muttered sourly.

"At any rate," Powell went on, "that gave the trio a chance to scatter and fall back to cover, then commence to try and wear us down with that gun battle you rode up on."

"*Thankfully* rode up on," North declared. "I hate to give vermin like them any kind of credit, but the blowhard who was doing the verbal taunting was uncomfortably close to the mark about us running low on ammunition. We were each armed for a quick bit of action if necessary, but hardly a drawn out engagement."

"Well you drug it out long enough. That's the main thing," allowed Lone.

"Indeed," agreed North. "Now, getting back to your vague familiarity with the name Powell, Frank has been doctoring the colonel on and off for a few years now. That's likely where you heard his name mentioned."

"To flesh it out a little more," explained Powell, "until recently I was traveling with Buffalo Bill's Wild West on its overseas junket. If you know the colonel as well as I've heard, then you know how he tends to utilize those about him in various ways. For that reason, on a number of occasions during our tour abroad—though I *am* a duly licensed medical doctor, I assure you— it was useful for me to participate in certain performances as White Beaver, Great Cheyenne Medicine Man. Hence the long hair I decided to grow in lieu of those itchy damn wigs I would have had to slap on otherwise."

"Looks good on you, Doc," Lone quipped. Then, eyeing North, he said, "Come to think of it, I heard you went on that overseas tour with the colonel, too."

"That I did. But strictly as an overseer of the Indian encampments at our different stops. So no need to try and conjure up any images of me in some kind of show get-up."

"Okay, I won't. Promise, Major." Lone looked thoughtful for a moment before saying, "I guess

I heard somewhere that Buffalo Bill's show had returned to the states. Reckon the part I didn't hear, though, was that any of the group had made it back hereabouts. Is the colonel here, too?"

The expressions of both North and Powell turned suddenly very somber.

"No, Lone, he isn't," North said in a carefully measured tone. "As a matter of fact, the troubling thing to report is that the colonel's whereabouts are . . . well, uncertain. The reason Dr. Powell and I are out this way, you see, is that we came looking to find you and solicit your help." His gaze rested heavily on Lone. "Under the circumstances, however, I suggest we first take time to clear this trash off the trail and deliver it to Marshal Dalrymple in North Platte. Then, if you're willing to hear us out, we can find some place to sit and present the situation from the beginning."

"Of course I'm willin' to hear you out. And if the colonel's in some kind of trouble," Lone grated, "you know damn well I'll be willin' to do whatever I can to help. Let's not waste any more time gettin' to it."

CHAPTER THREE

The first order of business when Lone, North, and Powell arrived in North Platte was to deliver the bodies of the three would-be robbers to Marshal Elmer Dalrymple, along with their report of what had happened. Needless to say, showing up leading the trio's horses with the grisly riders hanging face down over their saddles drew no small amount of attention from townsfolk. By the time they halted in front of the marshal's office and jail (with a highly indignant Ironsides now assigned to pulling the carriage), quite a gaggle of onlookers was accompanying them.

Dalrymple and his chief deputy, Keith Overstreet, eventually dispersed the crowd but not before they'd lifted the faces of the dead men and given anybody who was willing the chance to take a look for the sake of possibly identifying them. None were able to, including the lawmen. This gave way to a conclusion, at least for the time being, that the three were most likely saddle tramps new to the area who'd happened on North and Powell and marked them as prominent-looking targets ripe for the easy plucking of some quick cash and valuables. The only thing noteworthy about any of the failed robbers was that one of them only had three fingers on his left hand. Otherwise, their overall shabby appearance and the meager tally of coins and provisions that made up their belongings seemed to match as evidence of them being violent men in desperate need.

"If they was plumb strangers to the area, why'd they think it necessary to try and hide their faces?" somebody in the crowd muttered.

To which somebody else replied, "Must've read too many of those rootin'-tootin' dime novels where the robbers always wear bandannas wrapped around their mugs."

Overhearing this, Lone couldn't suppress a wry smile reflecting back to his initial reaction upon coming in sight of the carriage robbery in progress, how it made him think of a scene out of a dime novel.

Shortly after that the crowd in front of the jail was broken up. Dalrymple and Overstreet scattered the gawkers, telling them to return to their own affairs. The marshal then motioned for Lone, North, and Powell to follow him into his office so he could take down their statements; his deputy left to deliver the dead men to the town undertaker, saying over his shoulder that he would also stop by the Cody Ranch to arrange for one of the wranglers to bring a fresh horse to hitch up to North and Powell's carriage.

Inside the marshal's office, the necessary statements regarding the robbery attempt were quickly gotten out of the way. Then the conversation shifted to bringing Lone, along with Dalrymple, the rest of the way up to speed on what appeared to be the disappearance of Buffalo Bill.

In the years between the Indian Wars and the launch of what would become his world famous Wild West extravaganza, William Frederick "Buffalo Bill" Cody had called North Platte his home. During his time there he had, in partnership with Frank North and Frank's brother Luther, started several successful businesses and ranching operations. On a plot of land just north of town, Cody had built his own highly regarded Scout's Rest Ranch where his wife Luisa and their daughters stayed much of the time while Cody was traveling and making public appearances in response to his increasingly popular status as a frontier hero thanks to the hugely popular (and wildly embellished) writings of Ned Buntline. It was on these ranch grounds that Cody first staged his famous "Bust-Out 4th of July Rodeo Celebration" that eventually blossomed into the internationally renowned touring show that would make him one of the most recognizable figures in the world.

But none of that success or fame, all well known to those gathered in the marshal's office that afternoon, figured into the thrust of their conversation. In fact, some of the key traits nowadays most closely associated to Buffalo Bill—publicity and ballyhoo—were in sharp contrast to the meeting goals.

"Naturally, I was aware you gents had arrived in town and were staying out at Cody's ranch," the marshal was saying. "But since I also understood you were convalescing under Dr. Powell's care, Major, I held off bothering you until I got indication you were ready for visitors."

Dalrymple was a modest-sized man, two or three inches under six feet in height, lean and spare of build, almost frail looking. He was mild-mannered and generally soft-spoken but, for the unwary, there was a flintiness in his pale gray eyes that could turn steel hard in concert with nerves that had more than once proven themselves a match for troublemakers looking to test what was behind the badge.

"Mighty considerate of you, Marshal," North acknowledged.

It was explained to Lone on the ride into town that North had been injured in a horse fall over in Europe, accounting for the slight limp Lone had noticed. Upon returning to the states, Cody had insisted the pair stay as guests at his ranch (North having earlier sold off all his own holdings and property in the area while serving in the state legislature) where the major could finish healing under the watchful eye of Powell until Cody could join them there.

"What I *hadn't* heard anything about, though," Dalrymple continued, "was this other business involving the colonel."

North frowned. "That's not surprising, considering how the whole matter was hushed up after Sitting Bull's death and the subsequent canceling of Cody's mission. There was a smattering of newspaper coverage back east when the thing first got underway, but it was minimal due to many considering it just another of Cody's publicity stunts."

"You can bet it would have been a different story," added a brooding Powell, "if our mission had succeeded—had been *allowed* to succeed."

"Trust me, gentlemen," said North, "if my stint in government taught me anything, it was that the behind-the-scenes working of politics is a thoroughly nasty business. And my experience was merely at the state level. The higher up you go, the nastier it gets." He wagged his head. "I much prefer the more honorable way of facing your enemies on the battlefield."

Lone had been quietly listening and absorbing the discussion, saying very little up to that point. But he spoke now, asking, "The gent who originally requested the colonel come to the Dakotas and meet with Sitting Bull—was he in on the shenanigans that came next?"

"That would be General Miles, Nelson Miles," responded Powell. "He's head of overall army operations in South Dakota and closely involved with the Indian tribes housed on the reservations there. In answer to your question, no. I believe Miles was—and is—an honorable man who has genuine respect for the Indians. That very much included Sitting Bull, even though the old chief, after finishing his tour with Cody's Wild West, had returned to the Standing Rock reservation in North Dakota, not really part of Miles's jurisdiction."

"And *that*," interjected North, "was at least partly responsible for the ensuing 'shenanigans,' as you call them, Lone. Ted Laglen, the army major in charge of the Standing Rock reservation, is a petty, conniving, overly ambitious little jackass I had my own unpleasant dealings with clear back following the Battle of Tongue River. You can bet he wouldn't take kindly to Miles or anyone else, not even somebody the stature of Buffalo Bill, involving themselves in any kind of action that infringed into his area of command."

"What was more," Powell said, "Laglen had a personal grudge against Sitting Bull. In particular, he disliked the leniency he felt Washington had shown letting the chief go on tour with Cody in the first place, and then the sway Sitting Bull continued to have over his people after he returned. Laglen was convinced the old warrior was secretly encouraging the Ghost Dance movement as it spread into Nebraska and the Dakotas from where it originated in Nevada. He was determined to see Sitting Bull relocated down to the Oklahoma Indian Territory, believing that would knock him down in prominence and also be a major blow to help end the eastern Ghost Dance movement."

Starting to see the picture of how it all knotted together, Lone said, "So havin' Col. Cody show up to join with Sitting Bull and their efforts maybe helpin' to halt the eastern spread of the Ghost Dancers would've only added to Sitting Bull's high standing in everybody's eyes. And the way Laglen saw it, havin' the old chief elevated still more, never mind if it meant easin' the Ghost Dance problem, would make it a whole lot harder to force him to go where he didn't want to be."

"Exactly."

Dalrymple's forehead puckered. "Excuse me, but I'm getting a mite flummoxed. I've been hearing about these Ghost Dance rituals on and off for a couple years now it seems like. But, like you said a minute ago, Doctor, I thought they were happening out in Nevada."

"True that's where they originated," replied Powell. "Circle dances or round dances, of which the Ghost Dance is a specifically crafted version, have been practiced by numerous Indian tribes for many, many years. The movement based on the one we're talking about was started fairly recently by an influential Paiute medicine man called Wovoka.

"He had a vision during a moon eclipse. In this vision he was taught the proper way to perform the dance and told that if all the tribes of the Great Plains joined together and began holding lengthy dance ceremonies at set intervals, the great spirits would be reawakened and would join with the Christ God of the Whites to bring a new era of peace and prosperity to the land. The vast buffalo herds would return and the Red Man would be allowed to go about his old ways in the West, while the White Man would learn to be satisfied with practicing his ways in the East."

Dalrymple's expression remained troubled. "Man, I don't want to be the one making light of something that clearly has earned so much serious attention, but I gotta say, that is one wild, far-reaching vision! Ain't nobody but me stopped to wonder what kind of root ol' Wovoka was smoking or drinking the squeezings out of before he claimed seeing his vision?"

Powell frowned disapprovingly. "You're hardly the first to have expressed such thoughts. All I can tell you—because I have seen it with my own eyes—is that for every person who shares your ridicule and suspicion, there are a thousand Indians from more and more tribes every day, including the Sioux all up through the Dakotas and right here in your back yard, who have great faith in Wovoka's vision."

"Dr. Powell traveled with Col. Cody when they set out on the mission to meet with Sitting Bull," North explained. "He saw and experienced firsthand the mood of the Indians they encountered as far as their feelings toward the Ghost Dance."

Bitterly, Powell said, "We were at Four Mile Creek Camp—after being tricked and misled by soldiers Laglen sent to 'aid' us, though in hindsight were actually meant to *delay* us from reaching Sitting Bull—when a courier arrived with word that President Harris had rescinded General Miles's request for Cody's involvement. I may not be able to prove it, but I'll go to my grave believing that damned Laglen finagled the influence to cause that."

"That would be his way, no doubt about it," muttered North.

"At any rate, it left Col. Cody no choice but to turn around and head back. What influence he might have had on Sitting Bull and what influence the old chief might have had on the Ghost Dance movement, nobody will ever know. The meeting between the two never took place and, less than a week from when we got turned back at Four Mile, Sitting Bull was killed allegedly resisting arrest at his Grand River village." The doctor's gaze came to rest on Dalrymple. "So what that leaves us with, Marshal, no matter how you and others may feel about Wovoka's 'far-fetched vision,' is the way the people of the different Plains tribes feel about it. And I tell you again, a very large number of them are strong believers."

"I never said otherwise, and I never meant no offense," Dalrymple said with some tightness in his tone. "I was just stating my personal reaction to the details you laid out."

"Speakin' of those details," Lone drawled, "there's something about 'em don't seem to full add up."

"How so?"

Lone made a gesture. "This vision of Wovoka's. Ancient Injun spirits bein' reawakened to work with Christ bringin' peace and harmony to the land so's the Red Man and White Man can share it with no more fussin' and feudin' . . . If that was possible—and I ain't sayin' I don't find it kinda far-fetched my own self—where's the harm, the threat in it? Why is the army and the Indian Affairs folks so het up about lettin' the tribes dance and believe such a thing might come to pass?"

North and Powell exchanged looks.

Cutting his gaze back to Lone, North said, "You raise a good point. If all the ceremonies being conducted remained in line with Wovoka's teaching, that might very well be the case. Though even then, I suspect, there'd be some narrow-minded fools like Laglen who would still take exception."

"But helping to make sure his kind have something to wail about," added Powell, "is the misguided turn these eastern Ghost Dancers have decided to take. Thanks primarily to a young Lakota sub chief called Kicking Bear. Ever hear of him?"

Lone shook his head. "Can't say I have."

"I wish more people, especially those in his tribe, hadn't," Powell chuffed. "Unfortunately—and this is largely, though inadvertently, due to none other than Sitting Bull himself—a growing number have. You see, when interest in the Ghost Dance started spreading into the camps and reservations of the Sioux, many looked to Sitting Bull to advise on how seriously it should be taken. Wanting to understand more about it before responding one way or the other, the old warrior made the unwise choice of sending Kicking Bear to meet with Wovoka and bring back a report on the ritual itself and what its end goal was." The doctor paused, wagging his head in dismay. "But the interpretation Kicking Bear returned with, either through misunderstanding or outside influence or perhaps some deep-seated agenda of his own, maybe a combination of all three, was considerably different from Wovoka's vision."

"Different how?"

"Kicking Bear's version of the Ghost Dance, the one now catching on through the Dakotas and down into western Nebraska," North said, taking up the narrative, "is a far more aggressive program. It doesn't leave much room for the ancient spirits and Christ to join up and then bring about change slowly and peacefully. What it teaches is that a spiritual power will be created by the dances, and that power will be transferred to the true believers in order for them to rise up again and *force* the change back to the old ways. This even includes *Ghost Shirts* worn to repel the White Man's bullets. Ultimately, the peak of the ensuing battle will be a great supernatural upheaval that will peel back a layer of the earth like rolling up a carpet. Caught up and rolled away in this will be all the White Men and their evil customs and a wonderful new-old world will be revealed to the Red Man for him to live in alone and in peace."

Dalrymple's eyebrows lifted. "And I thought the first version was far-fetched."

Powell gave him another disapproving look. "Does that really sound so different from the End Days and the second coming of Christ as prophesied in the Holy Bible?"

Before the marshal had any chance to reply, Lone spoke up impatiently. "Alright. Enough of this. I know some of it has been necessary background, but it seems to me we're startin' to roam kinda far off course from what our confab here is supposed to be about—namely, the fact Col. Cody has gone missin'. I say it's time we cut a little closer to the bone on that. Start addin' up what we know and what we can speculate, then decidin' on some course of action for goin' to find him."

CHAPTER FOUR

Lone took supper that evening with Ma Sharples. They ate in the kitchen of the boarding house she owned and operated, finding a bit of privacy there from her other guests who had been served out in the main dining room and were lingering afterward in the adjacent parlor. As usual, Ma's fare was simple, plentiful, and delicious. Also as usual, Lone partook heartily with Ma looking on in approval.

"I like to see a man eat like a man," she declared. "Too often these days, when I serve my guests out in the dining room and the vittles are all dished up, everybody—including the men—picks so daintily and politely it's like they think there's some kind of shame in being hungry and wanting to chow down."

Lone grinned around a mouthful of mashed potatoes. "Reckon you never had that problem with the Sarge, did you?"

Ma rolled her eyes. "Lord no. That man could empty a plate quicker and cleaner than anybody I ever saw. Though once you started to get some size to you, you turned out able to give him a run for his money."

Back when Ma had been younger and known more as Adeline or simply Mrs. Sharples, the wife of a gruff career sergeant stationed at Fort McPherson, the Sharples had been one of the fort families who collectively raised Lone after he was orphaned as an infant when his blood parents were massacred in an Indian raid. Though he was grateful to all who looked after him during that time, he gravitated to the Sharples more than any other. So much so that years later, after he'd grown and gone to drifting when his stint as an army scout was finished, hearing how Ma (as all the locals now referred to her) was widowed and these days running a boarding house in North Platte beckoned him to her a visit.

Ever since, even though he still often went on the drift in pursuit of one thing or other, he always seemed to circle back to North Platte—much like Buffalo Bill—as the closest thing he had to a home base. Lone had long since realized that Ma's presence there and the mother-figure anchor she represented to him was the basis for this. And even if neither of them had ever put it in words, he also liked to think that his visits helped fill some of the emptiness she was left with after the passing of Sarge and the fact their marriage had never resulted in issue of their own.

As if reading his thoughts, Ma said as she pushed an oversized wedge of cherry pie in front of him, "But no matter how well fed I keep you, it's never enough to stop you from sooner or later wandering off on another adventure. This time you've only been back a few days and already you're telling me you're aiming to ride out again. I should have known when Frank North came around asking where to find you it would amount to no good."

"It will amount to good," Lone countered, "if Col. Cody is in trouble and I'm able to do something to help him."

"Seems to me there's a lot riding on that word 'if,'" Ma huffed. "If that rascal Bill Cody is in trouble, he likely deserves it. And if the whole thing is just another publicity stunt cooked up by him and that whopper-spinner Ned Buntline—which seems likely, you ask me—then all the more reason you need to be careful not to get caught up in such hooey."

Lone shook his head. "No, I don't think this is just a bunch of hooey, Ma. Not this time."

"Well don't expect me to hold my breath waiting to find out. Reckon I know Bill Cody as good as anybody." She paused, eyeing Lone tightly for a long beat before saying, "Then again, maybe my ability for getting the right read on a thing ain't as sharp as it used to be. When you left out all those months ago to bury Peg O'Malley up in the mountains and that pretty little Chinee gal went tagging along with you, I felt certain sure you and her was a match that would be sticking together. Sorry to hear it didn't turn out."

"I am, too, Ma," Lone said stonily. "We cared plenty for one another, you weren't wrong about that. But other things got in the way. My stubbornness about obligations I felt had to be taken care of before I could ever devote myself properly to her or anybody else, her culture once she got back amongst kinfolk—it all piled too high between us." He shrugged. "But we parted friends and the last time I saw her she seemed happy. I can live with that."

Ma looked at him softly, fondly. " 'Course you can. Man like you don't know no other way but to keep goin' forward." Then, after a slight pause, she added with a frown, "Even if it means chargin' forward on this Bill Cody chase that I still think there's something fishy about."

Lone smiled. "I appreciate your concern and I can't fault your suspicion. Believe me, I well know how the colonel, especially when Buntline is in the picture, can cook up a whopper to stir the interest of the public. This ain't got the feel of nothing like that, though. In the first place, there's no sign of Buntline bein' involved. In the second place, I don't believe the colonel would leave North and Powell hangin' to fret and wonder the way they are. Even if they didn't approve of him bein' up to something, he wouldn't exclude 'em from knowin' about it."

"Then why ain't they the ones lighting out to find him?" Ma asked with a scowl.

"Because they're simply not up to it. Leastways not travelin' fast and light on horseback, the way I'll be doin'," Lone explained. "Major North is still half stove in from his injury overseas. The little bit of activity he saw out on the trail today left him wore out and limpin' worse by the time we left the marshal's office. And Powell may have already done some travelin' with Cody but that was ridin' a wagon, not on horseback like I told you is gonna be called for this time. Besides, he needs to stick here and look after North."

"If Powell was traveling with Buffalo Bill, how did he manage to lose him in the first place?" Ma wanted to know.

Lone scooped up his first forkful of pie and said, "Losin' track of one another wasn't part of the plan. When the colonel heard about Sitting Bull gettin' killed, he took a notion to strike out on his own and go find out more about what happened. He was sad and angry and suspicious that sendin' for him to begin with was little more than a trick to make the old chief let down his guard. Cody meant to show everybody he wasn't gonna stand for bein' treated like some kind of joke to be dangled as bait, especially when it led to the death of his old friend."

Her expression an odd mix of concern and disfavor, Ma replied, "Too bad Bill didn't see the joke he started making out of himself a long time ago when he let Buntline sink his greedy claws in him. Parading him first on a Broadway stage and then filling page after page of magazines packed with ridiculous yarns about his adventures. If that wasn't enough, Bill only added to it with that gaudy Wild West show he's now gallivanting all over creation with."

"Maybe so," Lone brooded. "But those are things the colonel went along with and choices he made for himself. That don't give nobody else the right to take his name and sling it around for their own purpose. And for sure not to bring harm to others in the bargain. Remember, too, that behind all the showmanship and ballyhoo, Bill Cody is still a tough old cob who endured and accomplished plenty when the frontier was at its most rugged. He sets out to hold some scoundrel to account for doin' him wrong, I wouldn't bet against him."

"Reckon saying it that way puts it in sort of a different light," Ma allowed. "But it still don't answer why everybody is so worried about Cody 'disappearing.' Sounds to me like that's exactly what he set out to do—head off on a long hunt and not necessarily be heard from until he'd bagged what he went after."

"Only that wasn't the agreement between him and Powell," Lone countered. "When they parted ways after learnin' about Sitting Bull, Powell was to return to Scout's Rest and look after North while the colonel was supposed to check in regular-like with telegrams to keep them updated on his progress. But so far, goin' on ten days now, not a peep has been heard. Powell sent out a few inquiries to places where he might have showed up, but nothing panned out there neither. And the doctor and Major North have got to be careful about not lettin' on too much for fear of stirrin' up an even bigger fuss. Luckily, the colonel's wife and daughters are away visiting friends in Denver so they haven't even been told about any of this yet."

"Lord knows with her man away so much doing his shows and what not, Louisa Cody must be used to his absences. But getting back to you chasing after him, what makes you think you're going to be able to have any luck finding the old rascal from a saddle?"

Lone smiled slyly. "Because I figure two old scouts might think sort of along the same lines. Plus, I can go places telegraph wires don't reach. And, if need be, I got ways of askin' questions that'll make folks plumb eager to tell me things they might not be so willin' to share with somebody else."

"Makes me sorry I asked," Ma sniffed. "So when are you planning to head out?"

"I figured yet tonight. Sky's clear, there'll be near a full moon in a while. I already stocked up on trail supplies and Ironsides is waitin' down at the livery stable with a bellyful of grain and fresh hay, rarin' to go. We can cover a good stretch of miles by daybreak."

"That's crazy. I won't hear of it. I have an empty room. I insist you use it to get a good night's sleep before you leave. I'll see you off with a big batch of biscuits and gravy and also have some other vittles prepared for you to take on your mule-headed way."

Lone gazed into the eyes of the stout, gray-haired woman—eyes that always shone with kindness and caring for him, despite her outer facade of gruffness—and he knew he couldn't say no to her. When it came right down to it, his mule-headedness was no match for her stubbornness. Besides, a morning send-off of Ma's biscuits and gravy was mighty tough to turn down.

CHAPTER FIVE

Lone was on the trail next morning before the sun was fully risen above the eastern horizon. There was a crispness in the air that served as a reminder of summer's end and the rapid approach of fall, with winter not too far behind. Not that the coming of winter on the high plains was anything to look forward to, but the bite of this dawn nevertheless felt good and bracing on Lone's face and he was glad to be out in it and on the move once again.

As Ma had mentioned last evening, he'd only been back in the North Platte area for a few days. Less than two weeks. Most of that time had been spent out at the remains of the Busted Spur, the modest horse ranching operation he'd started a couple years ago with one-legged ex–mountain man Peg O'Malley. Somewhat ironically, most of the money used for the ranch's start-up had come from a job Lone and Peg did guiding an expedition of scientists and adventurers up into the vast Nebraska Sandhills—a job initially referred to Lone by none other than Buffalo Bill.

Despite a promising start, the Busted Spur operation then received a harsh set-back. While Lone was away on another side job to earn money for buying more stock, a gang of ruthless outlaws descended on the ranch, left Peg for dead, and stole the small herd they'd accumulated up to that point. Peg lived long enough to tell Lone, upon his return, what sparse information he could about his attackers and to make a dying request for burial in his beloved Colorado Rockies.

It had taken Lone the better part of a year to first honor his friend's wishes regarding a final resting place and then pick up the cold trail that eventually led him to track down each of the gang members and see to it they paid for what they'd done. Other incidents had also cropped up that delayed his return to North Platte and what was left of the Busted Spur. As more had time passed, Lone grew to recognize that some of his delay in returning was due to misgivings on his part as far as whether or not he had it in him to try and build up the Busted Spur again on his own. The notion of starting the ranch in the first place had spawned from two loners and roamers—him and Peg—deciding it was about time they put down roots somewhere. Now, with half the team gone, the notion no longer had the same pull.

Once he got back, spending days alone out at the place, walking the ground, examining the disrepair from a combination of neglect and the damage done purposefully by the outlaws during their raid, Lone couldn't find within him any inclination for remaining or rebuilding. The notion was gone. Like Peg, like too many other people and things he'd had to move on from in his life.

Having firmly reached that conclusion, he'd ridden away from the Busted Spur for the final time and was on his way back to North Platte to inform Ma, among other things, when he ran afoul of the robbery attempt on North and Powell. Lone had known Ma would be disappointed to hear he'd given up on sticking with the ranch, in her eyes meaning it would only prolong his wandering ways. So the good thing about him getting involved with this apparent disappearance of Buffalo Bill, even though she didn't approve of that either, was that for the time being at least it put off needing to mention anything to her about the other.

These were the thoughts rolling through Lone's mind as he rode, holding Ironsides to a steady, miles-eating pace that he knew the big gray could keep up all day and more if need be. The former scout was aimed on a general northwesterly course, not fully decided yet if he should try for Fort Robinson up near the border, where he knew several people and might gather some worthwhile information, or if he should bear more due north and go directly to the Pine Ridge reservation in South Dakota and try to seek out General Miles. The problem with the latter was that, given all the talk about how the Ghost Dance movement (of which he had much to learn) was stirring up the

Sioux, he didn't know what resistance he might encounter crossing their land before he ever got close to the general.

Lone's hunch was that Col. Cody's quest, because he was basically going rogue against federal orders to butt out, might also take him to one of these friendlier locales rather than Laglen's area of influence up in North Dakota. The only difference would be that, due to his well-known closeness with Sitting Bull, he'd probably have little trouble moving among the Sioux.

For Lone, either destination was at least a three-day ride. So he had plenty of time to make up his mind which one to settle on. And in the meantime he had a sizable chunk of rolling, treeless, grassy emptiness that was the Nebraska Sandhills to cross in between.

With the sun climbing higher and growing moderately warmer and the air hanging still and dry, he rode steadily on. Stopping only to rest and water Ironsides on occasion, he did his own eating and drinking in the saddle. Ma's breakfast kept his belly well satisfied until past noon when he ate one of the biscuit and sausage sandwiches she'd packed for him. Come night camp, he planned on putting a considerably bigger dent in more of the vittles she'd sent.

Then again, certain things seemed to be shaping up that might interfere with the simple pleasures of a peaceful camp and a good meal come day's end.

Because somebody—make that a pair of somebodies—was following him.

It had been about mid-morning when Lone first caught a glimpse of two riders on the move some distance behind him. But then they quickly lagged back and dropped out of sight, leaving him to think they were perhaps just some wranglers out rounding up strays for one of the cattle ranches scattered across the lower reaches of the Sandhills. A couple hours later, though, they popped into sight and promptly disappeared once again. And then a third time not long after.

By that point there was little doubt they were fogging his trail. Not drawing any closer yet not fading entirely away. Apparently not meaning to be spotted but doing a poor job of it. Trying to remain unseen out in the middle of all this open emptiness was a tricky task, particularly attempted against someone with senses honed as keen as Lone's.

But spotting the two men did nothing to answer the questions their presence now created. Why were they following him? Who were they and what was their intent? The first thing that sprang to Lone's mind was that it must have something to do with the Buffalo Bill matter. But since he'd been involved in that for less than twenty-four hours and only a handful of people had any awareness of this, how would the two riders know what he was setting out to do and what did it mean to them?

And if the men on his tail *didn't* have anything to do with the Cody situation—what other possibilities did that leave? Since Lone was following no established course or trail, the likelihood the pair just happened to be traveling the same way as him didn't hold up. And if they were looking to rob him of his horse and supplies, it seemed an awful lot of bother to go to for such a meager take, especially after letting it drag out so long and so far before making their play. Finally, seeing as how Lone had left a few enemies in his wake over the years, there was a chance the pair had reason to be hounding him for the sake of settling some past score.

The fact they hadn't closed on him by now, evidently believing their presence remained undetected, convinced Lone they had in mind one of two things: Either they were waiting to attack his camp late tonight when he was asleep and his guard relaxed; or they meant to follow him all the way to find out what his destination was.

Having decided this, Lone relaxed some and smiled a wolf's smile, letting Ironsides plod steadily on. Yeah, come night, things seemed to be shaping up so that his enjoyment of the food Ma had sent might be more limited than he'd been looking forward to. That was unfortunate, but he could work with it. He could also show great patience. Up to a point. So he'd ride out the day, waiting to see if his two shadows made any kind of move.

If they didn't, he'd be damned if he would wait any longer. It was easy enough to figure that once he stopped to make night camp, those on his back trail would do the same. And that's when they'd discover, after full dark descended, how not only could the span between their camps be covered in more than one direction, but few men could move more silently or effectively in the darkness than Lone McGantry . . .

CHAPTER SIX

Under different circumstances, Lone might have stopped to make camp a little earlier. But in this instance he wanted to use up as much daylight as possible and was looking for some particular conditions to the terrain before he reined up. He found what he wanted just as dusk was settling—a shallow depression at the top of a low, blunted hill. Spreading his bedroll against the northwest shoulder of the depression would give him a windbreak in case a blow came up during the night and also gave him a slightly elevated view for gazing out on his back trail. Plus, the fringe of yucca around the rim of the depression provided adequate fuel for a small fire and also cover for slipping out unseen if and when he decided to go visiting later on.

While he was stripping down Ironsides and then watering and serving him a portion of grain before leaving him to graze on the surrounding plentiful grass, Lone kept an eye peeled for any further sign of the men somewhere in back of him. He saw nothing. At least they weren't so incompetent they couldn't manage to stay out of sight most of the time. But they were nevertheless still there. He could *feel* them.

With Ironsides taken care of, Lone got some

coffee brewing and stretched out, propped on his upturned saddle, to leisurely eat an apple and another sandwich from the sack of goodies Ma had fixed for him. He was a good trail cook and in his time had probably taken as many meals beside a campfire as at a proper dining table. But he certainly didn't mind shirking meal prep duties in favor of somebody else, as long as good chow resulted. And coming from Ma, that was never in doubt.

The darkening sky was once again clear, the first faint glitter of a few stars starting to show. The moon would rise before too long. Not quite full, but close enough to provide good night illumination to maneuver by. That could work against Lone making a reconnoiter unseen, but conversely would be in his favor if his stalkers tried making their move first. Either way he had the advantage of knowing they were out there in the night while they, he believed, remained unaware he'd spotted them.

Lone finished eating and was working on his second cup of coffee. The small yucca-stalk fire, having served its purpose, he was letting die out. His gaze swept slowly, ceaselessly over the landscape back the way he'd come, across the rounded, pale green grassy humps rising and falling in and out of intermittent pools of shadows that slowly turned a deeper velvety black as the darkness of night thickened. Nothing moved, everything was still and silent. Except for occasionally lifting the coffee cup to his lips, this was true of Lone as well. He sat like a stone figure, just watching and listening.

Only when Ironsides emitted a soft warning chuff and scraped a forefoot one time on the ground did the former scout move. In a smooth, unhurried motion he set aside the coffee cup and, as his hand brushed back across his hip, its thumb flicked loose the keeper thong from the hammer of the Colt Peacemaker holstered there. Then Lone went motionless again, though watching and listening even more intently than ever.

A full minute passed before a tiny object, a pebble, arced through the darkness and dropped lightly to the ground a foot in front of the fire's few remaining embers. Lone's fingers tightened on the grips of the Colt but otherwise he remained still.

"I got your attention, McGantry?" whispered a calm voice from the yucca fringe above his head.

Lone replied, managing to keep his own voice steady. "You do."

"Good. Just hold easy, I'm a friend."

"Uh-huh. You one of the pair been followin' me all day?"

"Not hardly. But it's good to know you didn't miss spottin' them two skulkers. Considerin' your reputation, I'd be disappointed if you had."

"Glad not to let you down," Lone said, an edge

slicing into his tone. "You seem to have me at a disadvantage. I know you from somewhere?"

"We crossed paths once, real brief, a long time back," came the answer. "Name's John Burke. Arizona John Burke folks have come to call me, or mostly just Arizona Burke."

Lone relaxed a little. "You used to be friends with Bill Cody."

"Still am. Same as you. That's why I'm here. Say, you got any coffee left in that pot down there?"

"Some. Likely ain't very hot, though."

"Long as it's coffee, I'd sure be obliged to have a couple swallows. Okay I come down?"

Hand still resting on his Colt, Lone said, "Come ahead."

A moment later a shadowy figure came slipping lightly, quietly down over the shoulder of the depression a few feet to Lone's left. Standing there on the other side of the campfire embers, the figure reverse-melted out of the murkiness and revealed itself to be a man of average height, wiry build, clad in a fringed buckskin shirt and knee high moccasin boots with striped trousers tucked into them. The gent's face was wedge-shaped, cut by a thick mustache drooping down from under a sharply pointed nose and framed by dark hair spilling in long strings from under a battered, wide-brimmed hat. A gun belt with a black-handled Remington revolver holstered for the cross draw was strapped around his waist and in his left hand he casually gripped a Henry repeating rifle.

"I been smellin' your coffee for the past half hour and it was plumb drivin' me nuts," announced the man who had identified himself as Arizona Burke.

Lone gestured. "There's a spare cup there in my possibles pack. Help yourself to what's left."

Burke rummaged to quickly unearth the cup and then squatted down to pour it full of tepid black liquid from the pot. After taking a big gulp, he tipped his head back and emitted a satisfied sigh through a wide smile. "Ahh, nectar of the gods! You brew mighty fine coffee, friend McGantry."

"Once again, I'm glad not to disappoint," Lone replied dryly. "But now, before we go much farther with this friend stuff, what say you explain your remark about us both bein' one with Col. Cody and that bein' the reason you're here?"

"Seems reasonable enough," allowed Burke after another gulp of coffee. "The bare bones of it is that I showed up in North Platte this mornin' shortly after you rode out. I went straight to Major North and Doc Powell with the news I came to deliver. After I passed it on to 'em and they in turn told me about your involvement, we all figured you ought to be filled in as well. So I grabbed some fresh supplies and lit out to catch up."

"Considerin' your late start," said Lone, "that made for a fair piece of catchin' up."

"You're tellin' me. You don't push that big gray particular fast, but you're sure Hell and Jesus on steady."

"What you call coverin' ground," Lone quipped.

"Uh-huh. You sure did that." Burke tipped his cup high and drained it. "Still, I'd've caught up sooner if I hadn't run into the tracks of those polecats tailin' you. Figurin' who they had to be, I reckoned it was best not to let 'em know I'd joined the parade. So I swung out wide around and rode my ass off to get ahead of them and you both. That's why, in case you didn't notice, I came in just now from the front end."

"I noticed," Lone said. "Gotta give it to you, you caught me some by surprise."

"Not all the way, though. That big gray of yours"—Burke inclined his head toward Ironsides—"makes a pretty handy watchdog."

"Me and him been together quite a spell. We take care of each other," Lone explained. Then: "But let's back up to the part where you said you know who the skunks on my back trail are. How about fillin' me in some more on that?"

"Mase Baneford and Calvin Cully be their names," said Burke. "I know it's got to be them on account of the rest of the pack they was ridin' with—Roy Epps, Three-finger Jack Dahl, and Ben Eames—are layin' dead back in North Platte courtesy of tanglin' with you and Major North. I took a gander at the bodies and recognized 'em before I left."

"So these two are after me to get revenge for their pals?"

"Not necessarily. In the first place, the five of 'em wasn't nothing close to bein' pals. They was throwed together as part of a deal to save their individual hides and wouldn't give two shits about seekin' revenge for each other. Way I figure, all they cared about was holdin' up their end of the bargain they struck for their own sakes."

"Bargain?"

"With Major Laglen up in North Dakota. He's the one who scraped the five out of a brig and laid out this bit of dirty work as a trade for their release." With a sly smile, Burke continued, "You see, the major is feelin' kinda desperate these days what with havin' hisself in a puddle of hot water growin' steadily hotter over lettin' Sitting Bull get killed right under his nose and then this Ghost Dance craziness gettin' worse right along. So when he heard about Buffalo Bill not turnin' back the way he was supposed to even after gettin' word from Washington, Laglen was fit to be tied about what more the colonel might stir up if he went rootin' around loose."

"But why send his men after North and Powell then, and not directly after Cody?" Lone asked.

Burke spread his hands. "Because, like everybody else right at the moment, he don't have no idea where Buffalo Bill is. The telegrams Powell sent out inquirin' about the colonel is what alerted Laglen in the first place. So, figurin' Powell or North would be first to hear if anything turned up, Laglen sent his hounds to where they was."

"Mind me askin' how you got wind of all this?" Lone said.

"Because I was part of the colonel's outfit when he first started out for his meetin' with Sitting Bull. Me, Pony Bob Hallam, a fella by the name of Chadwick, and Doc Powell. While the rest of 'em got ready to head for the Standing Rock rez in North Dakota, Bill sent me to branch off and make a swing through the Pine Ridge to get a firsthand feel for how this Ghost Dance thing was takin' hold overall. So he'd have that to compare with the way Sitting Bull might try to paint it.

"Well, I never got the chance to hook back up with him and let him know what I found out. I was still at Pine Ridge when General Miles—a very pissed off general, I might add—sent word to the command there informin' that Cody's mission had been ordered off. So, with nothing particularly better to do and knowin' a little half-breed gal down across the Nebraska line in the Fort Robinson area, a sweetie who always welcomes me into her tipi when I pass through, I just hung around close for a while. I was still there when word came about Sitting Bull gettin' killed and then, not long after, about the colonel takin' a notion to strike out on his own, orders or not."

"And the part about Laglen sendin' out his hounds?"

Burke's sly smile returned. "You been around enough to see how it sometimes works in army ranks. Just because a commander is an idiot or a weasel don't make everybody under him the same. They may have to take orders but there are different ways of actually carryin' 'em out. In other words, General Miles—who is a smart and respected commander—has certain, er, *ears* you might say within the ranks of that fool Laglen."

"Ears that are connected to mouths."

"Right. So when Miles heard what Laglen was up to, he got word to me down at Fort Robinson and sent me to warn North and Powell, figurin' that was the best way to sooner or later reach Cody, too."

Lone's brows pinched together. "So what we all took for a robbery attempt on North and Powell yesterday may not have been that at all. More likely, Laglen's hounds were gettin' antsy and thought they could force some information out of Cody's friends."

"Ain't sayin' it's sound thinkin', and no way of knowin' if Laglen had a hand in it or not. But it makes even less sense any other way," said

Burke. "And the fact that the remainin' two, Baneford and Cullen, are now on your tail seems to back it up. Since they was gettin' nowhere skulkin' North and Powell, you pokin' your nose in and right away ridin' off must be givin' 'em cause to think you might be a surer lead to the colonel."

"If that's the case, if their plan is just to follow me and see where I lead 'em," mused Lone, "then they're not apt to make a try on my camp tonight like I been half suspectin'."

"Be my guess."

Lone frowned. "But I ain't much for the notion of continuin' on and leavin' 'em to dangle behind me like a dried turd on a horse's tail."

"Understandable," Burke said. Then, his mouth curving into another sly smile, he added, "If you don't mind a suggestion and the offer of some company, how about we ease back there in a little while and take a curry comb to 'em?"

CHAPTER SEVEN

At least Baneford and Cullen, under the impression they hadn't already been spotted, were savvy enough to pitch a cold camp for the sake of avoiding a night fire discernible for miles. The only thing they accomplished with this precaution, however, was to make it a trifle harder for Lone and Arizona Burke to locate the pair when they went backtracking in the dark, ghosting over the ground on moccasin-clad feet.

But locate them they did.

They found them on the back slope of a grassy hill. Wrapped in their bedrolls, fast asleep. No lookout posted, horses hobbled upwind and too far off to be much good as far as signaling any kind of warning. The savviness of the pair clearly had its limits.

Lone and Arizona pounced fast. Each took a stance over one of the men, kicking away the rifles and gun belts lying beside their bedrolls then leaning over to yank away top blankets and wake the polecat under it with a gun muzzle jammed against his forehead.

In the pale moonlight, the face of the hombre at the other end of Lone's Colt barrel appeared to turn paler still. At the same time, his jaw dropped slack and his bulging eyes rolled up and inward to gawk at the menacing nearness of .44 caliber death.

Through gritted teeth, Lone said, "Okay. You nosy sonsabitches been foggin' my trail all day—Now it's time to wake up and spill why."

The sagging chin quivered and the man stammered, "I—I don't know what you're talkin' about. We ain't foggin' nobody. Me and my pard are just passin'—"

Lone cut him short by lifting the Colt's muzzle off his forehead long enough to swat the barrel sharply across his ear. Then, shoving the muzzle back in place, he snarled, "Lyin' will only make this more unpleasant. For you, not me. You spout false again, you'll do the rest of your talkin' through a busted nose. Now think real hard to remember the question and then answer it straight this time."

The other skulker, the one under Arizona's gun, said out the corner of his mouth, "Don't let him hoorah you, Cully. Hold your ground. We ain't done nothing wrong."

"Sounds like your pard don't care much about you gettin' your head dented in, Cully boy," Lone observed.

"Maybe" said Arizona, "I oughta give this jasper his own taste."

Lone shrugged. "Suit yourself. If these hombres are bound to try and play it tough and stubborn, might be our quickest way is to just cut to it. I want to get some sleep yet tonight, so I'm in no mood to waste a lot of time with such sorry excuses for trail hounds. If crackin' a few bones don't do it, then I know some tricks with my Bowie knife that I guarantee will have 'em singin' like a couple of whippoorwills."

Arizona's man sneered. "You're bluffin'! You wouldn't carve nobody up just for—" That was all he got out before Arizona's pistol barrel cracked across the side of his head. But the blow quieted him only for a second before he wailed, "Ow! Goddamn, that hurt!"

"There's more where that came from," Arizona told him. "And if you're stupid enough to push it, that knife blade my friend mentioned won't be far behind."

"I ain't so sure these two old prairie wolves *are* bluffin', Mase," Cully said anxiously. "I think they just might be crazy enough to actually start carvin'. And I don't know about you, but I don't see my deal with Laglen as bein' anywhere near worth gettin' skinned over!"

"Shut your stinkin' mouth," Mase warned him. "You don't hold your mud, you'll make us both damned sorry."

Leaning closer over Cully, Lone smiled a cold smile and said, "Appears your pard is kinda simple minded. He ain't seemed to notice the two of you are already in pretty sorry shape. You gonna let him call the tune to make it worse, or are you gonna look out for yourself?"

Cully squeezed his eyes shut tight for a long moment. Then, opening them abruptly, he responded with a ragged sigh. "Okay. Alright. I admit we been followin' you."

Lone nodded approvingly. "That's showin' some smarts."

"You gutless cur!" Mase hollered.

Arizona gave him another hard rap and growled, "Keep quiet or I'll pound you out cold."

Glaring up at Lone, Cully said, "I'll answer your questions. I don't know a lot but I'll tell you what I do. Just let me sit up, okay? I don't breathe so good layin' flat on my back."

Lone considered briefly before lifting his Colt and taking a half step back. "Go ahead. Real slow and easy. One wrong twitch, your breathin' worries will be settled by a .44 slug."

Cully sat up, eyes never leaving Lone's Colt. He lifted his left hand slowly and rubbed the spot on his forehead where the gun muzzle had been pressed.

"Get to it. Start talkin'," Lone said.

Mase couldn't resist making one more try. "Don't do it, Cul—spit in his eye!"

Lone cut an annoyed sidelong glance, snarling, "Shut him the hell up!"

Arizona was raising his Remington to do just that when something caught his eye and caused him to instead holler, "Knife!"

Lone's split second of distraction to call for the silencing of Mase had given Cully the opening for an act of desperate resistance. From the bedroll folds at his right hip he pulled a long-bladed knife and thrust it straight for Lone's stomach. Only Lone's sudden twisting motion in response to Arizona's warning shout saved him from getting six inches of steel planted in his guts. Instead the razored edge of the blade was deflected by the buckle of his gun belt and managed to slice just a shallow gash up alongside his belly button. It still hurt like hell, though, as indicated by the roar of half-pain, half-rage it brought out of the former scout.

When Lone matched this roar by triggering one from his Colt, the combination of his initial twisting motion and his reflexive jerk from the knife gash caused the bullet to sail a hair's breadth wide of Cully's head and an equal distance above the shoulder of his knife arm. Before Lone could get the Colt re-aimed, Cully pulled back his knife and this time swung the blade in a hard downward sweep that laid open a long, deep slash across the front of Lone's right thigh. The former scout emitted another howl of pain as the wounded leg buckled on him and he toppled off balance. As luck would have it, he fell almost directly onto Cully, momentarily pinning the skulker's knife hand even as Lone's Colt was jarred from his grasp. The two then went rolling in a kicking, flailing entanglement, fighting for control of the knife clenched in Cully's fist.

While that was going on, another struggle broke out between Arizona and Mase. Arizona's shouted warning to Lone had given Mase his own brief, desperate opening and he seized it by lunging up and grabbing for his captor's gun hand. His fingers clamped on Arizona's wrist and he jerked down, trying to pull the standing man off balance. He succeeded, but only partially. Going with the tug for just a second, Arizona suddenly countered it by dropping his full weight and driving both knees into Mase's stomach.

Air exploded out of Mase in a great gush but he somehow managed to still keep his hold on Arizona's wrist. That ended up to his disadvantage, however, when his frantic yanking resulted in Arizona's finger tightening on the Remington's trigger and the gun discharged a round point-blank into Mase's heart. He was dead even before the smoke began curling up from his scorched shirtfront.

Half a dozen yards away, the fight there was more prolonged. Lone's leg was starting to cramp and he was steadily losing blood from the thigh wound as well as a lesser amount from the stomach cut. Cully wasn't an overly big man but he was stocky and hard-muscled and proving to be damnably determined. When Lone heard Arizona's Remington go off, he couldn't tell exactly what it signaled but it didn't really matter because he had his hands plenty full regardless. He knew the blood loss would start to take its toll soon and, even though he'd gone into this tussle the larger and stronger man, that advantage would then start to ebb. Plus, Cully still had the primary grip on the goddamned knife!

The pair kept rolling one way and then back again, locked together, driving elbows and knees relentlessly into one another. All the while the knife was locked in a fierce double grip between their faces.

At last, planting the knee of his good leg more securely than he'd ever been able to before, as he started to push into another roll reversal, Lone was able to shove his upper body higher and shift his face off to one side of their locked hands. This gave him an opening to slam forward as fast and hard as he could, smashing his forehead against Cully's cheekbone and eye socket. He heard bones crunch and felt hot blood spurt over his face. He also heard Cully scream. He drew back his head and slammed it forward again. And again. The crunch of bones turned into a pulpy squishing sound. Each time more blood spurted and each time Cully screamed.

When Lone drew his head back a third time, he held it back and finished the leg thrust that took him and Cully into another roll. Only halfway this time, leaving them lying on their sides. Gritting his teeth against the pain, Lone pumped the knee of his injured leg deep into Cully's crotch. When the man doubled forward involuntarily, Lone tightened the two-handed grip he had on Cully's doubled fists wrapped around the knife handle and shoved with all his might. Cully was now too battered to hold back the thrust. The blade sank to the hilt just above his Adam's apple. His one good eye bulged wildly and he made a bubbling sound deep in his throat. Then his head lolled to one side and the bubbling stopped.

CHAPTER EIGHT

"Lucky for you," Arizona was saying, "you got a thigh muscle like a slab of hickory. The blade laid a deep track, but not all the way through. My cauterizin' and stitchin' closed it up pretty good, if I do say so myself. No bleedin'. We'll have to keep an eye out for any sign of infection, otherwise I think it'll heal just fine. In time. For a while, though, it's gonna hurt like—"

Lone, his face scrunched with discomfort, interrupted him to say, "No, it ain't *gonna* hurt—it *does* hurt. Like holy blue Hell!"

They were now returned to their own camp. After getting Lone's leg wound temporarily wrapped and tied off tight to stanch the bleeding as much as possible before leaving the skulkers' camp, they'd ridden back on the confiscated horses of Mase and Cully (who were beyond needing mounts any longer). Upon arrival, Arizona had immediately stoked up a large fire—to provide better illumination for more thorough wound tending, to boil water, to heat knife blades for cauterizing. With his doctoring duties completed (including the cleaning and bandaging of the less serious cut to Lone's stomach), the old frontiersman was now awaiting a well-earned and much anticipated cup of coffee from the pot he had brewing on the edge coals.

In response to Lone's painful lament, Arizona said, "Go ahead and take another belt of that who-hit-John from the bottle there beside you. No need to be stingy now that we've got plenty more from the stash I found in the saddlebags of Mase and Cully. Ain't gonna do them no more good. You, on the hand, could use the pain dullin' and it'll also maybe help you grab a couple hours of shuteye yet before sunup. Soon as that pot's ready, you can bet I ain't gonna be pourin' *just* coffee into my cup."

"Always hated to see a fella drink by hisself," grimaced Lone as he reached for the whiskey bottle lying alongside the upturned saddle he was leaned back against, an upturned saddle with his injured leg stretched out in front of him. "And I ain't afraid to admit I could damn sure use a dose of pain duller."

Eyeing him as he tipped up the bottle and gulped deeply, Arizona said, "You gonna be up to ridin' first thing come mornin' with that leg givin' you fury?"

"Try and stop me," Lone declared, lowering the bottle.

Arizona grinned. "Reckon I'll take a pass on that."

Lone heaved a sigh. "The thing that makes me maddest of all ain't the hurtin' or the cuttin' up that caused it. I deserve at least part of that for bein' sloppy enough to miss the mealy-mouthed weasel havin' a hideaway knife. What really burns me is the ruination his blade did to my shirt and britches. Wasn't neither of 'em more than about seven or eight years old, just gettin' proper broke in. Now I got to replace 'em with stiff, itchy new duds."

"If Cully had been a mite quicker with his blade, you could've kept wearin' those broke-in duds with a nice dirt overcoat to go with 'em. Think about that," Arizona said.

" 'Druther not," Lone replied, scrunching up his face again.

Deciding the coffee was ready, Arizona poured himself some, leaving room in his cup to add a generous splash from the whiskey bottle Lone held out to him. Handing back the bottle and then holding the cup close so he could blow some cooling breaths onto its steaming contents, he said, "Thing makes me maddest about our tussle with those polecats—apart from you gettin' sliced up, that is—is how we had to kill 'em before we got any information out of 'em."

"You heard Cully confirm they was sent by Laglen."

"Yeah, but we pretty much knew that already." Arizona scowled. "Still leaves me powerful curious about what they was supposed to do if and when they succeeded in runnin' down the colonel. *And* I can't help wonderin' if Laglen don't have other polecats also out on the hunt for him."

Lone worked up a scowl of his own. "Makes it all the more important for somebody on the colonel's side to catch up with him first."

"You can say that again."

"But figurin' out where the ol' rascal took a notion to head for—not to mention something unexpected he might've run into on the way—leaves a lot of ground to try and cover."

"You ain't wrong on that. Even though most folks these days know him from those wild and wooly books about him and the 'show business' side he works so hard at, it wasn't too many years ago that he was ridin' these plains when every day was a for real fight to stay alive. And Bill made it through when a lot didn't." Arizona's eyes narrowed. "I wouldn't bet against him still havin' a measure of that same toughness and savvy."

"Me neither," Lone agreed. "And I think that's part of what he's out to prove."

His coffee having cooled enough to drink, Arizona took a big swallow and then said, "Also workin' in the colonel's favor is the fact he's travelin' with Pony Bob Hallam. Bob ain't no slouch neither when it comes to havin' some rough edges. Trouble is, he also ain't no slouch when it comes to passin' sly-like through a territory if he ain't wantin' to be noticed. Him and the colonel puttin' their heads together toward that purpose is bound to make it tough for anybody—

friend or foe, either one—to cut their sign."

Lone arched a brow. "Yeah, I figured from the start that was gonna be the hardest challenge—trackin' the colonel if he was bent on stayin' low for a while."

Arizona took another drink of coffee. "Yet you lit out like you had something in mind. Care to say what?"

"Fact is, my plan was kinda open-ended," Lone replied with a wry grin. "I been torn between headin' up to the Pine Ridge rez or first anglin' lower to the Fort Robinson area where I know some folks who might've caught wind of something I'd find useful. Reckon I was leanin' more toward Fort Robinson. But, since you only recently came from there and have also been in contact with General Miles up at Pine Ridge—without either of you havin' got any kind of bead on the colonel—don't make much sense for me to go ahead and try either place. Guess that leaves Standing Rock as a prospect. But damned if I can buy the idea of the colonel, no matter how bold he is, bargin' right up to 'front Laglen smack in his front yard."

"Me neither," agreed Arizona. "But there might be a third prospect worth considerin'."

Lone made a gesture. "Let's hear it."

"You ever had any dealin's with the Robideaux brothers?"

"Those Frenchies who used to run that tradin'

post south of Scotts Bluff? Sure, any number of times back when. But I figured they must be dead or at least out of business by now."

"Not quite." Arizona wagged his head. "Though his brother Joseph passed some time ago, ol' Antoine is still kickin' and still in business. He don't trade much with white folks these days on account of most East-West travelers use Mitchell Pass to the north where they have a wider range of businesses in the town of Scotts Bluff to get their supplies from. Antoine makes do mainly with business from Injuns who roam on and off the surroundin' reservations. He married a squaw, in case you didn't know, and it turned out she's got kinfolk scattered in every direction from Hell to breakfast.

"Point I'm gettin' to is that Antoine is in a prime position to hear all kinds of talk and rumors about what's goin' on amongst the western Nebraska and Dakota tribes—how strong the Ghost Dance movement's catchin' on, what are the feelin's about the murder of Sitting Bull, and so on and so forth. Add in the fact that Buffalo Bill used to be real good friends with Antoine and his brother, and it strikes me that if the colonel wanted to move on the sly and find some out-of-the-way old haunt he could trust as a spot to lay low and gather information, well, Robideaux's place just might cross his mind."

By the time Arizona had finished his spiel,

Lone's eyes were bright with excitement. "By God, man, you just tossed a mighty juicy bone to bite into! There ain't a hell of a lot more to think about. It flat sounds like too good a prospect not to check out."

Arizona regarded him. "You sayin' that as *Lone* McGantry, or are you open to havin' some company to go do that checkin'?"

"I suppose," Lone said after a broadly exaggerated show of consideration, "I could stand to put up with you a while longer. Especially since you're the one who's got the saddlebags with all the pain duller in 'em."

CHAPTER NINE

The next day was a tough slog for Lone. His leg wound hurt like hell. But he pushed through, driven by his quest and aided by frequent nips of "pain duller." Never to the extent of muddling his overall senses, just enough to counter the worst of the throbbing ache.

He and Arizona had started the morning with a big breakfast of bacon and beans, complimented by half a dozen of Ma's biscuits slathered in some strawberry jam she'd also sent along, all washed down with plenty of hot, fresh coffee. For the balance of the day they followed Lone's prior routine of stopping only briefly to rest and water the horses but otherwise staying on the move and taking their noon meal in their saddles. The fact Lone still had some of Ma's sandwiches to share made this, as proclaimed by Arizona, not much of a hardship at all.

The day was cool, under a thin, pale cloud cover. A mild breeze gusted against their faces as they rode. It was of no particular consequence now in the daylight hours, but if it persisted after the sun went down and the temperature dropped, it would carry a more uncomfortable bite.

With their destination now a point more due west than the course Lone had originally started out on, the pair adjusted their aim accordingly. By day's close, they calculated, they would intersect with the North Platte River which, flowing out of the Laramie Mountains in Wyoming, passed just above the area they were bound for. Riding the rest of the way within the river valley would mean smoother terrain and generally easier going for the remainder of the trip. It would also provide plentiful water and greener graze for the horses, including the two claimed as spoils of war which Lone and Arizona intended to sell and split the profits on as soon as an opportunity presented itself.

As they rode, they talked some. They got more directly acquainted after hearing limited past mention of one another. They naturally swapped a few Buffalo Bill stories, and also spoke of a handful of other colorful characters they'd each had encounters with. Though generally given to solitude and not one to easily or quickly make friends, Lone found Arizona passable company and the talking helped keep his mind off the misery in his leg.

They reached the river before dusk, as anticipated, and followed it a ways farther until stopping to make night camp. After a simple supper that finished off the balance of the fare Ma Sharples had made up, Lone stripped below the waist and sat in the water at the river's edge, his leg extended out straight on a flat rock just under the surface, and let the lazy current of the North

Platte flow soothingly over his thigh wound for a half hour or so. When he climbed back out, Arizona doused the track of stitches thoroughly with whiskey to help keep any infection at bay and re-wrapped the thigh in strips of torn blanket.

That done, Lone thanked him sincerely for his ministrations, polished off what was left in the dousing bottle, then crawled into his bedroll and slept soundly the night through.

Next morning and throughout the ensuing day, his leg felt steadily less miserable.

On the third day after their late night encounter with Mase and Cully, Lone and Arizona crossed the North Platte and angled toward Robideaux's Trading Post. The terrain changed drastically as they moved along the northern fringes of Wildcat Hills, a spine of towering, jagged escarpments that marked the heart of a miles long stretch of volcanic ash deposits and limestone rock outcrops abruptly splitting open the undulating high plains grassland nearly to the western edge of Nebraska's panhandle. The eastern tip of these ridges and buttes was the distinct cone of Chimney Rock, a marker on the Oregon Trail recorded in countless diaries of emigrants passing within sight of it. Due north were the equally distinct mounds of Scotts Bluff, so named after the ill fate of an early trapper to the area and now the location of a sizable town.

"Always kinda amazes me," Arizona mused as he rocked back and forth in his saddle, "how this big change in the landscape happens so sudden-like. After miles and miles of rollin', treeless Sandhills, bam!—all at once it turns to this. Makes me think ol' Mother Earth must've got a bad belly ache one day way back when and upchucked this string of rubble from somewhere down deep as a way of gettin' relief."

Lone grinned. "That's an interestin' notion I never heard before. But accordin' to a scientist fella I spent some time around a while back, one of them college professors who was educated in the ways of Mother Earth when she was just a filly, the upchuckin' took place a lot farther west, maybe even out in what's now an ocean. Some big ol' volcano blew its top and spat hot lava and what not in all directions. Part of it splattered here and cooled into these formations we're lookin' at."

"Is that a fact? I'll be dogged."

"Then again, it ain't like he was exactly around to see it. So that makes it just the speculatin' of him and a bunch of other high-minded types cut from the same cloth." Lone shrugged and flashed another grin. "Comes right down to it, I like your speculatin' about equal."

"Well, however they got here, looks like we're gonna have a good chance to look 'em over and ponder it some more. The way those high cliffs and the pine trees sproutin' out of 'em are startin' to throw long shadows," Arizona said, pointing, "dusk is settlin' pretty quick. No way we're gonna make Robideaux's before full dark. I'm for pitchin' another night camp here, then finish ridin' in fresh come mornin'. What say you?"

Though the pain in Lone's leg had grown steadily more tolerable, a long day in the saddle still left him plenty sore and more exhausted than he ordinarily would have been. So calling a halt at this juncture certainly didn't sound unappealing to him. He signaled as much with a nod. "You got my vote. Go ahead and pick a spot."

"Lone."

Arizona's tone, conveyed in just that single spoken word, snapped Lone wide awake.

It wasn't very late. Still the early hours of darkness. A slice of moon was on the rise in a sky shot full of stars and hung with a few strung-out cloud wisps. The dying campfire, mostly coals but with a few small flames still licking up here and there, glowed between the two men. Lone lay stretched out atop his bedroll, propped against his upturned saddle, coffee cup dangling from the crook of a forefinger. He realized he'd dozed off that way, making small talk with Arizona as the two of them had sipped whiskey-laced final cups of coffee before turning in.

Arizona spoke again in a low whisper. "Somebody movin' around out there in the dark. Can't quite tell how close. Your big gray senses 'em too, he's been doin' some pawin' and snortin'."

"Got it," Lone whispered back.

Slowly he set aside the coffee cup then reached down and slipped the keeper thong off the Colt holstered on the gun belt he hadn't yet removed from around his waist. An eye flick to one side assured him his Winchester Yellowboy was leaning close by.

After that he just settled back against the saddle bottom and waited. Ears pricked sharply, making sure to avoid glancing at the glowing campfire coals in order to keep his vision adjusted to the night's murkiness.

It wasn't long before the clop of approaching horses' hooves grew discernible. Arizona held up three fingers, signaling that many riders. Lone nodded in agreement.

Moments later a gruff-sounding voice called out of the darkness. "Hello the camp!"

Lone gave it a beat then called back. "We hear you. What's your business?"

"Just three weary travelers caught out late," came the answer. "Saw the glow of your fire, was hopin' it might mean a friendly welcome and some hot coffee you'd be willin' to share."

"We can be friendly enough, long as it cuts both ways," Lone allowed. "Come ahead on in, show yourselves."

CHAPTER TEN

The three riders reverse-melted out of the darkness and into the faint glow of the fire. They were a hard looking crew, something not particularly uncommon to the area. Gaunt, unshaven, shadow-cut faces showing the ravages of weather and the accumulation of more than a few years under conditions that aged men fast. All dressed in standard, well-worn trail garb and each well-armed.

Lone and Arizona had risen to their feet and stood awaiting the newcomers. They positioned themselves on opposite sides of the dwindling fire, barely within its glow, rifles held casually in one hand, muzzles angled downward.

The riders reined up and regarded them with flat, emotionless expressions. The man in the middle was tall and rangy of build, with a blunt-featured though not unhandsome face, prematurely gray sideburns and bristly brows of the same color over narrowed slate eyes.

Those eyes bored into Lone for a long beat, and then his wide mouth spread into a crooked, toothy grin. "Lone McGantry. I'll be damned," he said. "Didn't expect to be runnin' into you out here in all this big empty."

"I been known to pass this way on occasion,"

Lone replied. "You're the one who's kinda far off your range, ain't you, Benton?"

"Some might say that," allowed the man referred to as Benton. "But any who really know me, know that I go where the wind takes me."

Lone matched Benton's crooked grin. "Especially if it's blowin' away from the latest posse ridin' your dust, right? Last I heard you was keepin' the chasers plenty busy down Kansas way."

Benton shrugged. "What can I say? I got a hankerin' for a change in scenery. Plus, I also got a crick in my neck from lookin' over my shoulder all the time. Those Kansas posses ain't worth beans a catchin' what they chase, but they're hellfire stubborn about not lettin' up. I wanted to come some place where I could look straight ahead for a while."

"As in ridin' the straight and narrow trail? You expect me to believe that?"

Before Benton could answer, the rider to his left spoke up. He was a whip lean specimen packing a brace of ivory-handled Remingtons in showy holsters—a case of overcompensation, Lone judged, meant to offset a pinched, pockmarked face made even homelier by stringy chin whiskers, bad teeth, and beady, ratlike eyes. "This proddy," he said, "has got an awful snotty mouth on him, don't he, Ford? You gonna just let him run it like that?"

Ford Benton shot him a displeased sidelong glance. "Comes to runnin' a mouth, how about puttin' the brakes on yours and lettin' me handle this? Thing to know is that this here is Lone McGantry; Indian fighter, ex-army scout, hunter, trapper, and so on and so forth. In other words, a fella who knows these high plains and other wild places like the back of his hand. The other hombre, if I ain't mistaken, is called by Arizona John Burke. Him I don't know so well, but from what I hear is cut from a similar bolt. And both, just incidentally, also happen to be old and close pals to Bill Cody."

Lone's eyebrows pinched together. "What's Col. Cody got to do with any of this?"

Benton gave an indifferent shrug. "Nothing in particular. We just heard the old buff hunter was recently seen out this way. And now, runnin' into you two, made me think maybe you was ridin' with him once again."

"Reckon you thought wrong," Lone said.

"That's too bad. You see, young Slim here"— Benton made a gesture to indicate the lean hombre who'd spoken up before—"is kinda excited at the chance to maybe meet him. He's heard all the yarns and read a bunch of those storybooks about Buffalo Bill. Been jealous as hell ever since I mentioned how I had firsthand dealin's with the old rascal a long time back."

"Uh-huh. Guess you're talkin' about the time,"

Lone drawled, "Cody lent a hand to Bill Hickock when he pinned back the ears of your older brother Ferlon and that bunch he was ridin' with down Abilene way."

Benton's slate eyes grew darker, turning almost black. "Don't push it, McGantry. I'm tryin' to keep this friendly."

"Trouble with that," Lone told him, "is we never been friends and ain't likely ever gonna be."

"Maybe so. But, just to keep the record straight, the only reason Hickock and Cody got the bulge so easy on my brother's outfit that time was because Ferlon was sick as a dog with whore's drip and the rest of his men turned yellow cowards. I was just a tag-along pup at the time, didn't even have a six-gun of my own, so I couldn't do nothing to stop 'em. Hickock and Cody gave me a kick in the pants and chased me off with a warnin' not to follow my brother's ways. I didn't, leastways never endin' up in prison. Ferlon died behind bars from the drip when they wouldn't bother to doctor him proper. I didn't get the chance to visit him, not even once."

Lone eyed Benton tight. "So now, after all this time, you're out for revenge on the colonel?"

"Nobody said a damn word about revenge or any such," Benton objected. "That spot of past trouble got brought up by you, not me. I only set the record straight on it. And the only reason we're talkn' about Cody at all is because, like I told you at the outset, we heard he's been seen in the area."

That's when Arizona spoke up, saying offhandedly, "That why you got a man prowlin' in the rocks over yonder? Thinkin' maybe Buffalo Bill got hisself lost somewhere in 'em?"

"I don't know what the hell you're talkin' about," Benton huffed.

"Okay. Then, if he don't belong to you," Arizona said in the same off-handed manner, "reckon you wouldn't object if I was to plunk a bullet in him the next time he silhouettes his clumsy ass against a pale cliff face."

When Arizona started to raise his rifle, Benton was quick to stop him. "Hold it, you crazy old coot! You'd shoot a man that recklessly, without even knowin'—"

"Out here, knowin' a critter is skulkin' behind you in the dark is all you need," Lone snapped. "If that bumblin' jackass had worked his way around much closer, I'd've spun and done him myself—without warnin' him *or* you. So if he *does* belong to you, call him off. Pronto. And if he's the best you got for a scout, you'd better start shoppin' for a replacement mighty quick. Before this one gets himself and half your crew buried."

Benton's mouth twisted into a grimace and he

sat rigid in his saddle for a long count. Then, abruptly, he called out, "Colby! Get your ass out here, and be quick about it!"

After an uncertain pause, there came the sounds of rustling bushes and boots scraping carelessly on rock surfaces, coming from a pool of deeply shadowed underbrush that ran along the base of a tall, weather-seamed and sun-bleached rock cliff rising at a point diagonally behind where Lone and Arizona had pitched their camp. Emerging from the deep shadows came a tall, solidly built man dressed in all dark clothing. His hat hung between his shoulder blades, suspended by its chin string, exposing a headful of longish, shaggy brown hair atop a plain-featured face currently wearing a half-sheepish, half-angry expression.

"Hear he comes now," muttered the man who sat his horse on Benton's right, an exceptionally wide-shouldered number with a thick torso and a flat-nosed, gimlet-eyed mug that bespoke of going more than a few rounds in a boxing ring at some point in his life, "Mr. *'I can sneak up on an Injun and steal the war paint off his nose without him ever knowing it.'*"

Colby, the dark clad man, faltered in his step and glared fiercely at the speaker. "Don't start, Tucker, or I swear—"

"Knock it the hell off, both of you!" Benton barked sharply.

The two men refrained from further comment

but continued glaring at one another. Until Benton spoke again, saying, "Go on and bring up your horse, Colby. Looks like we won't be sticking around for a cup of coffee after all."

"Whatever you say," Colby responded, looking contrite once again. "But before we turn heel on these hombres, you might want to ask 'em why just the two of 'em need four mounts."

"How's that?"

Colby jerked a thumb in the general direction of the bushes he'd emerged from. "Off to the side there. They got four horses picketed. And it ain't like two of 'em are pack animals. I saw saddles and gear that marks 'em all as hayburners for ridin'. Struck me as kinda curious."

Benton frowned thoughtfully. "Yeah, it is, ain't it?" Cutting his gaze back to Lone, he asked, "You expectin' company, McGantry? Or—" and here his eyes lifted and swept searchingly across the high rocks and heavy pine growth spread out behind Lone and Arizona "—have you got some of your own boys posted up there in those rocks?"

Lone smiled. "Why not ask your scout? Did he see any?"

"Damn it, McGantry, I'm askin' *you*," Benton declared. "Me and my boys rode in here with no ill will and have been nothing but civil. Yeah, I sent a scout out ahead to look things over, simply because it makes good sense to be cautious hereabouts. All the same, you been needlin' me the whole way, and I'm about sick of it. Now it's a simple question—what's with those extra horses?"

Lone's smile faded. "Okay, here's a simple answer. Why there's four horses over there is the business of me and my friend. Period. If you want to believe it might mean we got a couple more friends with rifles up in the high rocks—you know, on account of how it makes good sense to be cautious hereabouts—there's one sure way to find out. Otherwise, since you already figured out there ain't no coffee gonna be served here anymore tonight, I'd say the best thing is for you fellas to just ride on."

Apparently deciding he now had leave to run his mouth some more, beady-eyed Slim was quick to say, "He's bluffin' his ass off, Ford. He ain't got nobody up in those high rocks, he's just tryin' to squirm out of havin' four to two odds stacked against him."

"I agree with Slim," said Colby, still standing on the ground in front of the mounted Benton. "I heard what you said about those two being old friends with Cody. What if they showed up to deliver—"

"Shut up!" roared Benton.

Though the command was directed at his two men, all the while Benton's eyes—dark and menacing—were glaring straight at Lone. The latter met this with a flat, cool gaze and for several tense beats the scene was held in the grip of that silent stare-down.

Until, finally, Benton released a long, hissing sigh out through gritted teeth. "Okay, McGantry," he rasped, "me and my boys will go ahead and take our leave. But only because we got bigger fish to fry and ain't got time to waste on the likes of you. So you and your pal should take this as a stroke of good fortune and, at the same time, a piece of strong advice. Comes around that we find either of you standin' in our way again, consider any good will or understanding all used up. Be prepared for things to go very bad for you, no hesitation, no questions asked. Got it?"

"Plain enough," Lone responded, the flatness of his gaze never wavering. "But you and your boys understand as well. It cuts both ways."

CHAPTER ELEVEN

"Well. That was interesting," Arizona drawled after Benton's bunch had ridden off and the rataplan of their horses faded into the night. "You expectin' any more old friends to drop by—maybe for a late night snack or breakfast in the mornin'?"

"I hope to hell not," Lone grunted.

"Good. I'll hope right along with you. But, at the same time, I got a hunch we may not have seen the last of that outfit."

Lone made a sour face. "Wish I could say I feel otherwise. But Ford Benton showin' up anywhere seldom means good news and his leavin' never comes soon enough."

"I've heard his name here and there, but never ran directly afoul of him before. Makes me kinda itchy between the shoulder blades hearin' the skunk knew anything at all about me," Arizona said. "Seems like you have a kind of history. How about the others ridin' with him—know any of them?"

"All except the mouthy, skinny one he called Slim. He's a new addition," Lone replied. "The one with the punchin' bag face is Tucker Wald, a thug from the old Poison Rabbit street gang in New York City. He's a tough nut when it comes to close-in fighting, a puncher and a bonebreaker with his bare hands, also good with a knife and belly gun. Only so-so at longer range shootin'.

"The one who was clatterin' around in the rocks is Colby Strauss, who claims to be an all-round veteran of the frontier, a tracker and Indian fighter who supposedly was in on the fight against Cochise at the Battle of Apache Pass. I'll leave it to you to decide, based on what you saw and heard tonight, how long you think his stumble-footed ways would *really* have lasted in Apache land. But, apart from that, several reputable witnesses have sworn to his dead-nuts accuracy with a rifle at long distances."

Arizona lifted his brows. "Sounds like Benton has built hisself a small army with a wide-rangin' set of nasty skills. A gunslick in Benton himself, a bone-crusher in Wald, a crack rifleman in Strauss. And to round it out—since here's where I can provide a bit of background—one more fast gun in the form of Toledo Slim Bevins, the scrawny rat-face with a lip almost as quick as his gun hand. I saw him in action over in Laramie about a year ago, and he's the real deal when it comes to skinnin' leather."

"That's encouragin' to hear," Lone quipped. Then, cocking an eyebrow, he added, "But 'Toledo'?"

Arizona spread his hands. "That part I can't enlighten you on. It's what he chooses to call hisself and, so far as I know, nobody has ever took exception to it—especially not after seein' him draw."

"So that sums up what we know about our recent visitors as individuals," Lone said, gazing out into the darkness that had swallowed Benton and his crew. "But what do we know about what it is they're truly up to in this neck of the woods, and how might it tie in with the disappearance of Buffalo Bill?"

"You think they're responsible in some way?"

"No, I didn't get that read off 'em." Lone wagged his head. "But I think they have an awareness, a gut or an animal instinct you could say, that something big must be cookin' for the colonel to be clear out this way minus a lot of hoopla. That's got 'em puttin' their sniffers to the ground in case there might be some way they can benefit from it."

"But not just for revenge on account of Benton's brother?"

Lone shook his head again. "No, that was more Hickock's play. Cody was just backup. All they did was wound Ferlon anyway. It was the whore who infected him and the lousy care he got from the prison doctor that killed him. Besides, way I heard, young Ford traced down the whore and got his revenge on her a long time ago."

"Real brave."

"Yeah. But that don't make what he's grown into any less dangerous."

"So what I'm hearin'," Arizona said resignedly, "is that we oughta split standin' watch the rest of the night."

"Uh-huh. And every night from now on, leastways until we know a helluva lot more about what-all's goin' on than we do at this point."

"Okay. I'll go first, call you to spell me in a few hours." Arizona turned and looked up at the rocks and pine growth rising behind their camp. "Shit. Wish we hadn't been just bluffin' about already havin' a couple riflemen posted up there."

"Just be thankful they served their purpose as good as they did," Lone told him.

"You really think the risk of somebody actually bein' there is what made Benton turn tail?"

Lone shrugged. "Not entirely, I don't figure. Mostly, I expect it was what he said about his mind bein' on havin' bigger fish to fry. But every little bit helps, right? So tell our phantom pards thanks if you see 'em on your way crawlin' up."

CHAPTER TWELVE

They showed up in the pale gray half-light of pre-dawn.

Lone had intended to give it another half hour or so before descending down from his lookout post to stir up a breakfast fire and roust Arizona. He'd found himself a reasonably comfortable notch in some high rocks and had actually rather enjoyed the hours of solitude he spent there on watch. Other than a measure of stiffness or an infrequent stab of sharper pain if he stepped wrong, the discomfort in his leg was growing steadily more tolerable. A convenient fallen tree trunk that he was able to prop the leg up on for most of the duration of his watch helped keep it that way.

The air was crisp, filled with the scents of pine and cedar, the quiet of the wee hours broken only by faint nocturnal sounds—trees creaking intermittently, the flutter and occasional call of birds, the rustle of squirrels and other small mammals. In the distance, a pair of coyotes wailed back and forth to one another. Thankfully, the dark hours had included no evidence of any closer, more dangerous predators like the cougars that gave these Wildcat Hills their name.

But dangerous predators come in all shapes and species. Sometimes individually, sometimes in packs. Sometimes slithering on the ground, sometimes on four feet—sometimes on only two.

Lone suddenly caught movement out the corner of his right eye—a dozen yards over and slightly lower than his position. Making no other motion of his own, he rolled his eyes hard in that direction and studied intently. A small shadow disengaged from a larger one, a heavy cluster of pine bushes. Moving smoothly, silently, the small shadow glided out onto a flat-topped point of rock that jutted out twenty feet above and directly over Lone's and Arizona's campsite. Only when the shadow stretched out and lay flat did it take discernible shape against the bare, sun-bleached limestone. It was an Indian brave, identifiable even in the murkiness by his fringed buckskin breeches and the feathers thrusting out from his headband.

Though his gaze remained locked and his entire body poised, muscles clenched tight, Lone nevertheless allowed a low, silent exhalation to escape through his nostrils. As he continued to watch, the brave (almost certainly a Sioux) stayed flat and still, his own focus wholly on the camp below. One hand was clutching a rifle he had carried forward and placed alongside his prone body.

Lone frowned. What was this scoundrel up to? To the best of his knowledge, this portion of the Wildcat Hills was well outside any nearby reservation boundaries. But the former scout also knew it wasn't all that uncommon for some Indian men, especially the younger bucks, to roam wide in search of better fishing and hunting; or sometimes just for the hell of it, simply to be daring. And with Antoine Robideaux being licensed to trade with the Indians, latitude for travel between the close Box Butte reservation and his post was generally allowed.

In times of less unrest, such an allowance might be of little concern. But Lone's understanding of current conditions—namely, the tension building in both White and Red ranks due to the Ghost Dance movement, all fueled hotter by the added suspicion and blame flying around in the wake of the clumsy arrest attempt and alleged inadvertent killing of beloved Sitting Bull—seemed more like a time to tighten such standards.

But did this lone prowler fit into any of that? Whatever his motives, Lone couldn't see how his presence here at this hour—armed with a rifle—could mean anything good. So far, though, he wasn't re-positioning himself or bringing the rifle up in a way that indicated he meant to use it. At least not right away. But if he intended to harm the two men he perceived to be in the camp below (Lone having left his blankets rigged to look like a second sleeper was rolled up in them), then what better time than now when both appeared to be deep in slumber?

As Lone was rolling these thoughts around in his head, a fresh stirring of movement jerked his attention sharply to his left. Sure enough, he caught a glimpse of another feather-sprouting silhouette popping silently in and out of a clump of rock and piney brush. He wasn't in sight for very long, but long enough to confirm he damn well was there—fifteen yards away, on a level roughly even with Lone's position.

Things had just taken a turn for the worse. Two prowling braves now, converging on the camp in a pincer-like maneuver. That made it clear beyond doubt they were up to no good. Yeah, the first one hadn't been in any hurry to raise his rifle and start taking aim because he was waiting for his pal to get situated. And now he was.

Shit. Lone's mind raced, trying to make a quick decision on what was the best course of action for him to take. He could easily eliminate the brave exposed out on the rock point with one shot. But then how would the second, less visible one off to the left react? If he caught sight of Lone's muzzle flash and tried to return fire on him, that would be one thing—Lone would be ready for that. But figuring the second brave was also armed, what if he was already drawing a bead on the camp, down on a sleeping, unsuspecting Arizona, and he went ahead and retaliated by going through with opening fire in that direction? Arizona would be a sitting duck.

Lone swore under his breath. Top priority had to be doing everything he could to ensure Arizona's safety. If that meant only driving off the two threats and not getting a chance to cut down either of them, then that would have to do.

Having made that decision, Lone didn't spend any more time second guessing it. Leaving the Yellowboy at his side because it would be more unwieldy for the circumstances, he slipped the keeper thong from his Colt and drew it from its holster. For what he had in mind, everything was well within range of a handgun.

Rising up just slightly and extending his gun arm, he triggered two quick rounds down at the camp, bullets gouging into the dirt a couple feet to one side of Arizona's bedroll. In concert with the roar of the Colt, Lone hollered, "Take cover, pard! Dig!"

The former scout had time to see a response to his warning—Arizona flinging away his blankets and rolling/scrambling for a pool of shadows—before he twisted hard to his right, simultaneously swinging the Colt and pointing it toward the rock point where the first brave had appeared. But the red devil was smart and double quick. He didn't attempt trying to get a shot off, either at the camp or return fire on Lone. Instead, he simply rolled over and dropped off the far side of the point where he'd been stretched belly down, disappearing into inkiness.

Lone held off wasting a bullet on a lost cause, recognizing he now had a bigger concern by having given the brave off to his left time to take aim on his powder flashes. To counter that, he immediately dropped low and pressed himself back as deep into his notch as he could fit.

The expected bullet didn't come.

What did, however, preceded by a brief rattle of dislodged pebbles and a blood-curdling war whoop, was a human form crashing heavily down onto Lone after launching from the rocks only a few feet directly above him. The attacker—a third Indian prowler, obviously—swarmed over him furiously. Knees and feet drilled into the former scout. A hard, bony fist pounded down on the back of his neck and the side of his head. Clenched in the opposite hand, a knife slashed blindly, savagely, accompanied by loud grunts and curses in the Sioux tongue.

The notch Lone had pressed himself in for the sake of evading a potential bullet suddenly became a trap he was almost helplessly wedged into by the furious assault. At the same time, though, the tight confines of the space also hampered what could have been lethal swipes from his attacker's knife. The blade clicked and scraped on the rocky walls that pinched the brave's arms too tight to his body, preventing him from thrusting more accurately. Even still, Lone felt the stinging bite of three or four cramped, shorter jabs slicing him open on the chest and shoulder.

He finally got himself braced and with a desperate burst of power and an enraged roar, he shoved out from the inner point of the notch and bulled forward, ramming a shoulder into the stomach of the flailing brave and hurling both of them out of the confinement in an entangled struggle. The fallen tree trunk that Lone had been resting his leg on caught the brave across the backs of his legs and unbalanced him the rest of the way so that both men ended up tumbling to the ground. They quickly broke free from one another and scrambled to their feet. Once again Lone found himself facing a man with a knife while the Colt had been jarred from his grip. This time, however, he had enough separating distance and thereby enough time to reach across his waist and pull free his own knife—the ten-inch Bowie he carried sheathed on his left hip.

The brave's eyes widened at the sight of the Bowie. Not from fear, but rather a moment of surprise followed by a flash of excitement for the challenge it presented. At these close quarters and in the growing brightness of dawn, Lone could make out the Sioux's features reasonably well. He was young, not far into his twenties. Lean and hard muscled and agile. His gaunt copper face was stamped as indelibly as a cattle brand with deep, seething anger and hatred for this

White Man poised before him; and all Whites everywhere.

Lone recognized the look all too well. For a long time he had carried the same brand in reverse—a hatred for all Indians, in particular those of the Pawnee tribe as a result of one of their raiding parties killing his parents when he was just an infant and leaving him the lone survivor, an orphan eventually raised to bear the name "Lone" as derived from how he'd begun his life. In time, however, a variety of experiences and an accumulation of what he hoped was wisdom, had changed him some. Made him more understanding, more tolerant in situations where he previously never would have been. Men like Bill Cody—himself a former Indian fighter—taught him that not all Indians were automatically enemies. And then came times when he served with fellow scouts of Indian blood who'd proven as true and trustworthy as any man he ever rode beside.

But no amount of acquired wisdom or tolerance could ever offset a gut level retaliation from Lone McGantry when he felt sufficiently wronged or threatened, not by beast nor man of any color. And the blood now dripping from fresh cuts inside his ripped shirt and the renewed fiery pain in his thigh, accompanied by the warm, sticky wetness of more blood telling him the stitches had been torn open, had him in a very retaliatory mood.

Though he knew a smattering of the Sioux tongue, Lone chose not to use it as he glared at his attacker and snarled, "Okay, you little red bastard—you came to play, let's play. Looks like your pals have run like scalded dogs, so it falls to me and you to see it through. Come on, go ahead and try me face-on instead of jumping on my back like some hydrophoby squirrel!"

There was little chance the brave understood a word of this, but he surely understood the taunting tone. And it wasn't like he needed any egging on to begin with. So his response was to emit another war whoop and immediately lunge for Lone, this time having more room to brandish his deadly blade.

He was fast and he clearly had experience handling the weapon, but neither was Lone a stranger to knife fighting. He leaned away from the lunge and then immediately twisted at the waist and attempted a counter slash of his own as the brave's thrust extended him momentarily off balance. But he compensated amazingly fast and squirmed nimbly away. The Bowie grazed a fingernail's thickness above the Sioux's shoulder, coming that close to drawing blood.

The two men circled each other slowly, knees slightly bent, torsos leaning inward, eyes locked. The area out front of the notch Lone had tucked himself into for a lookout post was an elongated oval of gravelly, packed dirt running about ten feet crossways to the front of the notch and extending outward only six or so. The ten-foot span gave way at each end to walls of sloping higher rocks and foliage; except for a washed-out trough running down at a forty-five-degree angle from one corner (where Lone had ascended), the six-foot span ended at the edge of a cliff dropping sharply down onto a jumble of jagged rocks several yards below. In other words, the fighting arena for the knife duel underway had some very restrictive boundaries.

The brave lunged again. This time Lone parried and their blades locked, hilt to hilt, for a long moment before they pushed apart and went to circling again. Lone could feel sweat starting to drip along with the blood inside his shirt. But of more concern was the blood running into his boot from the re-opened stitches in his thigh. Damn! He couldn't afford to let this drag out. He had to finish it before the leg started to cramp too bad and the blood loss began dulling his reflexes. Plus, he wanted to know if Arizona was okay. In spite of his confident-sounding taunt, he couldn't be sure the other two Indians had indeed turned tail. The fact there was no further sign of either of them was promising, but that could change any second.

This time Lone made a thrust and it was the brave who parried. When their blades locked again, Lone instantly reached up with his left hand and clamped an iron grip on the wrist of the Sioux's knife hand. Before the brave had any chance to try and jerk free, the former scout dropped momentarily into a still lower crouch then leaned close and raised his shoulder suddenly, levering his opponent's arm across it and yanking down hard on the gripped wrist. Forced to bend in a way it was never intended to bend, the arm snapped loudly at the elbow and the accompanying sound that came out of the brave was no longer a war cry but rather a screech of pain.

Lone kept pulling down, trying to force the man to drop his knife. But the tough, stubborn warrior refused. Even in his agony, he continued to fight. With his free hand he reached around to claw at Lone's ear and attempt to gouge his eyes. Cursing, shifting his weight, Lone abruptly bent forward at the waist and jerked out as well as down on the arm. This lifted the brave's feet off the ground, dragging him up across Lone's back and flipping him through the air in a kicking, wailing somersault that ended with his back slamming flat on the ground. The impact of this was enough to finally break his hold on the knife.

But the Sioux still wasn't ready to give up. With most of the wind knocked out of him, he nevertheless half-rolled onto one hip and then, using his good arm, pushed shakily to his feet. Lone took a step and stood before him, feet planted wide, Bowie hanging loose at his side. He wagged his slowly, once to each side. A silent warning: Let it end here, kid.

Only the brave wasn't having any. Lone could see it in his eyes—hatred burning too hot, from a rage fueled too deep.

With his broken arm dangling limp, the Sioux took a moment longer to steady himself—then came once more in a rush! As he did so he swung his good arm out ahead, flinging into Lone's face and eyes a handful of dirt he'd scooped up when pushing to his feet. It was one of the oldest tricks in the book and, though it caused Lone to turn his head to one side for a split second, it counted for little else.

Another old trick, one for countering a bull rush like the one the brave was attempting, if you're bold enough and quick enough, is to wait until the last possible instant and then dodge out of the way. Lone executed such a maneuver smartly, for good measure throwing in a downward punch to the back of the brave's neck as he barreled past. The punch was meant to knock him down again and convince him to stay there. Though the blow landed solid, the recipient's forward momentum was too great for him to drop right away. He staggered on for several more steps. Too many. He reached the edge of the cliff drop-off and was unable to stop, plunging on over and falling to his death with a final defiant war cry.

CHAPTER THIRTEEN

When Robideaux's trading post came in sight, Lone and Arizona drew rein and sat their saddles for a minute, gazing down on it from the crest of a grassy hill that gave way to a shallow, valley-like expanse lying in between. The morning sun was fully risen now, everything bright and cool. A faint breeze stirred the high grasses where they weren't smothered by numerous, various-sized rock outcrops. The latter were scattered cast-offs from the central Wildcat Hills mass that rose and tumbled just to the south.

The buildings of the trading post lay at the southeast tip of a narrow gap—Robideaux Pass—that slashed through a continuing series of tall, ragged ridges where the mass continued on, curving north before expanding into an amoeba-like sprawl that included the escarpments of Scotts Bluff due north and Bald Peak off to the west. Weathered and faded to a dull gray color, with streaks of wind-polished silver, the mud-caulked cedar planks of the post's main building formed a sizable, solid-looking, L-shaped structure with a flat, heavy-beamed roof. A small barn with a corral behind it, both looking to be in good repair, stood close by. Other sheds and buildings strewn about, however, appeared to be in much poorer condition, some on the verge of collapse. Additionally, there were a half dozen Indian tipis interspersed among these.

"Been awhile since I was out this way. Old place has seen better days," Lone observed. His voice had a definite weariness to it and he sagged notably in his saddle.

Arizona cut him a sidelong glance, concern showing in his eyes. "Right about now," he said, "appearances are the least of what you oughta be worryin' about. Thing you need to be hopin' for most is that Robideaux's squaw wife ain't up and died or run off and left him. By all reports she's a plenty powerful Sioux healin' woman, and the shape you're in you need all the healin' power you can get."

"I've pulled through worse than this, and some of it out in the middle of hostile territory where I had to lay low and get by on nothing but my own nursin'," Lone grumbled.

"I believe you. It shows. You get many more cuts and seams carved into that hide of yours, you're gonna look like one of them jigsaw puzzles the kids play with, takin' 'em apart and fittin' 'em back together again."

"Thanks to you, I currently *am* fitted back together. Mostly. And I'll say again how grateful I am for it." Lone scowled. "I'll also say again how goddamn sick I'm gettin' of knife-swingin' hardcases showin' up to keep ruinin' my shirts and whittlin' off pieces of me. From now on, anybody—and I mean *anybody*—gives me even the slightest hint of a stinkeye, I'm gonna just haul off and ventilate the sonofabitch with a couple pops from my .44. I swear."

Arizona cocked an eyebrow. "Might seem kinda extreme to some folks. But I reckon a fella's got the right to look out for hisself."

"Damn straight."

"Speakin' of lookin' out," Arizona drawled, "you happen to notice how somebody's been glassin' us ever since we left camp a while back? I seen the sun glint off a lens—telescope or binocs, I reckon—two different times now."

"Yeah, I saw it, too."

"Guess it ain't unheard of for an Injun to have a spyglass, but I'd say it ain't real common neither. So you figure it's probably your pal Benton and his crew?"

"Most likely," Lone allowed.

"Figure he'll follow us down to the Frenchy's?"

Lone considered for a moment. "If it's Benton, I doubt he'd be in a hurry to press nose to nose against us again right away. I think he'd be more apt to hold back, believin' we ain't tripped to him shadowin' us, and watch to see where we go, what we do next."

"Come up with any notion yet on why he's takin' such an interest in us?"

"Can't say I have. But since his spyglassin'

must have shown him our new travelin' companion by now"—Lone jerked a thumb to indicate the body of the dead Sioux draped over the back of one of the confiscated horses they were leading—"I expect his interest oughta be perked up all the more."

After his encounter with the knife-wielding brave, Lone had descended back down to camp and found an anxious Arizona awaiting him. Thanks to the warning shots Lone had fired and the other two braves having subsequently fled without joining the attack, the old frontiersman was unharmed. Upon being jarred awake and bullet-chased out of his bedroll, he quickly got the message there was danger at hand. Though not knowing the exact nature of the threat, he'd rolled out gripping his Henry rifle. Trouble was, he found no target to use it on except for the brave he spotted fighting Lone up in the high rocks—and he couldn't get a clean shot at him due to Lone shifting in and out of his line of fire.

Once Lone won his battle and was back in camp, the focus on who had or hadn't fallen to harm quickly became clear and in no time Arizona was again at work sewing and re-sewing and otherwise patching up Lone's wounds. All during this, the patient, gripping his reclaimed Colt tightly in one fist, remained grimly alert and watchful for a potential return of the fallen brave's comrades, possibly with reinforcements. Why this didn't occur was something of a mystery, inasmuch as at least one of the flushed pair was known to be armed with a rifle and Lone and Arizona as they were currently involved made uncomfortably vulnerable targets. But, for whatever reason, they were left alone—and gratefully so.

Coffee, jerky, and several gulps of pain duller downed by Lone passed for breakfast. After that, as soon as the horses were watered and saddled, they were back on the trail to Robideaux's. The decision to bring along the dead Sioux had been made in hopes somebody at the trading post might be able to identify him, for the sake of notifying his family and also to perhaps get an idea of why he'd been on the prowl the way he was.

"Don't much like admittin' to sharin' a feelin' with the likes of Benton," Arizona said sourly. "But I got a perked up interest too—an interest in findin' out what kind of reception we got waitin' for us down yonder, and what we're gonna be able to learn when we get there."

"Only one way to find out," Lone responded. "Let's ride down and see. What we came for, ain't it?"

Ford Benton lowered the spyglass he'd been peering through and frowned. "Yeah, they're goin' on to Robideaux's place. Just like we figured last night they must be headed for."

"But what about the dead Indian?" said Colby Strauss.

"What about him?" Benton snapped. "He's a dead damn redskin. Good riddance, that's what I say about him!"

"But why would they be haulin' him in with 'em?" Strauss persisted. "Those shots we heard just before dawn must have been when they tangled with him. He likely gave 'em cause, same as that pack of feather-heads who jumped us the other day did, after we'd already been set back on our heels by the hellcat who showed up out of nowhere. But knowin' how tensions are already strung banjo tight between Injuns and Whites all through this territory, why would any White Man parade around advertisin' they'd capped one of the devils? That's a sure way to fan the flames on both sides, maybe even serve as an advertisement for wantin' to get your hair lifted. Plain don't seem smart."

Toledo Slim sneered. "Maybe they ain't smart. Maybe they're plain dumb."

"No." Benton gave a shake of his head. "I told you I've had run-ins with McGantry in the past. And I've heard plenty more about him outside of my own dealings. I don't know why he's haulin' in that stupid Indian, but dumb he ain't. Just like him and Burke bein' old pals with Cody and now, out of the blue, the two of 'em showin' up in the middle of everything else that's goin' on around here ain't no simple coincidence."

"If they ain't been out this way lately, maybe they don't know how dicey things stand hereabouts," suggested Tucker Wald.

"But if they're fetchin' those spare horses to try and help Buffalo Bill get clear, like we suspect," said Strauss, "then they must have been notified somehow. And if they got enough notification for that, they should've got filled in on the rest of it too, don't you think?"

"What I think," grated Wald, "is that if your clumsy ass hadn't blown everything last night by stompin' around in those high rocks like a three-legged buffalo, then you could have stuck around for some up-close spyin' after the rest of us rode off—like was planned—and overheard enough about what they was up to to be *tellin'* us some things instead of only throwin' out questions."

Strauss's eyes flashed. "You want me to tell you something, Wald? How about I tell you to kiss my ass! If you think it's so stinkin' easy to—"

"God *damn* it, will you two knock it off!" Benton twisted around in his saddle and glared fiercely at the two men. "We're poised on the brink of the biggest-payin' job ever to come our way—maybe bigger than anything we could've ever imagined. Yet you two keep bickering like a couple of hog farm whores tuggin' on opposite ends of the same blanket.

"Well, you're *not* on opposite ends! We're all in this together. Yeah, we had a couple of missteps, first from the hellcat who caught us by surprise and then the ragtag redskins who poked their noses in right after. But ain't none of it that we can't get turned around. We know we trimmed Cody's horns pretty damned good in the process, too, and he can't have gone very far since. So I sure as hell ain't ready to give up, not on something this big." Benton paused and his glare turned to red-hot coals. "And I double-damn sure ain't willin' to let it slip through my fingers, especially not on account of men who've rode the river with me and I thought I could count on."

Wald and Strauss both hung their heads like scolded children.

Until Wald mumbled, "Dang it, Ford. You know we won't let you down."

"Same for me, Ford," Strauss added softly. "Same as Tucker said."

The heat never cooled in Benton's eyes. "Good. I'd hate to have to put a bullet in one or both of you if I thought otherwise. I'd hate it, but I'd do it in a heartbeat before I risk lettin' this opportunity be pissed away."

CHAPTER FOURTEEN

All at once, Lone was awake.

Feeling momentarily disoriented and uncertain of his surroundings, however, he made no sudden movement. Slowly, he slitted his eyes open and looked around. He was lying on a cornstalk mattress on a narrow cot in a small, dimly lighted room. There were two long curtains hung over the doorway and vertical bands of brighter light seeped through the seam that separated them and also along the edges of the door frame. The smell of tobacco and cook fire smoke hung in the air, mingled with a variety of other scents that were unfamiliar—though not unpleasant—to Lone.

Voices came from the other side of the curtains. Two men talking. One spoke with a French accent, the other was Arizona Burke. Okay. Sure. Lone started remembering more about how he'd ended up in the room. More about how he got here maybe, but not everything between then and now.

Not long after he and Arizona had arrived at Robideaux's trading post and gotten past the obligatory greetings followed by some jawing to explain the dead brave they brought with them, Robideaux's Sioux wife, Shining Water, had taken a quick look at Lone's injuries then promptly shooed him into this back room where she commenced tending to them. She started by making him drink a big mug of a tea-like brew that thankfully tasted much better than it smelled. Whatever it was, it was a hell of a lot more potent and effective than the pain duller whiskey he'd been gulping and it had him beginning to feel loopy even before the mug was empty. As if drifting in and out of a fog, he recalled being laid on his back while a warm, thick salve was smeared liberally on his lacerations, big and small. After that, the fog swirling steadily thicker, he had a vague recollection of Shining Water kneeling beside his cot with a simmering, smoking pot in her hands. She placed the pot under the end of the cot, directly beneath Lone's head. The smoke lifting up out of the pot mixed with the tea fog he was already wrapped in and together they took him to a place he only just now had returned from.

Lone pushed up on an elbow and then swung his feet over the side of the cot. Somewhat surprisingly, considering his memory of how the tea had affected him, he felt quite awake and alert. What was more, the soreness in his various wounds, including the re-torn and re-stitched slash on his thigh, was far less than he would have expected.

Looking down, he saw that the thigh was wrapped snugly in layers of what appeared to be thin sheets of some kind of treated animal skin. He also saw that, except for a leather breechcloth, he was naked. Looking around, his eyes having adjusted to the dimness of the room, he spotted his boots standing on the floor in front of a nearby wooden stool. Resting on the seat of the stool was his gun belt, complete with holstered Colt and sheathed Bowie, and his Winchester Yellowboy leaned against the wall just behind. At least, Lone thought, the closeness of these made him feel a little less naked.

But still . . .

Turning his face toward the curtained doorway, he called through to the other side, "Hey, Arizona! You see a pair of empty britches anywhere out there, bring 'em in here to me, will you?"

The curtains parted a minute later and Arizona stepped through with Antoine Robideaux right behind him. Arizona was grinning, Robideaux wasn't. The Frenchman, by Lone's reckoning, had to be pushing seventy. The years showed on his narrow, leathery face but otherwise he carried his banty rooster frame with a spryness, even a bit of a cocky strut that further meshed with the barnyard bird he made Lone think of. His attire—wide-collared white shirt, ornate vest, big red sash around his waist, and dark brown trousers tucked into calf-high moccasin boots—added even more swagger to his appearance.

Arizona paused only a few steps into the room.

His grin widened above the pile of neatly folded clothes he was holding in his upturned palms. "Well look at you," he said. "I swear, you're wearin' more of Shining Water's healin' salve than you are clothes. Stick a feather in your hair to go with that leather flap hangin' over your onions, you could pass for a runaway off the rez."

Lone made a sour face. "Real funny. Are those clothes for me?"

"They are. All supplied brand new by our host and his lovely wife who declared no amount of washin' or mendin' could save the ones you was wearin' when you came in, on account of 'em bein' too bloody and cut up."

"Well that's mighty generous," Lone said. He shifted his gaze to Robideaux. "I'm obliged. And also to your wife. Where is she, by the way? I'd like to thank her in person for her care to my injuries."

"She is gone on an errand and will not be back until near evening. It is certain she will want to check on you as soon as she returns," replied Robideaux. "You can thank her with praise for her healing skills and that will be quite sufficient. Me on the other hand, for the clothes M'sieur Arizona is presenting you"—and here the Frenchman's face finally showed a smile, spreading wide under his pencil thin mustache—"you can thank with reimbursement subtracted from the price we negotiate for my purchase of the horses and saddles you brought in. Is that not fair? Friendship is a wonderful thing, you understand, but when one has a business to run there are certain boundaries that must be maintained."

Lone grinned. "I understand perfectly, you old pirate. You'll do your damnedest to lowball us on what you pay for the horses then turn around and gouge me on what you charge for the clothes. That what you got in mind?"

Robideaux slapped a hand to his chest. "I am wounded!"

"No, that's my department," Lone countered dryly. "But you know what? Your wife did such a fine job of fixin' me up—finishin' what Arizona did to get me this far—I'm feelin' too good to squabble with you. I'm okay with whatever you and Arizona hash out on the horses and clothes. In fact, you can go ahead and do that while I'm gettin' cleaned up and into those duds."

Now Robideaux's smile turned into a frown. "Refusing the challenge of barter is a great disappointment. I will let you have time to reconsider while I go get some hot water so you can wash off the excess salve before donning your new clothes. Shining Water said to tell you to be sure not to remove the wrap from your thigh."

When the Frenchman had disappeared back through the curtains, a freshly grinning Arizona said to Lone, "I think you hurt his feelin's more by sayin' you was in no mood to haggle than you did by callin' him a pirate."

"Just tellin' the truth, that's all. In both cases."

Arizona placed the pile of clothes on the cot beside Lone then took a seat on the nearby stool after removing the gun belt and putting it on the floor next to the boots. Letting the grin fade and bringing an earnest gaze to rest on Lone, he said, "Speakin' of bein' hurt—how you doin', hoss?"

"All things considered, pretty damn decent," Lone told him. "I don't know what Shining Water treated me with, but it was mighty potent. How long was I out anyway?"

" 'Bout three, four hours."

Lone lifted his brows. "That ain't too bad. Felt like it must have been longer. You learn anything while I was under?"

"Oh, yeah. Antoine filled me in pretty thorough. Seems we've rode smack into a hornet's nest."

"Kinda expected that. In a way, we even hoped for it, didn't we?"

"Well in that case, we got our wish. And our decidin' to haul in that brave you killed ain't doin' nothing to calm down the buzzin'." Arizona paused long enough to hitch forward on his stool before adding, "But the good news in the midst of it all is that we were right about Col. Cody showin' up here. He did, and not so very long ago."

Needless to say this heightened Lone's attention. Before Arizona could continue, however, Robideaux came back in. He was carrying a steaming pitcher in one hand and a tall coffee pot in the other. Two tin cups also dangled by their handles from one of the fingers of the hand holding the coffee pot.

"Here is the hot water I promised," he announced. "I also brought fresh coffee I thought you might enjoy. And cups for you both." He carried these items over and sat them on a small stand positioned diagonally across one corner. "Help yourselves to the coffee. Then there is a wash basin, soap, and towels on a shelf below here."

"Much obliged. Again," said Lone.

Robideaux turned back to the doorway. "I will leave you alone for now. When you are ready, just come out. My oldest daughter will have a lunch prepared. After you've eaten, we will then barter about the horses and clothes."

Lone's mouth twisted wryly. "Okay. You win. Hard to be stubborn in the face of so much hospitality. But don't think that means I'm gonna go easy comes to the hagglin' then—remember, you insisted on it."

CHAPTER FIFTEEN

Once Robideaux had again left the room, Arizona poured cups of coffee for him and Lone then sat sipping from his while Lone proceeded to start rinsing off the excess salve from his body and otherwise getting washed up. When Arizona took a whiskey flask from the folds of his shirt and asked Lone if he wanted a splash of it added to his cup, the former scout declined, saying, "No. Whatever that grog Shining Water poured into me was, it's still doin' its job. This coffee is fine just the way it is."

There was no denying that the Indian woman's treatment of his injuries had Lone's discomfort level greatly diminished. Almost astonishingly so. Though standing and bending over the wash basin brought occasional pangs of pain, mostly to his thigh, they were fleeting and of no great consequence. Even the weakened feeling from blood loss that he'd noticed earlier during the ride from their night camp to the trading post seemed largely restored. None of which was to say he was in a hurry to engage in another round of hand-to-hand combat with anybody, but the recuperative strides he'd made in such a short amount of time were nevertheless noteworthy.

"So," Lone said as he began rinsing soap suds

from his face and other parts of his body, "let's get back to you tellin' me about the hornet's nest we rode into. And, more importantly, how long ago did Cody show up here and does Robideaux know where he headed next?"

"Okay. First the hornet's nest," Arizona responded. "Like you said, I guess that shouldn't come as a surprise. The spread of the Ghost Dance movement—especially the revved up version Kicking Bear brought back from Nevada—is spreadin' through the Dakotas and down here into western Nebraska like a wind-whipped prairie fire. And the murder of Sitting Bull, no surprise, has only fanned the flames hotter.

"Now. Since Kicking Bear originally got sent by Sitting Bull out from the Standing Rock rez up in North Dakota and that's also where Sitting Bull ended up gettin' killed, you might figure that'd be the main hot spot for things."

"Seems reasonable," Lone allowed.

"Uh-huh. Thing is, it turned into *too hot* of a spot for some of those involved. We already knew about how Major Laglen's stubbornness when it came to clampin' down on Sitting Bull as what he saw to be the main way for puttin' an end to the Ghost Dancers backfired on him and put him under pressure from his higher ups when the old chief got killed."

Lone made a sour face. "Yeah, and we saw a pretty clear example of how Laglen's tryin' to wiggle out from under at least part of that pressure by the hounds he sent after North and Powell, and then me."

Arizona took a drink of coffee then said, "By the sound of it, they may not be the only hounds he sent out to try and save his ass. What's more, it happens there's another fella feelin' a squeeze brought on by the Ghost Dance craziness and the killin' of Sitting Bull."

All washed and dried now, Lone turned back to his cot and began sorting through the clothes supplied for him to get dressed in. "Keep goin'," he told Arizona.

"The second fella I'm speakin' of is none other than Kicking Bear, the young sub chief who reported back from his visit with Wovoka havin' a whole different take—for reasons nobody has quite been able to put a finger on—as to how the whole Ghost Dance thing is supposed to work." His brows pinching together, Arizona gave a puzzled shake of his head. "It's the damnedest thing. Accordin' to Robideaux, even while Kicking Bear's notion is growin' more and more popular on one hand, on the other there's those who blame him for playin' a part in Sitting Bull's death by drawin' harder attention from Major Laglen. Upshot bein', Kicking Bear seems to've dropped out of sight for a while until tempers sort of level off. And where do you reckon some folks suspect he's gone to ground?"

Lone's head popped out of the collarless cotton shirt he'd just pulled on. He scowled in thought for a moment as he shoved his arms through the sleeves, and then he saw what Arizona was dangling. "Somewhere around here, you sayin'?"

"That's right. Namely, a healthy little stretch of real estate called the Wildcat Hills."

"That's a healthy stretch alright."

"Keep in mind it's only a suspicion. But it's a strong enough one to have sent the colonel and Pony Bob Hallam off to check it out. The colonel's thinkin' was if he could catch up with Kicking Bear and have a sit-down with him, a pow-wow like he was plannin' with Sitting Bull, maybe he could get the straight of where this warlike angle to the Ghost Dance came from. And then maybe find a way to convince the young hothead, especially now that he's bein' hit with some backlash, to tame it back down more like Wovoka's original vision before things turn into another bloody war the Injuns can never win."

Lone grinned wryly. "Buffalo Bill never thinks small, does he?"

"Wouldn't be Buffalo Bill if he did."

"How long ago did him and Pony Bob head out?"

"Three days. Nary a peep since. Not from them, nor any direct sign of Kicking Bear neither. Not unless you're inclined to count our visitors from last night, that is."

"What's that supposed to mean?" growled Lone, growing slightly annoyed at Arizona's habit of circling around a point before finally getting to it.

"Means that Robideaux's oldest son, Trace they call him, recognized the Sioux brave we brought in as bein' from one of the villages on the Box Butte rez just north of here," Arizona answered. "It's well known, you see, that the suspicion or rumor or whatever you want to call it about Kicking Bear goin' to ground in the Wildcats has spread through the villages on the rez. And a lot of younger bucks in 'em—you can picture the kind, the restless ones champin' at the bit to challenge traditions and the word of the elders every chance they get—have made no attempt to hide their eagerness to want to throw in direct with Kicking Bear. To protect him if need be, and also help push his version of the Ghost Dance. The elders have so far kept it from the local agent and for sure from the cavalry detail now stationed in the area, but a lot of those bucks ain't been seen for a while."

Lone said, "So that suggests the three we tangled with were probably some of the renegade pups who jumped out of limits."

Arizona made a catch-all gesture. "Seems likely. I'm guessin' they must have seen the light of our campfire durin' the night, or maybe just smelled the smoke. In any case, something drew 'em to us. And even though we were way the hell out on the fringes of the hills, us just bein' there was enough to make 'em decide we might pose a threat to Kicking Bear so they closed in."

"Damn young fools," Lone muttered.

"Like we ain't all been there at one time," Arizona grunted. Then he continued, "The reason Robideaux's wife is away right now is that she's accompanyin' their son returnin' the dead brave to his village. They both know the family. Though I don't see where there's much doubt, their visit will confirm whether or not the deceased was one of the bucks known to have skipped out. If so, it won't help the family's grief any but they'll have to lay at least part of the blame for what happened to him on his own actions."

Lone gave the old frontiersman a look. "You really think that'll make much difference on where they lay the brunt of the blame?"

"No. 'Course not. Why do you think I said at the outset that our haulin' in the dead buck didn't do nothing to calm the buzzin' of the hornet's nest we rode into?"

Lone stood up and began buttoning his new britches about his waist. "Come to reflect on it, you also said something about Major Laglen sendin' out more hounds to cover his ass. And just a minute ago you mentioned a cavalry detail stationed nearby. How many goddamn hornets are in this nest we're bumpin' up against?"

"Plenty. And the rascally ol' nest kicker we came lookin' for is burrowed right in the thick of 'em. All we gotta do is find him, dig him out, then yank him clear without gettin' our asses stung off."

CHAPTER SIXTEEN

Emerging from the back room, with Lone now outfitted in new duds anchored by his own comfortable boots and the added comfort of his gun belt strapped back in place, he and Arizona were directed to a cloth covered dining table in an add-on alcove that jutted out from one end of the store's main central area. The latter boasted a wide array of supplies filling nearly every inch of floor space, not to mention numerous counter tops and wall shelves. Once seated, they were served lunch by Robideaux's daughter, a pretty, copper-skinned lass of seventeen or so with striking eyes and long, lustrous black hair. The Frenchman joined them for the simple but delicious meal of roast pork, seasoned greens, fresh-baked bread, and tall glasses of cold buttermilk.

While they ate, Robideaux helped Arizona fill in some remaining details about the tense status of things locally as well as related matters ranging across a wider swath of the territory. Though his input came largely from second hand reports, the sources for these had been culled and refined over many years, giving Robideaux trust in the reliability of what he passed on.

The 30-man cavalry detail stationed halfway between the trading post and the Box Butte reservation was out of Fort Robinson from up north, and had been in place for less than a week. It was under the command of one Lt. Gregory Reeves and had been sent in response to the rumors of Kicking Bear being on his way to the area and the escalation in tensions it was expected this might cause.

"I had some dealin's with Lt. Reeves up Deadwood way a number of months ago," Lone replied to this news. "At the time he was under the command of Capt. Red Trimball, a fella I first served with back durin' my scoutin' days. Good man. From what I saw, Reeves seemed a competent and reasonable sort as well."

"Oui. That also fits my impression of the lieutenant," agreed Robideaux. Then, the corners of his mouth quickly turning downward, he added, "Unfortunately, I cannot say the same for his second in command—quite an opposite specimen by the name of Sgt. Skinner."

Lone shook his head. "Don't know that I ever ran into him."

"Consider yourself lucky," said Arizona sourly. "I butted heads with that loud-mouthed, foul-tempered jackass just a couple weeks ago when I was layin' over at Fort Robinson, like I told you about. Malachi Skinner. Can't handle his liquor, which is why he keeps gettin' busted back in rank, and he hates all Indians except for the young, vulnerable females he's able to dazzle with cheap trinkets in order to have his way with, then sobers up and berates and humiliates 'em because he hates himself for layin' with what he calls 'red trash whores.'"

"Sounds like a real charmer," Lone grated. "Surprised he's still got his head, let alone his scalp."

"Day's comin'," Arizona muttered ominously.

"I hope it does not happen during his time here," Robideaux said, his frown deepening. "I hope that for many reasons, but among them is the fact there are already too many Whites in the area who mistrust and dislike me for trading with the Sioux. Much as Sgt. Skinner might deserve a harsh comeuppance, that kind of thing happening now would not only inflame the whole territory but, for me personally, would likely force the closure of my business. I am too old to uproot and start over. I would end up finishing out my days on the reservation with my wife and her family."

"Sorry to hear you'd be facin' that after all the years you've stuck it out providin' necessities to folks venturin' this way," said Arizona earnestly. "But knowin' your wife's family would be there to take you in ain't all bad is it?"

"Not entirely, no. But still far from desirable. On the other hand, having a young, impressionable daughter of my own"—and here the old Frenchman's gaze drifted to rest fondly on his fetching daughter as she went about her chores in the other room—"the remotest hint of the possibility that pig of a sergeant might look at my Tomeeka and even *think*..."

"Hey, let's back up a corn row or two," Lone interjected when Robideaux's words trailed off. "Apart from veerin' off on a thing too disturbin' to dwell on and something we ain't about to let happen, we're also roamin' pretty far off course from our main purpose for bein' here. If we're able to run down Col. Cody—and maybe help flush Kicking Bear in the process—then all the quicker we can send those soldier boys and their piece of crud sergeant back to Fort Robinson and off Robideaux's doorstep."

Arizona grinned. "You ain't careful you're gonna start soundin' as big-thinkin' as Buffalo Bill, and makin' the doin' seem as easy as in one of those wild Buntline yarns."

Lone blinked with mock innocence. "You mean some of those yarns ain't the Gospel?"

"Only as preached by Ned Buntline," Arizona told him. "And while his sermons might be entertainin', I wouldn't count on 'em guidin' you particularly close to the Pearly Gates."

Maintaining his somberness in the face of this bit of banter, Robideaux said, "There is no doubt that assuring the safety of Col. Cody is of great importance. I tried my best to discourage him and Pony Bob from ever venturing into the Wildcat

Hills. My greatest fear, you see, was not that he might encounter Kicking Bear. No, that would actually be the preferred thing. Because Kicking Bear had been mentored by Sitting Bull and well knew of the friendship and respect between the old chief and Cody, I think he would at least meet with the colonel and not be in a hurry to do him harm.

"But, in the first place, I am not fully convinced Kicking Bear is even in those hills. Whether he is or not, should Cody and Pony Bob run into a pack of the young hot-bloods who *have* assembled there—such as the ones you two encountered—then I fear the result might be far different. It is entirely possible the bloodthirsty young fools would not even recognize Cody, or go ahead and do him harm even if they did. The fact you report they have rifles will no doubt embolden them even more, making it increasingly worrisome."

"*Some* of the bucks up in those hills have rifles," Arizona amended. "Far as what me and Lone can say, only one for certain sure. Still strikes me as curious that neither the one with the rifle nor the other one Lone spotted sneakin' up on our camp ever followed through after the third one jumped Lone. Leaves me thinkin' they only had the one gun amongst 'em and it wasn't enough to give those other two the courage to stick with the fight once they lost their advantage of surprise."

"That may be," Robideaux allowed. "And it is somewhat more encouraging to hear they may not *all* have firearms. Still, they are sufficient in number even with just traditional weapons to be of considerable danger—to Cody as well as others."

"You don't have to convince me of that," Lone said wryly. "It boils down all the more for us needin' to find the colonel and gettin' him the hell out of there."

"What about that cavalry detail?" Arizona asked. "Do they know about the colonel goin' up in there? Are they plannin' to go in themselves—after him or Kicking Bear, either one?"

Robideaux shook his head. "When Cody heard there was an army detail close by, he wished for them not to know of his presence. In fact, I believe it hastened his decision to go in search of Kicking Bear. As for the soldiers proceeding in direct pursuit of Kicking Bear, my understanding is that their orders for the time being are to hold and observe and to engage in action only in the event of an outbreak of violence."

"That sounds typical for some desk-bound commander packin' more stripes than savvy," Arizona snorted derisively. "Send men out with orders to hold their fire until the other side opens up first. Play it fair and noble, even at the cost of more lives."

"This is one time I'm kinda glad they are

playin' it that way," said Lone. "If we go in after the colonel we're gonna be plenty busy as it is, dodgin' hot-bloods and tryin' to cut sign you can bet Cody and Pony Bob will have done their damnedest to mask. We don't need to be worryin' about trippin' over soldier boys to boot."

"Can't find no fault with that thinkin'," Arizona allowed. "Trouble is, havin' no soldier boys to trip over may still not be the end of it."

Lone started to question his meaning, but then abruptly remembered. "Major Laglen sendin' out more hounds from up Standing Rock way. That what you mean?"

"As a possibility, yeah," Arizona answered. "That's the talk, right, Antoine?"

"The talk, yes. Another rumor floating on the wind," Robideaux conceded. "While also another I am not fully convinced of, at the same time the reports persist of Major Laglen's increasing desperation to salvage his reputation and possibly career. So one cannot simply dismiss what a person in that position might resort to."

"I like the thought of him doin' plenty of squirmin'," Arizona said. "Thing I don't quite get, though, is what he figures to gain by sendin' men down here."

"Two things, the way I see it," Lone responded. "We know how much trouble Laglen went to, pullin' political strings and what not, to stonewall Col. Cody's attempt to meet with Sitting Bull.

Since that ended up turnin' to shit, the last thing he wants now is for Cody to meet with Kicking Bear and maybe still have some success gettin' him and his Ghost Dance notions tamed down some. That'd make the major look even worse. I'm not sayin' he's desperate enough to try and kill the colonel or anything, but he has even more at stake now than he did before to get him out of the way. And if Cody comes up totally empty, it'll leave him lookin' more like what a lot of folks suspected from the start—that he's just a foolish old gas bag seekin' show biz publicity and one more piece of past glory. Plus, anything he says to defend himself against Laglen's shenanigans will make *him* appear the desperate one."

"Such a thing we cannot allow!" declared Robideaux.

"Yeah, that's kinda the whole point of me and Lone bein' here," Arizona reminded him.

"The other thing Laglen could be aimin' to gain by sendin' men this way," Lone continued, "is obviously tryin' to get his hands on Kicking Bear. Since he needs so bad to control how things get presented, he'd want to avoid any direct involvement from other commanders like Niles up in South Dakota or Hassett at Fort Robinson—jurisdictions be damned."

Arizona snorted. "Like any of them would want to cooperate with that snake anyway!"

"Maybe not. But don't ever think they wouldn't

like to get their own hands on Kicking Bear," Lone told him. "So let's jump back to the hombres Laglen might be sendin'. Last time, for the ones who showed up in North Platte, you had names and backgrounds on each of 'em, Arizona. Rumor or not, have either of you"—his eyes cut back and forth between Arizona and Robideaux—"heard anything in the way of identities for this new batch?"

Before he got any kind of answer in words, Lone could see on the faces of the pair that neither had anything.

The best Arizona could come up with was, "Whoever they are, if there's any truth to the rumor at all, the only thing you can count on is that they won't be out of regular soldier ranks. Just like Cully and Mase and the others, they'll be hardcases who made the mistake of gettin' out of line somehow and then made the worse mistake of lettin' that give Laglen leverage over 'em. And you already got a taste of how determined and dangerous owlhoots operatin' under pressure from Laglen can be."

The muscles at the hinges of Lone's jaw bulged visibly. "Yeah. And I also recently got a taste of how determined and dangerous a hot-blood buck operatin' under the spell of Ghost Dance promises can be. Makes our hike up into the Wildcats takin' shape as a real interestin' picnic, don't it?"

"These names you mention I do not recognize. However, I do recognize the kind of men you are describing," said Robideaux. "They pass through from time to time, stopping briefly for supplies, often in a hurry to move on and clearly avoiding the larger selections and other attractions of Scotts Bluff where there are also the watchful eyes of lawmen."

Lone cocked a brow. "Speakin' of such, you seen any men like that lately? In particular, four of 'em—hard-lookin' and heavily armed, led by a tall, rangy hombre with whitish hair and flinty eyes? The others might've called him 'Ford'?"

"Oui," Robideaux said with a nod. "They were here only a few days ago. Same as usual, wanting supplies and then to move on. They did ask about any Indian trouble in the area, seeming a little anxious about that."

"Were they here when Col. Cody was?"

"No. No, they came and went before he and Pony Bob arrived." Robideaux gave the answer but then his mouth pulled tight, considering, before he added, "Though the four did leave only a very short time ahead of the colonel. They weren't here inside the store at the same time, but it's possible they may have encountered each other on the outside."

"And while the four hardcases were here, did they mention or ask about Cody in any way?" Lone wanted to know.

The Frenchman's head wagged. "No, not at all."

Arizona scowled. "You ain't thinkin' that Benton and his bunch might be the ones sent by Laglen, are you?"

Now it was Lone's turn to shake his head, a firm back and forth motion. "No. That don't seem at all likely, or even possible. Benton's only recently up from Kansas, I don't see how there can be any connection between him and the major. Except for 'em both havin' an interest in Cody. We know the why of that when it comes to Laglen, but what the hell is Benton up to?"

Before anybody could venture a response, the attention of all three men seated at the table was suddenly drawn by the sound of heavily clumping boots and loud voices confronting Robideaux's daughter, Tomeeka, out in the main store area.

Robideaux quickly rose to his feet, saying, "Excuse me, I must go see what this is all about."

CHAPTER SEVENTEEN

"Well, well. Here's the Frenchy himself. Finally showing up to take care of some of his own business, instead of leaving it to his pretty little daughter or wife and son."

This was the greeting Robideaux got as he approached the sales counter out in the center of his store. It came from a barrel-chested, bow-legged man standing before the counter, feet spread wide and meaty fists planted on his hips. He wore a U.S. Cavalry uniform with sergeant stripes on its sleeves. Sergeant Malachi Skinner. Just short of forty, with a fleshy, florid face shot full of tiny scarlet veins flaring out from either side of a bulbous nose and reaching across bloated cheeks. The classic signs of a heavy drinker, backed up by the murkiness in his eyes. Eyes that, behind the murkiness, darted restlessly, quick and suspicious, and containing an unmistakable spark of innate meanness.

"What are your interests here today, Sergeant?" Robideaux inquired in a cordial, businesslike manner.

Behind the counter, his daughter appeared visibly ill at ease though somewhat relieved by the arrival of her father. The two soldiers flanking Sgt. Skinner stood motionless, hands hanging at their sides, expressions blank.

"Oh, there's plenty here I find interesting," drawled a smirking Skinner in response to Robideaux's inquiry. As he said this, his gaze lingered meaningfully on the fetching Tomeeka. Then, abruptly, the smirk disappeared and his gaze hardened as he cut it back to focus strictly on Robideaux. "But what I'm most interested in right at the moment is what the hell is the big idea of you trying to hide the killing of a renegade Indian and thinking you could sneak his body back to the rez—and on top of that being chickenshit enough to use your wife and son to do the dirty work?"

Robideaux's nostrils flared indignantly. "Neither I nor any member of my family have engaged in any form of 'hiding' or 'sneaking'! I take offense at the accusation and demand either an immediate apology or for you to leave my property at once!"

Skinner swelled to his full height, several inches over that of Robideaux. "*You* demand?" he bellowed. "Who the hell do you think you're talking to, you little pipsqueak?"

"I ain't sayin' as a pipsqueak, mind you, but I can sure take a crack at answerin' otherwise."

This response came not from Robideaux, but rather from Arizona Burke as he sauntered leisurely out from the dining alcove with Lone at his side.

His words caused Skinner to wheel half around, fists tightening and raising reflexively. As soon as his eyes touched on Arizona, they became an angry glare and his mouth twisted menacingly. "Burke!" He spat the name like it was a bad taste he wanted rid of. "You piece of wore out prairie trash, I thought I'd seen the last of you when you turned tail up at Fort Robinson a couple weeks back."

Arizona set his jaw. "Real shame how disappointin' life can be sometimes, ain't it? You was wrong about seein' the last of me just like you're wrong if you think my leavin' the fort when I did amounted to me turnin' tail—sure as hell not on account of the likes of you. I left due to an important job I was sent to take care of."

"An important job that leads you here to this palace of dried out, tick-infested so-called supplies fit more for a burn pile than even as barter to a pack of equally vermin-infested redskins?" Skinner taunted. "You're good at runnin' your mouth, I'll give you that. Almost as good as you are at runnin' away from a fight."

Arizona expelled a ragged breath out through his teeth. "Okay, you insultin' tub of guts, if you want to hack out what's stuck in your craw the rest of the way and settle our differences once and for good, let's step out back and get it done. My only question is"—and here the old frontiersman's eyes swept from side to side, taking in the two troopers standing with Skinner—"how many of you yellow-legs will I have to settle with at once?"

"There ain't no date on the calendar to mark the day I'll need backing, especially not from a couple of stumble-footed clods like this pair, to settle any personal score of mine," Skinner replied in a growl. "But now I'll turn the question back on you: What about that squinty-eyed slab of beef standing alongside you? I've seen in the past his sneaky, glory hound way of sliding into the middle of a fracas and taking all the credit for the outcome. I face off against you, am I gonna have to watch out for him trying to club me down from behind?"

Lone didn't waste any time answering the question for himself. "Mister," he grated, "I don't know who the hell you are or what you think you know about me, but you seem to be tryin' awful hard to insult everybody in the joint and earn yourself a good shuttin' up. I don't want to horn in on anybody else, but I'd be plumb happy to be the one to handle the chore."

"Yeah, you wouldn't remember me," responded Skinner. "Like I said, you're too much of a glory hound to notice the slobs you step on and over to get to the front where you can glom a bigger piece of the credit. I'm talking specific about that situation up in Deadwood a year or so back when I was once again part of a detail under then Lt. Reeves and we had the Scorch Bannon gang pinned down and primed to knuckle under. But who shows up at the last minute to sashay in and claim the big wrap-up but you and that other slick piece of work, Capt. Red Trimball! That clear enough now, McGantry?"

"What's clear," Lone answered, "is that you got a real twisted, self pityin' way of lookin' at things."

"To hell with you! I know what I know. The truth only cuts one way and sometimes it hurts." Skinner's glare returned to Robideaux. "But the main truth needing to be got to right now, Frenchy—never mind these other two troublemakers for the time being—has to do with that dead Injun your son and squaw wife are sneaking back to the reservation without bringing them to our post or to the regular Indian agent. You might have got away with it if one of the local ranchers hadn't spotted them and delivered the news to me and my men out on patrol. You denying what the rancher reported?"

"I am denying, as already stated, that I or any member of my family attempted to 'sneak' in some manner," insisted Robideaux. "Frankly, we did not consider your army post as it has been in place for such a short time. As far as Indian Agent Baker, we have long enjoyed good relations with him and had every intent, either directly or via the tribal chiefs, to make sure he was notified of the death. The reason my wife and son took the boy's body was because they recognized him and know his family. They thought it kindest to break the news in person and deliver the body as soon as possible for proper burial preparations."

"Oh, that's mighty heartening to hear your concern for being proper," Skinner said in a snotty tone. "But somehow you didn't seem to think it was important to notify the *proper* authorities!"

"I already explained that," Robideaux told him.

"Uh-huh. But you know something you *ain't* bothered to explain? Since the body needed to be took back to the rez at all, the buck had obviously jumped out of bounds, right?" The suspicious glint in Skinner's eyes shone brighter through the murkiness. "Oh, yeah. That also leaves the unexplained little detail of *how* the buck ended up dead?"

There was a beat of heavy silence. Until Lone said, "I killed him, that's how."

CHAPTER EIGHTEEN

Once again Malachi Skinner wheeled half around, his mouth sagging open as if in disbelief. When he managed to get the gawping hole closed, he sputtered, "What'd you say?"

Keeping his gaze and his tone flat, Lone replied, "You heard me. You asked how the Sioux brave ended up dead, I told you. I killed him just before daybreak this morning, when him and two others closed in on our camp a couple miles east of here on the fringe of the Wildcat Hills."

"Jesus Christ on a crutch, man!" the sergeant exclaimed. "Don't you know this whole territory is a powder keg ready to be touched off by the slightest spark on account of those crazy Ghost Dancers? You think killing a young buck and then parading his carcass around like a damn victory banner don't have the makings of possibly being that spark?"

Lone said, "Didn't you catch the part where I said there were three Indians who jumped me and Arizona? Two got away. You really think it would have been better for us to just ride off and leave the dead one behind for the others to put on display and use to stir up even hotter feelin's against us bloodthirsty Whites—or for us to bring him in so we could explain what happened and why?"

"You think that's gonna make a difference? You think it's like presenting evidence in a court of law?" Skinner wailed. "We're talking a bunch of heathen savages here. All they're gonna hear is that one of theirs got killed by a pair of drifters who don't even belong in the area."

"And the brave I killed didn't belong where he was either," Lone pointed out. "And he sure as hell didn't belong tryin' to gut me with a knife. What was I supposed to do—hold still and let him carve on me so I wouldn't tip the balance of touchy feelin's everybody else is teeterin' on?"

"Ain't like it woulda been a big loss."

"You go to hell."

"This thing busts open thanks to you being so kill happy, that's where more than just me might end up," Skinner muttered.

"If you're truly interested in tryin' to keep things from bustin' open," spoke up Arizona, "then instead of showin' up here to bully the Robideauxs why ain't you reportin' back to your post and gettin' your commandin' officer involved? Him and Indian Agent Baker could hightail it out to the rez and try to put a lid on things before they *do* get out of hand."

"The day I take advice from the likes of you is the day Ol' Scratch himself is shoveling ice cubes instead of hot coal in the furnaces of Hell," sneered Skinner.

Arizona shrugged. "Then I don't suppose you'd

care to hear—'cause I'm bettin' none of your so-called military intelligence knows it yet—about how some of those renegades formin' up in the Wildcat Hills have got their hands on repeating rifles."

Skinner frowned thoughtfully at hearing this. Then, grudgingly, he muttered, "I can't argue that no time should be wasted getting word back to the lieutenant about something like that. Is it straight, or are you trying to play me for a fool?"

"Don't rate yourself so high. I wouldn't joke about something like that, not even to get at you."

Skinner turned abruptly to the fresh-faced young trooper on his left. "Blessing, saddle up and make dust back to our post. Report immediately to Lt. Reeves. Tell him everything you heard here so he can take whatever subsequent action he feels appropriate. Also inform him that I'll be following along shortly with McGantry and Burke in my custody."

"Yessir, Sergeant." The trooper snapped a salute and turned to leave.

"Hold on a minute, sonny," Lone advised.

Skinner branded him with a fiery glare. "What the hell! Nobody countermands my orders to my men!"

"Have it your way. I was just tryin' to save the lad from makin' a false report," said Lone.

A confused looking Trooper Blessing hovered partway to the door.

"What are you talking about a false report?" Skinner demanded. "Are you saying what you claimed before was a lie?"

Lone wagged his head. "Not quite. The false part is that me or Arizona is goin' anywhere with you—and sure as hell not in your custody."

"I'm ordering you as an officer representing the United States Army!"

"And I'm sayin' you got no authority to order either of us in any way, shape, or form," Lone told him. "We ain't in your ranks, we ain't at war, and no martial law has been declared for this area. So that leaves us just a couple hombres free to come and go as we please."

"And we don't please to go with you," added Arizona.

"But you admitted to killing a man—at least you did, McGantry!"

"That's a matter for the law—if there was any around," Lone stated. "And if there was, then it'd be a matter of self-defense." He jabbed a thumb indicating Arizona. "I got a witness, the dead Sioux don't."

"The absence of any law is exactly what gives me—the army, that is—jurisdiction over the matter," proclaimed Skinner.

Lone wagged his head again. "Sorry. I don't see it that way."

"Suppose I *make* you see it that way?"

"You can always try." Lone's voice was like

sandpaper on stone. "But you'd be advised to call in more troops before you do."

A tense quiet gripped the room.

Until Trooper Blessing, still poised partway to the door, said nervously, "Sarge? Am . . . am I still supposed to be taking that message?"

"Yes, goddammit! You should already be gone by now," barked Skinner. "Get your ass moving—and deliver the report exactly like I told you!"

Once Blessing was gone, Lone said, "You're a determined cuss, I'll give you that. But you're settin' yourself up to look kinda silly in front of your commandin' officer when you show up empty-handed."

"Maybe." Skinner's mouth stretched in an odd, somewhat sly smile. "Then again, if you two insist on not cooperating, maybe what I'll accomplish is to make Lt. Reeves as pissed off at you as I am. In that case, he'll be more apt to give me the backup I request to pay you another visit and next time make sure you show the proper respect."

"Skinner," Arizona grated, "you could take me in face down over a saddle, if you was able, and it wouldn't mean you ever got an ounce of respect out of me."

The sergeant's smile held fast. "Under those circumstances, I'd still come away fully satisfied."

"Well unless you're figurin' to make a play with the one man you got left," said Lone, "the circumstances here and now are such that you ain't likely to go away very satisfied at this time. So call it, this has drug out far enough. Either make your try, or be on your way. We got other business to tend to."

Now Skinner's mouth turned down at the corners. His eyes drifted slowly back and forth between Lone and Arizona, measuring the two roughhewn men, considering. For a scant moment there seemed to be a glint of readiness, as if he might actually be considering to try and use force against them. At the same time, the trooper beside him looked highly anxious about such a prospect.

And then the moment was past.

Half of the sergeant's mouth lifted in an attempt at a face-saving sneer. "Okay," he said. "You can have it your way for now. Enjoy it while you can. 'Cause this ain't over, not by a damn site. You ain't seen the last of me."

Neither Lone nor Arizona said anything, just stood looking back with flat expressions.

Only when Skinner turned toward the front door, shoving the hapless trooper ahead of him, did Arizona speak. "You and me seein' each other again is a guarantee, Skinner. We got unfinished business apart from all of this," he said. "But, in the meantime, get it clear in your head and make sure the soldier boys reportin' to you understand likewise—the Robideauxs are no part of any beef you got with me or Lone. I know your bully-boy tactics all too well. I hear they suffer any ill treatment on account of us, I swear I'll hunt you down and put an end to your bullyin' once and for all."

Skinner halted in the middle of the doorway. His hands once more balled into fists at his sides and the shoulder muscles across his back bulged visibly. He stood like that, motionless for a long beat, then abruptly plunged on through and disappeared.

Once the sergeant was gone, Antoine Robideaux put a protective arm around his daughter and said softly, "Your words were meant to ensure our safety, M'sieur Burke, and for that I am grateful. I just hope they did not instead fuel a more certain retaliation."

CHAPTER NINETEEN

"Please. I beg you to at least wait for the return of my wife that she may further tend your wounds. Plus, we never completed our negotiations on a price for the horses you brought in against the cost of the clothes you were provided and the supplies you are now taking."

So spoke a very distraught looking Robideaux as he stood out front of his trading post's main building, craning his neck to peer up at Lone sitting his saddle high astride Ironsides. Alongside the former scout, Arizona was also mounted and ready to ride.

Grinning down at the Frenchman, Lone said, "Come on, Antoine, you know that proper hagglin' is an art that can't be hurried. Takes time to do it right. And time is something Arizona and me are in short supply of right now. We ain't got it to waste on that slob of a sergeant in case he comes 'round again, maybe bringin' Lt. Reeves with him. More important, we ain't got it to waste for the sake of Col. Cody on the chance he's in some kind of trouble up in those Wildcats. We got to try and find him, the quicker the better."

Robideaux looked forlorn. "I understand. But the day is already well into the afternoon. Won't you consider remaining through the night, allowing Shining Water to once more treat your injuries, and then ride out fresh in the morning?"

"That's temptin', Frenchy. But no, it's best we go now. We can be started up into the Hills by night camp," said Lone. "I for sure mean no affront to Shining Water. Tell her that. And tell her again how obliged I am for all she did to help me.

"Now as to the barterin', the hagglin', I'll tell you what. You've got the spare horses, we're leavin' 'em here until we get back. That gives you collateral. No matter how the hagglin' scalds out, the horses are surely worth more than the stuff we're takin'. So you got no risk of endin' up on the short end. Then, when we get back, we'll all sit down and haggle our asses off. How's that sound?"

"Lone's right," Arizona chimed in. "We need to head out for findin' the colonel pronto-like. Besides, we've caused you and your family enough trouble. The sooner we're gone, the sooner you'll be rid of us bringin' any more your way."

Robideaux appeared to relent somewhat, though still looked worried. "The trouble you will leave behind, however, is that which I will have to face from my wife when she discovers I allowed M'sieur Lone to depart before he is better healed. Actually, I question the decision myself." He glanced uneasily over at Lone then back to Arizona. "Though I also understand and share in the concern for Col. Cody, do you not agree it would be wiser for your friend to remain here the night—especially considering the rugged conditions you both will immediately be encountering?"

Arizona grinned crookedly. "You want to talk rugged encounters? Look into my partner's eyes and tell me if you'd care to be the one to try and stop him from doin' something his mind is made up on."

"No, I don't believe I would," Robideaux admitted. "Very well. All I *can* do, then, is wish you godspeed." His gaze shifting to Lone, he added, "And when you return, be prepared for a bartering session of epic proportions."

"Lookin' forward to it, Frenchy," Lone assured him.

Moments later he and Arizona had swung their mounts around to face the central mass of the Wildcat Hills and were riding in that direction at a gallop.

"Back toward the heart of the Wildcats, eh? This late in the day, and without those two spare horses?" Ford Benton frowned at the report received from Tucker Wald who had just descended from an elevated point in the jumble of ragged rock outcrops located a quarter mile northeast of Robideaux's trading post. Wald held a collapsed spyglass in one hand, indicating the watch duty he'd been taking his turn at up on a higher ledge.

Benton, Strauss, and Toledo Slim were occupying the temporary camp they'd set up at ground level in the cluster of natural concealment, seated on chunks of fallen rock situated in slashes of shade thrown by the sun now sinking lower in the western sky. Their horses grazed close by, hobbled to keep them in place behind the rocks and out of sight of the trading post.

"So what's going on?" said Toledo. "If they ain't taking the spare horses—like we figured they must be bringing to Cody—then what the hell are they up to?"

"Maybe their purpose for showin' up here ain't got nothing to do with Cody after all," suggested Wald.

Benton gave a firm shake of his head. "No. I ain't buyin' that, not for a minute. Two old pals of Cody just happening to ride in for no particular reason in the middle of all this shit that's stirring? Uh-uh, that's just plain too much coincidence to swallow."

"I agree with Ford," said Strauss. "Those two showing up here don't wash no other way but to have something to do with Cody."

"What about those soldier boys who came and went from the trading post so fast?" asked Wald. "You said McGantry used to be some kind of hotshot army scout, Ford—could it be he talked them into lending a hand with whatever him and his pal are up to? Maybe that sergeant went back to the post and is gonna come back with reinforcements."

"If that was the case," said Toledo, "why wouldn't McGantry and Burke wait for 'em instead of taking off like they did?"

"I don't know the answer to that. There's too damn much we don't know the answers to," Benton growled. "But what I do know is that Buffalo Goddamn Bill is still somewhere up in those Hills. We let him slip away once, we can't afford to again. And the more time passes and the more crowded things get, including that hellcat and those stinkin' Injuns we ran into before, the more risk there is of losin' out. I'll take the blame for holdin' off after we ran into McGantry and Burke, thinkin' we'd let them lead the way back to the old bastard. But I'm seein' now how I overlooked the obvious and put our chips on the wrong color."

The other three men exchanged puzzled looks.

"What're you saying, Ford?" asked Strauss.

"I'm saying that moth-eaten trading post over yonder has got some answers we failed to consider," replied Benton. "Comin' out of there is where we first saw Cody, remember? On his way *in*. Then McGantry and Burke make a bee line there first thing when they show up. Hell, even the army passes in and out. Don't you see? That little French weasel is right in the middle of it all, with his snout stuck in everything. I'm thinkin' we need to pay him another visit and get him to snort back out some of what he's breathed in. I got a hunch he gave a clue to McGantry and Burke on where to find Cody, and I got an even stronger hunch we'll be able to *persuade* him to share it with us, too."

A nasty smile splitting his battered face as he ground his scarred right fist into the palm of his left hand, Wald said, "I can practically guarantee that Frenchy will share anything you want to know."

Benton rose to his feet. "Okay, let's get to it then. Strauss, you split out and hang a tail on McGantry and Burke, just in case. I don't want to lose them just yet. Make damn sure they don't spot you. Leave markers for us to follow. We'll catch up as soon as we're done with Robideaux."

From where he sat in a canvas chair behind a folding table inside his tent, Lt. Gregory Reeves gazed up at Sgt. Skinner as the latter stood before him, giving his report. As he listened, the expression on the commanding officer's handsome, clean-shaven face remained impassive. Only when the sergeant was done did the lieutenant's brows pinch slightly tighter before he said, "While I don't share your overall low assessment of Lone McGantry, Sergeant, I'll admit to being disappointed he wasn't more forthcoming about this matter of killing a renegade Indian. I was looking forward to discussing that lack of judgment with him when he arrived here, in accordance with the message you sent Trooper Blessing ahead to deliver."

Sgt. Skinner's face reddened with a mix of anger and frustration. "I'm afraid I gauged things wrong and jumped the gun by sending that message, sir. I didn't expect the resistance I got from McGantry and his friend Arizona Burke after I ordered Blessing on ahead. With only one green trooper to back me and the safety of the Robideaux family to consider if I'd tried to push the matter too hard and things got out of hand, I . . . well, I thought it best to hold off and present the situation for your consideration, sir."

"Under the circumstances, you did the right thing," allowed Reeves. "But it makes me all the more determined to have that talk with McGantry."

"I was hoping you'd feel that way, sir," Skinner was quick to respond. "Let me take two or three men I know to have sufficient sand, we'll go back there and—"

Reeves stopped him with a raised hand. "Hold on a minute, Sergeant. You appear a little too eager. Having shown good judgment once, I question whether the sting of coming away empty-handed might not have you less inclined to do so again."

"In the line of duty, sir, I always try to show good judgment."

"Try, perhaps," Reeves countered. "But we both know there've been a number of times in the past where your temper, sometimes helped along by your fondness for alcohol, has gotten in the way of that."

Skinner's mouth pulled into a straight, tight line but he held his tongue.

"Furthermore," Reeves went on, "I recall hearing about a disturbance back at the fort a few weeks ago involving yourself and one Arizona John Burke. That would be the same individual you just identified as accompanying McGantry, would it not?"

"Yeah, the same," Skinner said sullenly. "But the past matter between me and Burke was a personal one and has nothing to do with the current situation. Like you said, he was with McGantry when they brought the dead Injun in, a witness to how it happened. He's also the one who claimed some of the renegades up in the Wildcat Hills have got their hands on repeating rifles."

"Information like that, if true, is certainly worth learning more about."

"That's what I thought also."

Reeves leaned back in his chair and hung a

heavy gaze on Skinner. "I'll be honest with you, Sergeant. When I was assigned to lead this patrol and establish a temporary post to try and keep a lid on the escalating trouble in this area, I objected to having you as part of it. My objection was denied. So we're stuck with each other, you and I. So far you've done nothing to warrant my initial concerns. On the contrary, you've conducted yourself commendably."

"Appreciate you saying so, sir."

"Therefore, for the sake of not tempting any disruption to that status, I intend to accompany you back for a further discussion with McGantry and Burke." The lieutenant stood up. "Corporal Hiner can handle things here in our absence. I've already sent Blessing on to notify Agent Baker of these recent developments and instructed him to do the initial follow-up out on the reservation. Probably best he does that alone anyway. Then he's to meet with us here afterwards, and in the meantime we will have made our trip to Robideaux's. From there we'll be able to compare notes on how things stand overall."

"Sounds like that ought to cover everything, sir," said Skinner.

Reeves nodded. "I'm glad you think so. Now go pick out six troopers who suit you to accompany us. I'll notify Corporal Hiner and have a horse saddled and made ready for me. We'll ride out in five minutes."

CHAPTER TWENTY

The meaty smack of calloused knuckles driving into thinly padded flesh and bone produced an instant half gasp, half groan of pain from the bloodied lips of Antoine Robideaux as he sagged weakly against the front edge of his store's sales counter. Four feet away, forced to look on from where she was being held fast in the strong grip of Ford Benton, Tomeeka issued her own tormented outcry over the abuse to her father.

"Damn, Tucker, I could hear a rib crack from that one clear over here," said Benton. "Take it a little easy on the old man. You break the stubborn fool in half, he ain't gonna be able to tell us anything."

"Aw, I'm just softening him up," Wald protested. "I know what I'm doin'."

"If you know so much," Benton snapped, "then why ain't you got more out of him?"

"You're the stubborn ones!" Tomeeka wailed. "He's already told you all he can, all he knows. What else do you want?"

With his fingers wrapped tight in her long, inky hair, Benton jerked the girl's head back sharply. "Sayin' Cody went up into the Wildcats and McGantry and Burke went after him don't tell us shit! Hell, we already knew that much when we got here. But *where* in those Hills? How do we find 'em? Those are the things we're wantin' to hear!"

Still sagging against the counter, held upright only by Wald's left fist wrapped in his shirtfront while the ex-pug's right loomed ready to do more damage, a battered Robideaux lifted his bruised, lumpy face and rasped between puffs to regain his breath, "You don't understand . . . the Wildcat Hills stretch . . . for miles. Ridges and cliffs, buttes rising and tumbling away . . . trackless canyons. No pattern, no way of knowing what path anyone going into them might follow . . . or where they might be found."

Benton's lips peeled back, baring his teeth. "So you expect us to believe that Cody and McGantry and Burke, and maybe Kicking Bear plus a handful of renegades from the rez, are all just roaming around in there. Half of them trying to avoid being found while the other half is on the hunt for them. Is that it? So our best bet is to just plunge in and hope we pick up the right trail or maybe just get lucky and bump into somebody we're interested in? You expect me to settle for a crock like that? I oughta kick in one of your ribs myself, just for you thinkin' me that big a fool!"

"Hey, Ford," Toledo called from the front doorway where he was keeping watch in case any unwanted customers showed up. "Before you stove in the old man any more, how about giving the girl a taste? I've seen tough nuts in the past who wouldn't crack under their own pain but would spill plenty quick at the threat to a kin or loved one."

"You scum!" Robideaux hissed at the suggestion.

Still keeping the Frenchman propped up, Wald turned half around and said to Benton with an anguished look on his face, "I ain't never roughed up no female before, Ford. Reckon I could if I had to, if you said it was necessary, but I gotta say I sure don't care for the idea."

"What about that bounty huntin' bitch from the other day—the hellcat who queered everything when we had Cody already nabbed once?" sneered Toledo. "We all ended up pouring lead at her! Yet now you're saying you'd never 'rough up' a female?"

"That was different! She was fightin' like a man, throwin' back lead as good as she got—we had no choice," Wald argued.

"Well maybe we got no choice now either. Not if we want to cut to it and find out something worthwhile without wasting more time we can't afford."

"I still don't like it," Wald said firmly.

Toledo's sneer stretched wider. "Don't worry, big fella. If you ain't got the stomach for it, you can give those pounders of yours a rest. Come over here and take the watch, I'll deal with the squaw." His eyes took on a menacing gleam as he paused for a moment to watch Tomeeka squirm in Benton's grip. Then: "You know what pretty women fear worse than pain? A mar to their precious beauty, that's what. A visible scar. And I found out a long time ago that a simple little thing like the front sight on a six-shooter can do some nasty, permanent damage to a smooth, pretty cheek."

Even Benton winced at this. "Christ, Slim. If that's how you treat your women, no wonder that female bounty hunter showed up wanting you so bad."

The gleam in Toledo's eyes burned brighter. "Don't worry, that bitch ain't seen the last of me. One of these days I'll let her have her wish and catch up. Then she'll find out."

Toledo's words trailed off as something outside suddenly drew his attention. Twisting around in the doorway, he raised the spyglass he'd been holding down at his side and quickly sighted it to one eye.

"What is it? What's going on?" Benton demanded.

"Looks like we got company comin'. Big dust cloud off to the north," Toledo said, leaning his upper body forward as if to shift closer to the magnified sight he was peering at. "Aw, shit. I can make out blue uniforms. We got a pack of soldiers, at least half a dozen or so, headed straight for us!"

"That tears it. We got no choice but to light a shuck, boys," growled Benton.

Wald gave Robideaux a hard shake, causing the Frenchman's loose hanging arms to flop limply against his sides like a marionette with the strings cut. "What about this stubborn old bag of bones? You want me to finish him so he can't blab?"

"No. I got something useful I *want* him to blab," replied Benton. Dragging Tomeeka roughly along with him, his fingers still wrapped in her hair, the gang leader took a long step over to stand in front of the bleary-eyed Robideaux. "Take a good look, and listen even better, Frenchy. We're taking your daughter with us. When those soldiers show up, for her sake you'd better make them understand this: They give us some room, we'll release her unharmed once we're in the clear. But if they give chase and try to run us down—we'll start leavin' her off *in pieces!*"

Tomeeka gritted her teeth and choked back a sob.

Robideaux's eyes rolled up to look at her and the torment in them was far greater than any physical pain from the beating he'd endured.

Benton viewed this with satisfaction. "He got the message," he announced. "Let him go—we need to make dust outta here!"

CHAPTER TWENTY-ONE

Lone and Arizona sat their saddles at the upward-sloping base of a tall, flat-faced butte a short distance within the western reaches of the Wildcat Hills central mass. The natural cream color of the sandstone face was presently tinted a pale rose hue by the setting sun. The same wash of fading light threw long, distorted shadows out ahead of the two mounted men.

"Well, there she be," declared Arizona. "A big, lumpy, wild sprawl of scarps and cliffs and twisty canyons waitin' with open arms. Waitin' to swallow us up, churn us this way and that, then hopefully—somewhere in the churnin'—dump us somewhere near to Col. Cody."

Lone cocked an eyebrow. "You make it sound not too different than steppin' into a slow twistin' tornado and hopin' to get dropped out in reasonably good shape."

"Wait'll we get deeper in. You'll see that's a comparison not too far off."

Lone cast a sidelong glance. "You sound like you've been deep in before."

"Matter of fact I have," Arizona conceded. "Some years back, as one of the more lunkheaded escapades from my misspent youth, I let a one-eyed old prairie dog by the name of

Schonover convince me there was gold to be found in the Wildcats. Never mind nobody had ever found a lick of an ounce before, he claimed to know better. So I coughed up money for a grub stake and in we went.

"Long story short, we spent most of a summer, all of the fall, and a good chunk into winter traipsin' and climbin' and diggin' with no results but blisters and sore feet. I finally bailed out ahead of a blizzard I could see was formin' up to come in a ripper, Schoony cursin' my back the whole way. I couldn't convince him to come with me. Far as I know, nobody's ever heard from him since."

"Maybe we'll run into him," Lone suggested dryly. "One of those crazy old hermits, sittin' on a whole pile of gold he's been accumulatin' and hoardin' all this while."

"If we do run across him," Arizona chuffed, "he won't be nothing but a dried up skeleton with his finger bones wore off and a magpie nest in his empty skull. Which, come to think of it, I half deserved myself, back when I was empty-headed enough to fall for his stupid yarn."

Lone grinned crookedly. "Not smart like both of us are bein' now, right? Chargin' into a pile of rocks you say is gonna turn us every way but loose in order to chase down one of the prime yarn spinners of all time. All for the sake of wantin' to make sure he's safe from his notion to jump backward out of a soft life of pretend adventures in show business and once more try to be who he was in the wild old days. Add in a hornet's nest of renegade Indians, a pack or maybe two of hardcases up to no good, and now a handful of U.S. Cavalry soldiers we've managed to piss off. Boil it all down, maybe we ain't got a very strong case for showin' good sense after all."

Arizona mirrored his grin. "Could be. But that ain't gonna turn us back, is it?"

"Not hardly. Come on, let's find a good spot for night camp."

An hour later thy were sprawled to either side of a crackling fire, scraping their tin plates clean of some re-heated boiled potatoes and slices of roast pork they had procured from the Robideauxs before departing the trading post. Acquired goods whose cost would eventually be part of the bartering/haggling session the wily old Frenchman was so insistent on.

"Too bad we didn't think to bring a jug of that buttermilk Antoine's daughter served at lunch," Arizona said as he wiped his plate clean with a final piece of bread. "I hadn't had buttermilk in a month of Sundays and that sure hit the spot. Left me cravin' more."

"Be something to look forward to when we make it back," Lone told him.

"Already got it marked in mind as something

to make sure of." Arizona set aside his plate and poured himself a cup of coffee. "Truth of it is, though, buttermilk's only really good when it's nice and cold. So even if we had bought some in a jug and kept it from spoilin', it would've been half warm and not near as tasty."

Lone gave him a look across the top of the flames. "You've really put a lot of thought into this buttermilk thing, ain't you?"

"Guess I got what you'd call an active mind," Arizona explained with a shrug. "Besides, it keeps me from worryin' about gettin' my hair lifted or catchin' a renegade arrow or takin' a bullet from some no account bushwhacker. Thinkin' about other things, like buttermilk, soothes me."

"I'd figure you'd find it more soothin' to think about things like your half-breed sweetie up near Fort Robinson, the one with the welcome mat always spread for you in front her tipi."

Arizona made a face. "Under different circumstances, that might well be the case. But runnin' into Malachi Skinner earlier sorta threw thoughts of her off the rail. Until I settle things with that side-windin' snake, I got no call to think good thoughts about my Twyla. Just a-fore I got called away from the fort, you see, I found out Skinner had tried to have his way with her in the manner I told you and Robideaux he has a habit of doin'. She managed to fend him off, thankfully, but until I make the sonofabitch pay for botherin' her, I can't put it to rest. I managed to get a piece of him one night before I had to leave, but others broke it up before I got full satisfaction."

"I didn't realize your differences with him ran so deep or so personal," Lone said, scowling. "I can see where he's an easy critter to dislike. Didn't take spendin' much time around him to feel an urge to belt him one myself. Just for the hell of it. But you got real cause, so I'll make sure not to get in your way. Be happy to hold your coat for you, though, any time you say."

"I'll be sure to keep that in mind." Arizona took a drink of his coffee. "But, first things bein' first, we gotta get this little job of work involvin' the colonel took care of."

"Yeah, there's that," Lone agreed. Reaching to pour himself some coffee, the movement stretched him in a way that caused him to wince slightly.

Observing this, Arizona said, "How's the leg holdin' up? From what I've seen, you ain't looked to have been favorin' it too much."

"It's tolerable," Lone answered. "Can't say it feels as good as it did when I first woke up on that cornstalk mattress back at Robideaux's, but I can manage. The rest of the scrapes and cuts mostly just itch from scabbin' over."

"You know, Tomeeka sent along a jar of her ma's salve and even the fixin's for a dose of the healin' grog if you want me to brew up a cup."

Lone shook his head. "No, I can't afford the effect of that grog. We'll both need to stay extra alert at all times from here on out. I wouldn't say no to a splash of pain duller in this coffee, though, and before I turn in I was thinkin' maybe I'd peel back that hide wrap on my thigh long enough to smear some salve on the cut before re-wrappin' it."

"Sounds like a good idea," Arizona said, holding out the whiskey flask for Lone to add some to his coffee. "When you're ready, I'll lend a hand with the wrap if you want."

"Be obliged." Lone tipped a generous dollop into his cup, handed the flask back. "Though I expect you must be gettin' mighty sick of nurse-maidin' me by now."

"I've had worse chores," Arizona said with a shrug. "And if it's part of what it takes to get Col. Cody out of a tight and back to safety, then so be it."

"I hope the old rascal appreciates what a good friend he has in you, Burke," Lone said earnestly.

"And I could say the same for you," Arizona countered. Then, with a wry smile, he added, "But bein' good friends with good intentions don't amount to a whole lot unless said intentions get successfully carried out. You happen to have a plan for how we're gonna do that?"

CHAPTER TWENTY-TWO

"What's with the girl?" Strauss wanted to know as soon as Benton and Wald, in response to his signaling them, swung their horses into the thick cluster of ponderosa pine where he waited. Mounted double with Wald was Tomeeka, her wrists lashed behind her back with a piece of rough twine and a longer length of same running from where one end was knotted around her throat to where the opposite end was clenched in the ex-pug's left fist.

"Never mind her for right now," Benton responded. "What about McGantry and Burke—you didn't lose 'em, did you?"

"Hell no. I wouldn't be stopped here twiddlin' my thumbs if I had." Strauss twisted in his saddle and pointed toward the high, flat-faced butte that rose up in the fading light of dusk three hundred yards away. "They're about three quarters of the way around to the back side of that butte, camped for the night."

"You positive of that?"

Strauss's head bobbed. "Swear it. I followed 'em in—careful-like, of course, at a distance—until I saw for sure they was stopped and stripping down their horses. Then I eased on back to here, where I could safely hail you fellas when you came along."

Benton didn't say anything for a minute, scowling as he swept his gaze across what he could see of the sprawling, rugged expanse of high rocks and jagged break-aways that he knew stretched on for miles. When he spoke, he said, "This ain't where Cody and Pony Bob went into the Hills when we first followed them, is it?"

"No, that was another quarter mile or so to the south," Strauss said.

"So these birds ain't trying to track them exact, then."

"Don't look like it," Strauss allowed. "After this long, no matter how good a tracker anybody claimed to be—not even Buffalo Bill himself, except maybe in those storybook adventures they write about him—that'd be most near impossible."

"So," Benton said, dragging the word out thoughtfully as he continued to scan the uninviting terrain ahead, "that means either McGantry is going in strictly on a poke and hope basis, or he has some particular destination in mind, a place he expects to find Cody." Here his eyes cut suddenly to Tomeeka. "A place I still think your goddamn old man told him about!"

Initially the girl flinched under his hard glare. But then she quickly regained a measure of composure and her own eyes flashed as she said, "You foolishly cling to your false beliefs, and refuse to accept that my father told you all he knows."

"The only bit of foolishness I'll own up to," Benton growled, "is that I brought along the wrong Robideaux as hostage. I should have grabbed your old man and left you to convince those soldier boys I mean business. Shit! Then we'd've had more time to work on the old buzzard until he finally spilled."

"What's this about soldier boys?" Strauss asked, looking alarmed.

"We had some unwanted visitors show up back at the trading post," Wald explained. "Slim spotted a fair-sized cavalry patrol headed in right when I was in the middle of trying to get the old Frenchy to talk. We had no choice but to light a shuck. We snatched the girl as a way to keep the blue coats from following too tight, gave the old man to understand and pass along what would happen to her if they didn't hold off."

"That was good thinking."

"Been better, like I just said," growled Benton, "if I'd opted for the old man instead."

"Don't be so sure. They might have been more willing to risk harm to a man over a girl," Strauss pointed out. "This way, as long as they're giving us breathing room, it ain't all bad."

"Here comes Slim now," said Wald. "He hung back to watch, he'll be able to tell us if they're giving chase or not."

"So far, so good. Those cavalry boys are staying put, just like you warned 'em to do, Ford," Toledo reported a minute later, after he'd galloped into the pine grove and checked down his horse.

"Well at least we got that much of a break," said Benton, though still looking disgruntled. "The thing now is to milk it for all it's worth and finish playing the hand we've been dealt."

Wald said, "So now that she's served her purpose, we gonna go ahead and let the girl go?"

"The hell she's served her purpose. Not all the way, not yet," Benton declared. "Long as we got her, we got a cushion between us and those blue bellies. Means we keep them off our asses while we fall back to our plan of lettin' McGantry and Burke lead the way to Cody."

"You mean we take her on into the Wildcats with us?" Wald asked.

"Damn it, it ain't a matter of *where* we take her," Benton said, his voice strained with impatience. "It's a matter of *how long* she's able to do us any good."

Strauss frowned. "You think the soldiers will even follow us into the Wildcats? Every indication so far is that they've been steering clear of there. I got a hunch those are their orders."

"I don't give a damn what their orders are or where they do or don't go," Benton stated. "Long as the girl keeps providing a cushion between us and them and we're able to stay on the track of McGantry, we can make this work. We get hold of Cody again, he'll give us an ace to play against every damn hand anybody tries to lay down opposite us!"

"Sounds like you got it figured pretty good, boss," drawled Toledo. "But what if we're overlooking a high card—not an ace maybe, but a high one all the same—that we could be playing right now?"

Benton eyed him. "You know I don't like riddles. What are you driving at? Spit it out."

Toledo inclined his head toward Tomeeka. "We been treating the daughter there like Little Miss Innocent, all teary eyed and loyal to her daddy but not knowing nothing on her own. What if that ain't the truth at all? What if, instead, she's a nosy little heathen half-breed brat who sticks her nose into everything she can? You know, like most women."

Benton scowled. "You thinking she might have overheard something about where Cody and Pony Bob were headed that day we first saw 'em leaving the trading post?"

Toledo spread his hands. "I'm saying it's maybe something to think about, that's all. Been my experience that most women, even the quiet and shy actin' ones, got a way of knowin' what goes on under their own roofs. And if you want to find out for sure what this one knows, my offer to do some convincing in my own special way still stands."

"Sounds to me," Wald was quick to speak

up, "that the thing you're interested in the most is scarrin' up another pretty woman. That's a goddamn sick itch for a man to have, if you ask me. I don't like bein' no part of it."

"Nobody asked you, and nobody invited you and your queasy gut to join in," Toledo snapped back.

"And nobody but me says how we are or ain't gonna go about things," Benton reminded everybody sharply. His gaze settling on Toledo, he added, "Your idea may have some merit. I need to think on it. Right now ain't the time or place, regardless." Then he cut his eyes to Wald and said, "I understand your reluctance, Tucker. If I decide to give Slim's idea a try, it won't be a decision I make lightly. But if I do, then that's how it's gonna go. Understood?"

Wald held his eyes for a long count before looking away. "Yeah, Ford. If that's the way you call it, then a-course that's how it'll be," he said quietly.

Benton nodded. "Okay. Thing we got to do now is see to our own night camp. It should have some concealment in case the soldiers try to sneak a scout ahead to try and monitor us. They're bound to do that sooner or later. So we need to try and fog our trail as best we can while staying close enough to McGantry and Burke to be able to pick up their sign again when they go back on the move in the morning. Most of that's gonna fall to you, Strauss. You up to it?"

"I won't let you down, Ford. Believe me, I understand how much is riding on this. Come on, follow me. I got a good spot already picked out for us to make camp."

Six people were gathered in the dining alcove off the main store area of Robideaux's trading post. All wore grim expressions that seemed to suit the deepening shadows of dusk seeping through the windows on the back wall of the room. Robideaux himself was seated at the table. His wife sat on a chair hitched up beside him, leaning close as she silently completed ministering to the cuts and bruises marking his battered face. One eye was swollen nearly shut, already turned a greenish purple; particularly noticeable amidst the rest of the visible damage was a split, also badly swollen bottom lip and a walnut-sized lump in the middle to his forehead. Not visible but still evident as further damage was the way the Frenchman sat hunched over to one side, indicating cracked or broken ribs.

The four other persons in the room, all men, remained standing. Each appeared concerned and somewhat ill at ease. Except for Trace, the Robideauxs' nineteen-year-old son. He looked concerned naturally, but rather than remain still like the others he paced restlessly, agitatedly back and forth behind his parents. He was tall and lean, hard-muscled, with darkly handsome features that at the moment were twisted by anger and frustration.

"I can't believe everyone is just *holding* here, doing nothing but standing around talking," he fumed, speaking in a clear and concise English that he and his sister had learned from the nuns at a nearby Christian mission, since abandoned. "*Look* what those foul dogs did to my father—*think* what they may be doing to my sister! Yet with armed and mounted soldiers available just outside the door, no pursuit is taking place!"

"Try to take it easy, son," advised Lt. Reeves in a level tone. "I know that's hard. Trust me, it's hard for us, too. But you heard what those men told your father—if we act too hastily, give them reason to react even more desperately than they already are, then things could turn still worse. I shouldn't have to spell out how."

Trace's face twisted with torment and a low groan escaped out of him. "But isn't there *something* we can do?"

"Listen to the lieutenant, my son," Robideaux said, the words thick-sounding through his damaged lips. "I looked into the eyes of those devils. Evil eyes all. But one especially, a young one who spoke with pleasure of what he would do to your sister if provoked . . . The damage to me is already done. We can't change that. So we must take every precaution to spare Tomeeka from such suffering."

Bracketing Reeves were Sgt. Skinner and Indian Agent Tom Baker, who had returned from the reservation with Shining Water and Trace. Baker was a long, lanky number, ruddy-faced from exposure to sun and wind, with pale blue eyes and a narrow mouth with lips that always appeared slightly pooched, as if in vague thought about something.

Speaking now, he said, "Lt. Reeves is a very competent officer, Trace. He and his men are committed to doing everything they can to get Tomeeka back safely. You must understand, however, that in addition to their own wishes and instincts they have military procedures they must follow."

"The only instincts and procedures I care about are those which will free my sister and punish the dogs who took her and before that beat my father!" Trace replied hotly.

Speaking again, gently but firmly, Baker said, "You and your mother were just out at the reservation with me. The two of you went with kindness to return the slain body of Blue Eagle to his family and with the wisdom to counsel them not to let their grief turn into blind anger, especially during this turbulent time. You helped greatly to quell what might have been—and may still be if cool heads don't continue to prevail—an ugly reprisal. I implore you to keep a cool head yourself. Don't you see? If you now rail too strongly for immediately striking back at Whites who harmed your family, it may be viewed as license for the family and friends of Blue Eagle to also strike back."

"Only it's not the same thing at all!" Trace insisted. "Blue Eagle played a direct part in causing the harm he met with. Those who killed him were acting in self-defense. But the curs who took my sister and did this"—jabbing a finger to indicate his battered father—"did so with no provocation, surely not from those they harmed. Such men, no matter their color or that of their victims, must be hunted down. Not only to be made to pay for deeds already done, but also to be stopped from committing more."

Reeves regarded him, an unmistakable measure of respect showing in his expression. "If all men thought and spoke that sensibly, young fellow, this old world would be a hell of a lot better off. Unfortunately, that's not the case. So all we can do is the best we can with what we've got."

"What does that mean?" Trace challenged.

"For starters, I've sent a rider back to our post with instructions to get off a message to Fort Robinson via the telegraph line tap we have set up there," said the lieutenant. "The message will be an update on recent events here, and will include a request by me for the fort's best scout and tracker, a man named Abe Timkin, to be dispatched to us post haste. If he leaves right away and rides the night, he should be able to make it by mid-morning.

"Once Timkin arrives, I'll assign him to immediately commence scouting for a patrol to be sent in pursuit of the raiders who struck here, took the girl hostage, and have the announced purpose of hunting down Buffalo Bill. What they have in mind if and when they catch him isn't clear, but I think it's reasonable to figure it's not anything good. And the same doubtlessly holds true for anyone attempting to get in their way."

Baker said, "You realize the pursuit of Cody shows every indication of leading up into the Wildcat Hills, right?"

"I gathered that, yes."

"Then I'm sure you also gathered there are rumors of Kicking Bear having taken refuge in them as well. So did your request for Timkin happen to include a secondary request—one for the lifting of the restrictions that have kept you from going into the Wildcats before now?"

Reeves showed an exaggerated frown. "Damn. In all this excitement, I plumb don't remember if I did or not. But if Timkin locks on the scent of those jackals tomorrow and that's indeed where they're headed without yet giving up the girl, then I guess I might have to put to the test that old saying about it sometimes being better to ask for forgiveness than for permission."

CHAPTER TWENTY-THREE

"Last night you asked if I had a plan. Well, here it is. Leastways part of it," said Lone as he fed a couple more leafy twigs into the smoky fire over which Arizona was frying strips of bacon in a skillet. A pot of bubbling coffee sat out on the edge of the coals, filling the crisp morning air with rich aroma.

Waving his free hand back and forth to push some of the smoke away from his face, Arizona responded, "This bacon was already cured and smoked, you know. No need to go to the extra trouble. And as far as your plan, is the idea to wrap us in some kind of smoke screen so we're hid from anybody who might mean us harm bein' able to draw a clean bead on us once we commence our search through this rock pile?"

Lone reached for the coffee pot and poured himself a cup of the brew. He was pleased to find the stretching motion caused only a minor pang of discomfort to run through his leg. Last night's fresh application of Shining Water's salve then re-wrapping it in the thin sheets of animal hide was continuing to work healing wonders.

"Actually," he said, "my plan is sort of the opposite of that. You made us crawlin' through and over this miles-long rock pile, as you call it, in hopes of gettin' lucky and stumblin' on Col. Cody sound like a mighty unappealin' long shot. So I came up with the notion—instead of just us doin' all the work of huntin'—how about givin' the colonel a reason to come huntin' for us?"

Arizona's brows pinched together. "Okay. What reason would that be?"

"Plain old curiosity is one that comes to mind. It's known to be a pretty powerful draw."

"Uh-huh. It's also known for gettin' a certain cat in some serious trouble. And these *are* the Wildcat Hills, remember." Arizona eyed Lone through the smoke. "Don't you reckon if the colonel is already in some kind of trouble, like we figure, he's likely to lean real hard to the cautious side, no matter how curious he finds himself?"

"That's the thing," said Lone. "Neither him nor Pony Bob showin' back up after enterin' in here four or five days ago is what's got us all thinkin' they're in some kind of fix. So what could that be? You boil it down, I see only three possibilities. One, they're dead. Ain't pretty to think, but even Robideaux said it's possible some of those young hot-blood renegades might be worked up enough to do something like that. Two, they had a run-in with the renegades and have been forced to hunker down, lay low until they get the right chance to break free. Three, they got injured, maybe wounded in a skirmish with the renegades or maybe hurt some other way—a bad fall or some such—and are forced to lay low because of that, waitin' until they're well enough to travel before tryin' to make it out."

Arizona listened, frowning thoughtfully as he followed along. When Lone paused, he said, "Okay. That much sounds reasonable. But if they're alive and have already got cause to be layin' low, hunkered down, what you got in mind for us to do that will somehow draw 'em out?"

Lone made a gesture indicating the smoke rising up from their fire. "I say again—things like this, as a start. Smoky campfires whenever we stop to take on some grub, walkin' out in the open when we come to a clearing, maybe even skylinin' ourselves from time to time. Hell, maybe takin' a shot at some fresh meat if given the chance. In other words, we do the opposite of stalkin' quiet and tryin' *not* to draw attention to ourselves, the way trackers and hunters normally would."

Arizona swung the skillet off the flames and by now was looking at Lone the way he might look at somebody who'd just suggested they climb up the smoke column and eat their breakfast up where the view was better. "Well I sure caught the part about goin' the opposite of normal in what you just laid out," he said as he began forking equal amounts of bacon onto tin plates Lone held out that already contained pieces of bread and some apple slices. "But where it took me to wonderin' was if you got up in the middle of the night and snuck some more of Shining Water's grog after all. 'Cause what I heard"—and here he lifted his gaze to regard Lone square on—"sounded to me like somebody not talkin' all the way clear-headed."

Continuing to hold out the plates for Arizona to pour some bacon grease onto the bread for softening and flavoring, Lone's mouth stretched into a wide, wry grin. "So you got some concerns about my plan, that what I'm hearin'?"

"Only the part that leaves out horns for us to toot or a big bass drum to pound on while we march along. You know, the little touches that would be sure to bring the renegades flockin' to finish what those first three only started yesterday morning. Or did you forget that particular detail—that the colonel and Pony Bob ain't the only ones we reckon to be roamin' around in this rock pile? There ain't only the renegades, neither. Remember that spyglass was on us when we was approachin' the trading post yesterday mornin'? We got reason to suspect Ford Benton is still sniffin' somewhere behind us, up to some kind of no good. What about that?"

"I ain't forgot none of it," Lone said around a bite of bacon. "I also ain't forgot that you and me happen to have a fair amount of bark on us in the event anybody comes lookin' to try and scrape some off. And I never said advertisin' our presence should be took as a sign we'd be easy pickin's. In fact, anybody who took time to think about it might be smart to consider our bold display is a statement we ain't afraid of no Ghost Dance bullshit or Benton's crew, neither one."

Now Arizona looked more thoughtful. "Confusion to the enemy, eh? Ain't that some kind of military tactic, or the claim of some famous general—probably a dead one?"

"Could be," Lone allowed. "In fact there's another military saying and sometimes tactic that comes to mind, one I happen to know Cody is fond of. It goes: 'Ride to the sound of the guns.' He got that from his friend and personal hero, George Custer. It was an approach that won Custer some key battles and plenty of glory in the Civil War."

"Too bad he didn't stick to that—ridin' to the sound of guns instead of to the sound of war whoops," remarked Arizona. "You happen to have any sayings or tactics that come from somebody still alive after followin' 'em?"

Ignoring the sarcasm, Lone said, "The whole point of what I'm suggestin' is that us proceedin' in such a wide open way is bound to draw attention. Yeah, part of it will likely be from those lookin' to do us a hurt. Any skunk of any stripe willin' to step up to try their luck, I'm bettin' we can hold our own against. But what

I'm also bettin' is that, if they're still alive, it will draw the attention of Cody and Pony Bob, too. *We* will be the sound of guns they're willin' to ride toward.

"Don't you see? Anybody stalkin' meanin' harm is gonna be slinkin' around in the usual way. Us actin' different will make us stand out as *bein'* something different. It oughta at least be cause enough for 'em to poke out their heads for a look-see. They do that, they'll recognize us and come forward instead of burrowin' in deeper. You beginnin' to understand at all how I'm thinkin'?"

Arizona tore off a big bite of bread and worked it slowly, thoughtfully around in his mouth. After washing it down with a swallow of coffee, his gaze came to rest on Lone and he said, "Surprisin' as it is to hear myself say, I'm blamed if your idea ain't beginnin' to make a cockeyed kind of sense."

"That's a start. Better than seein' no sense in it at all."

"I been worried all along," Arizona admitted, "how, if the colonel and Bob are gone to ground for whatever reason, hidin' and not wantin' to be found, they're surely savvy enough to make it tough for anybody to root 'em out. Your way presents a possibility for gettin' around that—drawin' 'em out and givin' 'em cause to, like you said, come huntin' us."

Lone cocked an eyebrow. "The down side, like

you said, bein' who else we might cause to come huntin' us in the process."

"Already been covered," Arizona said, looking stern. "I'll throw my dice same as you—we stay sharp and frosty like we know how to be, I'm bettin' we can hold our own against Benton's crew or any ragtag bunch of hot-blood pups or anybody else who tries to get in our way."

"Reckon that settles it then," Lone stated. "Let's finish our breakfast and then toss our dice out ahead into this rocky sprawl and see what turns up."

Half a mile away, within the reaches of the Wildcat Hills but off to the south of where Lone and Arizona had camped, Ford Benton and Colby Strauss stood frowning at the column of smoke rising from the distant campfire. Toledo and Wald, freshly crawled from their bedrolls and also frowning, came shuffling up behind them. Tomeeka, still tethered to Wald, had no choice but to also come along. She shivered in the brisk morning air despite the blanket draped over her shoulders.

"What is that? Campfire smoke?" asked Toledo.

"Yeah," Strauss bit out.

"From who? McGantry and that other old prairie rat?"

"Got to be," said Strauss. "That's right where

I saw them making camp, partway around to the back of that tall butte."

Wald's face bunched with annoyance. "What the hell? We freeze our asses off in a cold camp last night and again this morning—while they're hunched around a *warm* fire?"

Toledo glared at Strauss. "You're the one who said we'd have to get used to making cold camps from here on. To keep concealed best we can from the Injuns, you said. And you said McGantry and his pal would be doing the same."

"It only makes sense that they would. That they should," said Strauss.

"Then why the hell ain't they?" Wald demanded.

"How is he supposed to know why they're doing what they are?" intervened Benton. "I agree with Strauss that it don't make sense, that it ain't a smart thing. And I'm also holding that we're not going to be as dumb. In other words, get used to cold camps 'cause that's what we'll be sticking with. And since those fools look to be cooking breakfast, it must mean they're getting ready to go on the move pretty soon. So we'd better do the same. Chow down on some beef jerky and hardtack and consider it your breakfast before saddling up. All except you, Strauss. You'd better mount up right away and go check on those two. You'll have to do your eating from the back of your horse."

• • •

Lt. Gregory Reeves emerged hastily from his tent at the cavalry outpost, still buttoning the front of his blouse. His unshaven jawline bristled at the touch of cold morning air. Straightening his hat atop a tangle of uncombed hair, he came to a halt before the two men who stood waiting for him.

One of them, Corp. Hiner, posed smartly at attention, snapped off a salute. "Scout Timkin, just arrived from Fort Robinson, sir," he said, presenting the man standing next to him.

The latter, a towering individual with rugged, weathered facial features, dressed from head to toe in well-worn buckskins topped off by a battered Boss of the Plains hat was not, as a civilian scout for the army, required to salute. But, as a show of respect to Reeves, he did so anyway.

The lieutenant returned the salutes, saying to Hiner, "At ease, Corporal." Then, his face splitting with a wide grin, he set his eyes on Timkin and said, "Damn good to see you, Abe. Good God, man, if you left on receipt of my wire, you made remarkable time."

Timkin flashed an easy grin of his own. "Your message sounded kinda urgent. So"—reaching up to fondly pat the neck of the hard-ridden dun whose reins he held in his off hand, obviously the animal he'd arrived on—"I picked me a good horse and knocked on it as hard as I could."

"Well, I'm grateful. Because, yes, we do have something of a dicey situation here. A couple of them, actually," Reeves admitted. "Come on, I'll explain more thoroughly after you've turned your horse over to Corporal Hiner and we repair to my tent. Corporal, take Timkin's animal and make sure it gets tended to properly."

Once the corporal had smartly saluted and then led away the horse, Reeves then turned back to Timkin and said, "Now then, Abe. I'm sure you won't say no to some breakfast and hot coffee. Come on, I'll have meals sent in and I can update you while we eat."

CHAPTER TWENTY-FOUR

Lone and Arizona spent the morning working their way deeper into the Wildcats. The terrain was everything hinted at by viewing from a distance and from Arizona's more detailed description—and still more. By turns ruggedly treacherous then starkly beautiful. Flat, towering walls of cream-colored sandstone stitched by gnarled growths of pine; grassy patches of meadow ringed by cedar and birch; twisty canyons slicing off at odd angles with jagged rims like rows of broken teeth that had once lined monstrous prehistoric jawlines.

The sun had at first risen in a clear sky, warming away the initial early chill. But a sooty cloud cover moved in after a couple hours, stalling the warmth and leaving the air still and cool.

The two searchers stayed always at least a dozen feet apart, alternating riding in the lead, never presenting themselves as targets too closely bunched together. Their eyes were constantly scanning the ground, as well as to the sides and especially the heights. Watching for sign or any hint of movement or indication of eyes looking back at them. The marks of unshod ponies showed a few times, even a handful of moccasin prints, but they were all old and blurred and quickly faded into no discernible path or trail.

Twice the going was rugged enough to warrant dismounting and walking their horses. These occasions tested Lone's wounded leg and he found that, while there was some strain, it was nothing he couldn't manage.

It was as they had just ascended out of a shallow gully and were emerging to an expanse of flat, rocky ground studded with chunks of large, irregular-shaped boulders that they heard the first gunshot. It came from somewhere beyond the flat expanse, where heavy pine growth began again due ahead but crowded on either side by tall, sloping buttes.

Lone checked down Ironsides, going rigid in the saddle as his right hand reached reflexively to touch the butt of his Winchester Yellowboy where it poked up from its saddle scabbard.

Arizona pulled up alongside him. "That what I think it was?"

"No mistakin' it," Lone said.

A corner of Arizona's mouth lifted. "We gonna gallop toward it—ride to the sound of the gun?"

"I ain't George Custer and you ain't the Seventh Cavalry," Lone grunted. "I'm thinkin' we'd best just—"

He didn't finish due to the reports of two more gunshots, coming in quick succession. And accompanying them, faintly but unmistakably, could also be heard the shrill yipping of war whoops.

"Though it ain't altogether unheard of," drawled Arizona, "Injuns don't generally shoot and yip at one another."

"Nope. They don't," agreed Lone. He reached again for the Yellowboy, this time yanking it free and jacking a round into the chamber. "I'd say whoever they *are* shootin' and yippin' at is somebody we probably oughta take an interest in."

"You got me convinced," declared Arizona, swinging out his Henry.

Wasting no more time before gigging Ironsides into motion, Lone said, "Let's go find out then. Stay wide from each other and try to work close to those boulders in case you have to take cover behind one of 'em before we make it across that flat!"

They went ahead in that manner, fanning apart and then sweeping forward through the intermittent boulders. Their horses' hooves rapped loudly on the rocky surface. Also filling the air was the sound of more gunshots and more whoops, each growing closer and more frequent. Lone's trained ears could make out the reports of both pistol and rifle fire. Other than the fact Indians seldom favored handguns, he wasn't sure what to make of this.

When he and Arizona were halfway across the

flat, Lone spotted a solitary figure rushing out of the pines up ahead. The figure was on foot, running in long, smooth strides, twisting around periodically and extending an arm to fire a shot to the rear. There was something about the runner, his gait, his lean shape, that struck Lone as a bit unusual. But he didn't have time to dwell on that before the first of the man's pursuers—half a dozen Sioux braves, also on foot and running—burst into view.

The braves charged with fierce intent, eyes blazing in copper faces. Two of them were armed with rifles, the others with bows and spears. The spear carriers were running the hardest, trying to get closer before making their cast at the quarry, while the riflemen fired as they ran and the bowmen paused momentarily to launch arrows. Bullets whined through the air and cracked on impact, kicking up spurts of dust and rock shards at the runner's heels. Arrows rattled hollowly against the boulders.

Reaching one of the latter, a buckboard-sized slab bleached bone white by decades of sun exposure, the runner ducked in behind it and set himself to take more careful aim at his pursuers. He cranked off two quick rounds, causing the Sioux to scatter in response, either dropping flat to the ground or finding a boulder of their own to dive behind. Unfortunately, neither shot scored a meaningful hit. What was more, it then became apparent that those were the last two in his wheel when the shooter began frantically discharging spent casings and thumbing in fresh loads. Even though he did this with practiced nimbleness, it provided enough time for the braves to rise up and renew their rush.

But not for long.

So intent had the attackers been on the runner they were chasing that they'd failed to take adequate note of the horsemen closing in from the opposite side of the flat. This changed suddenly and drastically when Lone and Arizona, firing from their saddles, opened up with deadly accuracy. Two shots roared and two Indians sprawled dead.

Lone's target had been one of the spear carriers who'd made it to within twenty feet of where the runner crouched. The brave flung his arms wide as the bullet tore through his lungs, hurling his spear into a wild end over end spin, then fell dead before the weapon dropped to the ground.

A dozen yards behind that warrior, one of the bowmen dropped to a knee and hurriedly released a retaliatory arrow toward Lone. The missile sailed wide by mere inches. But the bullet Lone sent by way of his own retaliation didn't. It punched into the center of the brave's chest, lifting him up off his feet and knocking him into half a backward somersault before dumping him dead on the hard, unforgiving ground.

All during this, Lone was aware of Arizona's Henry barking busily and out the corner of his eye he'd seen two more Sioux bite the dust. That made five out of the six. Sweeping his eyes over the scene, Lone saw the last one, one of the bowmen, hotfooting in retreat, trying to make it back to the pines with Arizona pounding hard on his heels.

Lone relaxed slightly in his saddle, reining Ironsides to a halt. He levered a fresh round into the Yellowboy just in case and made another scan across the flat, closer in this time, touching on each of the fallen Indians to make sure they showed no signs of life. None did. Satisfied, he then cut his gaze to the runner behind the boulder.

The latter had straightened out of his crouch by now and taken a step forward, coming to rest with feet planted wide only a short distance away. Lone locked eyes with the gent—and got one of the biggest jolts of his life!

The "gent" wasn't a man at all. The person Lone found himself suddenly gawking at was a woman. Not only that, she was one hell of a special woman he happened to know very well.

"Velda? Velda! What in holy blazes are *you* doin' here?" he blurted.

Velda Beloit smiled crookedly and said, "Close your mouth, McGantry, you look stupid with it hanging open that way. You don't want to ruin the image of a White Knight riding in to save the day by rescuing the fair maiden, do you? White Knights are supposed to remain unflappable after performing even the most daring of deeds."

Lone scowled. "I ain't certain what unflappable even means but I sure as hell don't claim to be no White Knight."

"And neither am I exactly a fair maiden," countered Velda. "But I can still have my illusions, damn it. And you, you big lunk—you and your mighty gray steed, even though he's supposed to be white, along with the sidekick who rode in with you—make up the closest thing to a White Knight rescue I'm ever likely to encounter. So shut up and let me express my gratitude!"

Suddenly she was slammed tight against him, her face pressed hard to his chest, her arms flung up around his neck and shoulders. She clung like she never wanted to let go. Gently, hesitatingly, Lone wrapped his arms around her in return. It didn't take long before he became pleasantly yet uncomfortably aware of the ample female curves possessed by this person mashed so surprisingly against him.

Lone wasn't sure how long they stood like that. On one hand it didn't seem like very long, on the other it seemed like quite a while.

Until there came the nearby clop of a horse's hooves—not Ironsides'—and Arizona was clearing his throat nervously before saying, "Uh . . . excuse me?"

CHAPTER TWENTY-FIVE

Velda Beloit was a bounty hunter of considerable renown.

Before becoming such she had been the chief deputy to a Kansas sheriff who also happened to be her widower father. Raising her, an only child, Sheriff Beloit had taught her the skills of riding, shooting, and tracking over more traditional "girly stuff." And while Velda grew lovely and curvaceous in appearance, it was these less traditional traits that defined her and gave her purpose to the point of taking on the deputy job. Familiar with her accomplishments, none of the town's citizens had any problem with the hiring. In fact, after her father was killed in the line of duty, the role of sheriff could have been hers for the asking.

It was the pursuit of her father's murderers, however, and the subsequent legal restraints she ran up against in the forms of technicalities like "jurisdiction" and "due process" and other hindrances that eventually caused her to discard her badge altogether in order to mete out justice on her own terms. From there, the lure of bounty work and the pursuit of other fugitives who often managed to elude capture via similar legal constraints and complications took a tight hold and that's how Velda had been making her way ever since.

She and Lone had crossed paths several months back when a lowdown skunk Velda was on the trail of tricked Lone and stole Ironsides in the process of fleeing her. Naturally, that put Lone hot on his trail too. With a common goal and some tough challenges standing in the way of achieving it, it only made sense for the two of them to join forces. They'd succeeded in the end, but not before some unexpected twists and close calls forged a strong bond and measure of respect between them. There'd been a shared, unspoken physical attraction, too, the glimmer of a romantic spark that might have flared into more if Lone hadn't been tormented at the time by recent losses and the obligation he'd felt to resolve a prior relationship he'd left hanging fire for too long. That resolution turned out cold and empty, but by then he and Velda were traveling in different winds.

Only now, here she was again. Here *they* were, thrown together again.

The first order of business after Arizona rejoined them and broke up the embrace was to get off the wide open flat to somewhere that had better concealment and cover in case any more Sioux showed up. For this, they opted a return to the shallow gully Lone and Arizona had emerged from just before hearing the first gunshot.

Once better situated and after giving Velda some water to drink and allowing her a minute to catch her breath and regroup, Lone made necessary introductions. He included a quick recap of his and Velda's past dealings together. While he was talking, she reached up and released the mane of chestnut hair that was shoved up inside her hat, explaining she'd done so to keep it from getting tangled and snarled while passing through the pine bramble. Arizona watched with open fascination as she shook the long tresses loose and finger-combed them away from the sides of her face.

When Lone was done with his introduction, Arizona, still gazing at Velda, said to her, "Ma'am, you are plumb pretty enough to make a fella turn to crime just so there'd be a chance of you bein' the one to chase him down." When she blushed in response, he added, "Though I gotta say, a couple minutes ago—when I rode up and saw you and Lone huggin' on one another—I'd've been happy no matter what you looked like, just so long as you turned out to be a gal."

Lone scowled. "What the hell kinda crack is that?"

Arizona's eyebrows lifted. "What was I supposed to think with her hair pushed out of the way like that? Tell me you didn't reckon it was an hombre we saw runnin' from those Injuns, same as me. So put yourself in my stirrups, then, when I turned back and saw what I seen."

Velda chuckled. "Take it easy, fellas. Though I've never been the frilly dress type and at the moment am doubtlessly more frazzled than usual, I'm still all girl. So there's no problem. Just to make sure, I promise to leave my hair loose, okay?"

Both men took a moment to run another appreciative gaze over the speaker. All girl indeed. Despite the six-gun strapped to her hip and the attire of trousers and shirt, the shapeliness that filled out said attire (the oddity Lone had noted when he first saw her running, but hadn't added up at the time) was plenty conclusive. Not to mention the *feel* of that shape Lone had recently experienced pressed against him. Add in a pair of flashing eyes and the finely chiseled facial features now framed by a thick foam of hair and, yeah, you had more than just a girl, you had a whole lot of woman.

"None of which," Lone grated, continuing to feel annoyed for reasons he didn't fully understand, "yet gets around to answerin' what I asked you at the start. What in blazes are you doin' here?"

"Besides running for my life from a pack of howling Indians, you mean?" Velda's eyes flashed even brighter. "Prior to that, what brought me here in the first place is what takes me most places I go—hunting down a skunk with a bounty on his head."

"Here? In the Wildcat Hills?"

"I don't get to choose where they run. All I can do is chase after 'em."

"But wasn't you aware of the Injun trouble all through this area—the craziness stirred up by the Ghost Dance?" asked Arizona.

"I'd heard rumblings about the Ghost Dance, sure," Velda allowed. "But I didn't know it had resulted in any actual hostilities, not here in the Wildcats or anywhere else." She paused, her brows pinching tighter. Then: "That is, I didn't know any of that until three days ago."

"What happened then?" Lone wanted to know.

Velda's eyes darted anxiously back and forth between the two men. She paused a moment longer, taking a quick breath and releasing part of it before saying, "You're not going to believe this, but do you know who else is here in these Hills? None other than Buffalo Bill Cody!"

"Well that's a hell of a thing!" barked Ford Benton, from where he'd called a halt to his small column of men. "All that shootin' had to mean some kind of run-in to big trouble. And it couldn't be nobody but those damn fools McGantry and Burke, could it, Strauss?"

Colby Strauss, sitting his saddle a few paces ahead of Benton, grimaced at the question.

"Don't see how," he answered. "Sound might bounce a little funny in all these rocks, but that came from up ahead, about where they oughta be. Besides, who else is there in here other than them and us and the Injuns?"

"How the hell do I know?" responded Benton, craning his neck to rake a displeased glare at the surrounding terrain. "All these goddamn ridges and cliffs and canyons, you could cram Hell and half of Georgia in here and never see hide nor hair again. No tellin' what else you might find."

From back at the end of the line, Tucker Wald said, "If that *was* McGantry and Burke tanglin' with Injuns, from the sound of it there must've been quite a passel of the red devils. What if those two came out on the losin' end? That'd wreck the hell out of them being able to lead us to Cody."

Benton pulled a long face. "I wouldn't be too quick to count out our quarry. I keep tellin' you McGantry is a leather tough S.O.B., and Burke not much different. We'll be finding out how they fared soon enough. No matter, we'll keep on searchin' for that old bastard Cody, regardless. If there's redskins now with their blood worked up fresh, means everybody's gonna have to keep our eyes peeled extra sharp. Especially you, Strauss. So go ahead on point. Get to it."

As Strauss headed out, Toledo Slim called from his position in line behind Benton. "Just as a reminder, boss. Particularly if those two prairie rats did bite the dust, we still got the possibility of another lead we can try for. The more I see the smirk on this squaw's face when she thinks nobody is lookin', the more I'm convinced the little bitch knows something that could be useful to us. Just give me a handful of minutes to do what I know how to do, I swear I could have it out of her!"

Benton didn't say anything right away. He just glared some more at all the damnable rocks rising and falling endlessly in every direction. Then, over his shoulder, he told Toledo, "Let's wait 'til we find out for sure what that shooting was all about. Then we'll see. I gotta admit, though, I'm growin' more inclined to let you go ahead and do what you're hankerin' so bad to get after."

Toledo smiled. "I can wait."

Antoine Robideaux's good eye, the one not still puffed shut by the beating he'd endured, sagged with sadness as he gazed up at Lt. Reeves. "The sky above grows as gloomy," he said in a dismal tone, "as the hearts of my wife and I at the continued absence of our daughter. So much tension and trouble in the air, so many bad experiences of late, and now this dreadful emptiness on the inside and nothing but a cold gray without—could these be signs from God, some punishment for which He seeks atonement?"

The lieutenant shifted uneasily in his stance. "I'm not sure how to address that, Mr. Robideaux. I'm not really qualified. But I'm pretty sure God doesn't work that way. How I learned, trouble and bad occurrences come from the other fella."

"I was taught that also. And I want to continue to believe," Robideaux said. Then he added, "But times like these test a man's faith."

This exchange was taking place out front of the Frenchman's trading post. Robideaux sat on a wooden bench off to one side of the front door, a brightly patterned blanket draped over his shoulder. His wife, Shining Water, stood silently behind him. It wasn't yet noon. Reeves was recently arrived, riding at the head of a ten-man patrol; he and Abe Timkin, who stood dismounted beside the lieutenant, made twelve in total.

In a sincere, consoling tone, Reeves said now, "I have great empathy for what you and your family are going through, Mr. Robideaux. And, in your place, I suspect my outlook might be equally as bleak. But I implore you not to give up hope, at least not on the matter of your abducted daughter. As you can see"—here gesturing toward Timkin towering beside him—"I have returned as promised with the tracker I told you about. We're prepared to leave at once in pursuit of her safe return."

"We'll do our darnedest to bring her back safe and sound," Timkin said earnestly.

Robideaux nodded. "My wife and I are most grateful. I know you will do all you can. The evil of the men who took our daughter is unquestionable and I know that you are risking the safety of yourself and your men by going after them. We will pray for you. Please take great care."

"We have every intent to," Reeves assured him.

"One more thing," said Robideaux. "During the night, sometime in the small hours, my son Trace was so unsettled by the situation that he felt the need to ride out on his own quest for Tomeeka."

"Damn it, man, why didn't you stop him?" Reeves demanded, unable to hold in check a sudden burst of agitation. "Him being out there in the middle everything is a complication no one needs! I hope you understand that if trouble breaks out, I won't be able to guarantee his safety."

Speaking for the first time, Shining Water said in a soft yet firm voice, "Our son is a strong-willed young man, a brave who could no longer merely stand by when he saw cause for taking action. He rode out of here expecting no guarantees other than the one he made to himself that he would not stop until his sister was safely returned."

CHAPTER TWENTY-SIX

For the second time in only a matter of minutes (or maybe a third time if you counted the sudden embrace), Lone had been jolted by Velda.

"Buffalo Bill!" he echoed hoarsely. "What do you know about him? You sayin' you know where he is?"

"Matter of fact I do," she replied somewhat smugly. "If you close your mouth—you're doing that stupid looking dropped jaw thing again—I'll tell you all about it. It's a corker of a story, one that would fit right in with the kind of wild tales spun by Buntline and others. But this is real and where it stands now is that Bill's in a tight spot and needs help."

A corner of his mouth quirking up, Lone said, "Now here's something *you* might have trouble believin', but that's exactly why me and Arizona are here."

Velda's smug look faded. She looked Lone straight in the eye for a moment, then said, "No, I don't have trouble believing it at all. You wouldn't joke about something like that. I don't know how or why but, yes, I can see you're here to help him. And thank God for it!"

"'Spect there's lots of hows and whys to

cover," spoke up Arizona. "But I 'spect most important of all is how bad a fix is the colonel in and how far away is he?"

"He's hidden in a relatively safe place for the time being. About an hour, hour-and-a-half back the way I just came," Velda said, "depending on how much ducking and dodging we might have to do to avoid any more renegade patrols. As far as his condition, he and Pony Bob are both injured. Bill—pardon the familiarity, but that's what he insists I call him so I've gotten used to it—has a broken leg, Pony took an arrow to his side. We got the arrow out, but I've been worried about infection setting in. Neither of them are in any shape to travel over this terrain on foot, and our horses were either killed or run off. That's why I finally decided I had no choice but to try and make it out to get help. I was aiming for that cavalry outpost north of the Frenchman's trading post."

"Well we ain't no cavalry," Arizona drawled. "But we're here and we're willin' and we ain't half bad in a scrap. Plus, we can save you a heap of walkin'."

"You sure can. And you'll do just fine!" Velda exclaimed.

"Reckon that settles it then," allowed Lone. "Like Arizona said, there's still a lot of whys and hows to cover. But we can do that just as well while we're on the move." He glanced up at how the sky's sooty overcast was thickening into a darker gray made up of heavy-looking clouds sliding in from the northwest. "By the look of that sky we're gonna get some rain before the afternoon is done."

"Looks like," Arizona agreed. "Won't make the goin' any easier when it hits, though it might be helpful in other ways."

"I can't imagine how," said Velda. "But if we reach Bill and Pony Bob ahead of it, then we'll be okay. I left them tucked away in a nice, dry cave."

"Okay, let's make for it." Lone toed a stirrup and swung up onto Ironsides. Once in the saddle, he extended a hand down to Velda, saying, "You've already had yourself a good hike and a run, come on and double up with me. You know from the past that this big ol' gray can handle it."

A moment later Velda was snugged up behind him, pressed to his back this time, with her fingers laced over his stomach. "Don't worry, I won't squeeze too hard," she teased.

"Just be ready to swing your gun hand free in case we run into some more unfriendly company," Lone told her.

"Speakin' of such," grumbled Arizona, "I ain't lookin' forward to re-crossin' that bare flat again. 'Specially since I let that last red devil get away into those pines. I don't so much expect he'll be in there layin' in wait by hisself, but we don't know how far he'd have to go to round up some more of his pals."

"Unfortunately, probably not very far," said Velda. "They're pretty thick all through here. Bill figures there's close to four dozen of 'em gathered in these Hills around Blunt Nose."

Lone scowled. "Blunt Nose? I thought Kicking Bear was the chief pile of dung all the young hot-bloods was flockin' 'round?"

"That was just a ruse—a rumor cooked up and circulated by Kicking Bear and Blunt Nose—to draw attention down in this direction while Kicking Bear continues to spread his Ghost Shirt nonsense in a wider span up north. Bill and Pony captured a young buck one day early on and got that much information out of him before he slipped away from them."

"Blunt Nose. Seems like I oughta know that name," said Lone, frowning.

Arizona nodded. "Yeah, it goes back a ways but I 'spect you've heard it before. Blunt Nose is the younger brother of Yellow Hand, the war chief who led the breakout of warriors from the Spotted Tail rez right after Custer went down. Col. Merrit and the 5th rode to stop 'em, with me and Cody scoutin' for him. We 'fronted 'em at Warbonnet Creek. Remember?"

"I do now," Lone said. "The Battle of Warbonnet Creek. Heard the tale many a time—a big piece of the Buffalo Bill myth when Cody galloped ahead and fought a duel with Yellow Hand. Killed him and scalped him right there in front of God and everybody, wavin' his bloody prize and shoutin' 'First scalp for Custer!'"

"I was there. That's the way it went," Arizona confirmed. Then, smiling ruefully, he added, "And I've seen it about a hunnert times since in the re-enactments the colonel does as part of his shows."

After hearing this exchange, Velda said, "Bill indicated there was some kind of bad blood between him and this Blunt Nose. But he never went into details on the why of it."

"Well you just heard 'em," Lone told her. "While the colonel made peace and even became friends with Sitting Bull and a number of other chiefs since the Indian Wars, sounds like he don't figure he can count Blunt Nose among 'em. And havin' him here stirrin' up the local hot-bloods instead of Kicking Bear must have put a serious kink in any plans to arrange a pow-wow for the sake of tryin' to calm down the Ghost Dance business."

"I can't say how Bill thought about that. Though he doesn't strike me as the type to give up easy," said Velda. "But whatever he had in mind got knocked sideways by other things that came along to put him in the fix he's in now."

"That list of other things that came along and what in blazes you're doin' in the middle of 'em,"

Lone grated, "still has a lot of blank spaces. But first things gotta get took care of first. That means makin' it back across that flat. Then you can take over leadin' us to the colonel and Pony Bob and startin' to fill in some blanks along the way."

"You really think getting across that flat is worth so much concern?" Velda wanted to know.

"Only if our escaped friend from the first time we tried might be waitin' for us with some new pals in those pines or up in the base rocks of the buttes ahead on either side." Lone chuffed. "Otherwise it'll be a nice stroll across one of the few level chunks of ground in this whole goddamned rock pile."

"You don't have to be so snotty just over getting asked a question. Try to keep that in mind when I ask another one. How do you plan to proceed?"

Staring straight ahead at the distant pine growth, Lone said, "I figure we'll just tear across like Billy-bejeebers. If there's any red devils waitin' for us on the other side, we'll ride right down their throats and give 'em a taste of the same lead that already sent five of 'em to the Happy Huntin' Ground."

Arizona, who'd also climbed up into his saddle, rolled his eyes over at Velda, and said wryly, "He's pretty much locked on this notion that the best way to deal with a thing in his way is usually to go straight at it."

A faint smile curved Velda's mouth for just a moment. "Yes. I remember that about him."

"Alright, hang on," Lone said over his shoulder. Then, cutting a quick glance Arizona's way: "Same as before. Fan apart, sweep close to the boulders in case you need to sudden-like make friends with one of 'em. Let's go!"

So up out of the gully they went. Spreading out when they broke onto level ground and then gigging their mounts into a hard gallop. Pounding hooves rumbled loud on the rock-slabbed surface. Past the sprawled bodies and past the large boulder where Velda had earlier taken cover, eyes at all times sweeping ahead, muscles tensed to grab for their guns at the first hint of trouble.

But none came. Nothing happened. They made it across the flat without incident. Once within the pines on the other side, they checked down their horses and gave them a minute to blow and relax. But none of the three riders did so; not completely, not yet. Eyes continued to sweep and search, within the dense greenery now, ears perked for any discordant sound in the sudden quiet following the clatter of the crossing.

As some of the tension visibly eased out of his shoulders, Lone twisted partly around in his saddle and said to Velda, "No remarks on all that turning out to be for nothing?"

"You think I don't understand taking precautions, for crying out loud?" Velda responded somewhat tartly. "You think I don't take any in my line of work and then sometimes feel a little silly afterward if they turn out to have been unnecessary?"

"Better to feel a little silly than a lot dead," Lone pointed out.

"Yeah, that's the general idea. I get it. I also get that we need to keep being cautious if we mean for all of us to make it through this in one piece."

"Like you said, that's the general idea."

"In that case, how about we get a move on?" said Arizona. "I feel an itch between my shoulder blades from bein' in the middle of all these trees and bramble worse than when we was back there in the open. I've spent too much time out on the plains, I guess, where you can see what's comin' at you—even if you don't like what it is."

"Talk to the lady," Lone advised. "She knows how to get us to the colonel. The quicker we reach him, the quicker we can all put this whole nest of pissed-off Sioux behind us."

Velda pointed. "On through that gap between those buttes. This particular patch of pine thins out after about a half mile or so, then we'll drop into a narrow, snaky canyon for a while. A stretch of high ground will come next and then another, larger canyon, almost a small valley. Up in the high rocks on the back side of that is the cave where we'll find Bill and Bob."

Setting the horses in motion, Lone said, "What the devil drew you so far in? And what, I ask yet again, brought you here to begin with?"

"I already told you I came on the trail of a wanted owlhoot. By the time I caught up with him he'd joined with a handful of others cut from the same cloth, though I didn't recognize any of them from any dodgers I'd come across." Velda made a disgruntled face. "Them becoming part of the mix was the first complication. Then, while I was trying to figure out how to cull Bevins out of the pack—"

"Wait a minute," Arizona interrupted. "Did you say 'Bevins'? As in Arthur Bevins—a scrawny, rat-faced gunslick who calls hisself by the unlikely handle Toledo Slim?"

"Why, yes. That's the one. You've had dealings with him?"

"You could say that."

"We could say more than that," Lone amended. "Happens we recently crossed paths with that whole bunch he's now ridin' with. The rest of 'em, in case you ain't already figured it out, are Ford Benton, Colby Strauss, and Tucker Wald. Benton's the leader. They're law benders and hardcases all. In the past the other three mostly operated down through Kansas. What piece of bad luck for Nebraska bought 'em up this way I can't say."

"I can't claim to know what brought them,"

Velda said. "But as of a few days ago, I can sure tell you what they had in mind once they were here."

"Probably gonna be something I'll be sorry to hear, but let 'er rip."

Velda gave it a beat. Then: "They were out to kidnap Buffalo Bill!"

CHAPTER TWENTY-SEVEN

"Kidnap?" echoed Arizona. "What put a crazy notion like that in their heads?"

"What puts most notions in the heads of owl-hoots?" Velda countered. "Usually looking for some way to try and make money."

"You gotta admit," said Lone, scowling, "that nabbin' Buffalo Bill would sure give a body some negotiatin' power for that very thing. We're talkin' one of the most famous and recognizable men in the country—hell, maybe the whole world after that European tour he just finished. You figure in the wealth that fame has brought him in recent years, his properties and his business partnerships like with the Wild West show and all the books and stage plays and what not handled by Buntline . . . There's a whole lot of folks who'd come together and cough up a sizable chunk of money, for their own interests if no other reason, to get the colonel back in one piece."

"You say it that way," Arizona grunted, "it sounds like a mighty bold and gutsy undertakin'. A lot bigger one than you'd figure for a scrubby bunch like Benton's."

"I'd say it was more a matter of luck and timin' than any big master plan," said Lone. "The colonel practically handed 'em the chance, him traipsin' around out here on the frontier with only Pony Bob sidin' him, and Ford Benton bein' enough of a schemer to recognized what an opportunity it presented. And I'm sure Benton havin' a long-standin' personal grudge against the colonel didn't hurt."

"Sounds like I have some caching up to do," said Velda.

So Lone gave her a quick rundown on the history between Benton and Cody and Hickok. "Not that that has anything directly to do with this kidnappin' thing," he concluded, "other than, like I said, it adds in a personal grudge angle. But the real trigger, I'm speculatin', was as simple as Benton's bunch runnin' into the colonel and Pony Bob as they was comin' out of Robideaux's tradin' post. Arizona and me got that much from talkin' to Robideaux himself. I don't know how quick the idea hit Benton from there but, like I also said, he's a natural born schemer and seein' the colonel vulnerable that way must've been enough to kick him into gear."

"Which meant," said Arizona, "he'd've had to follow the colonel and Bob into these Hills, since something else we got from talkin' to the Frenchy was how the colonel was headed straightaway into here to try for his pow-wow with Kicking Bear."

"And *I* followed Benton's bunch in," Velda

tacked on, "still anglin' for a way to separate out my man Bevins."

"Christ. Y'all had a regular parade goin' on."

Ignoring the remark from Lone, Velda said, "When I lock on a skunk's trail, I pride myself on being dogged—some would say stubborn—about not giving up until I run the culprit to ground. This is one time, though, where I'll admit if I'd realized what a rugged, endless jumble of rocks and gullies and more rocks that these *'Hills'* actually proved to be, I might have turned back."

"Why didn't you?" asked Lone.

"Because just when I was about ready to, I caught up with them. Caught up with Benton's bunch not long after they'd gotten the drop on Bill and Pony Bob."

Lone twisted partway around in his saddle. "Wait a minute. You sayin' those polecats actually had the colonel captured?"

"That's right. At least they did until—"

Velda's words were halted by the shriek of a war whoop and the distinct whistle-buzz sound of an arrow streaking in and passing only a fraction of an inch under the lobe of Lone's right ear. Had he not twisted around a moment earlier, it would have struck him full in the throat.

"Look out!" Arizona blurted as the missile sailed across a couple feet in front of his horse's nose and thunked into a nearby pine trunk. His Henry rifle was in his hands an instant later and he was jacking a shell into the chamber.

Reacting in a different way, Lone kicked his right foot free of its stirrup and pitched to the left out of his saddle. In the same motion he swept his arm back and around and pulled Velda down with him. They hit the ground and rolled, each clawing to draw the Colts from their holsters. By the time they stopped rolling and had begun squirming around flat on their stomachs to face the direction the arrow came from, Arizona's Henry was barking and throwing lead the same way.

Another arrow cut the air in response and whizzed by just half a foot wide of the old frontiersman.

"Get the hell down!" Lone hollered.

Arizona cranked off another round before complying, then skinned out of his saddle on the far side and also hit the ground. His horse and Ironsides both wheeled and galloped clear of the fray.

Velda said, "That last arrow came from just to the right of that pointy boulder poking up out of those bushes. I think there's only one—but he's on the move!"

Sure enough, a flash of copper skin and a feathered headband appeared a moment later on the opposite side of the pointy boulder and another arrow immediately followed, accompanied by another yipping war whoop. This time the arrow sliced in at a low angle and buried its tip in the ground mere inches from Lone's shoulder.

"Looks like he's got it in for you in particular, Lone," Arizona called.

"I got no problem sharin' him," Lone growled in response.

Seconds later that's exactly how it worked out. The attacking brave adjusted his position in the bushes once again but did so too hastily, too sloppily. A faint shivering of the bramble caught the eyes and gunsights of the three skilled shooters on alert for it, so when the brave rose up this time with drawn bow he was instantly and simultaneously hammered by slugs from two Colts and a Henry rifle. The arrow, released by dead hands, fluttered harmlessly away and the archer was slammed back out of sight, issuing a final gurgling sound that was far from a war cry.

Lone, Velda, and Arizona rose slowly to their feet, guns still held at the ready, eyes and ears still alert, sweeping and listening intently to make sure the man they'd just gunned *was* the lone threat.

After a minute, Arizona said in a half whisper, "You reckon that was the one got away from our skirmish back on the flat?"

"Be my guess," Lone replied.

Velda scowled. "But that doesn't make much sense, does it? One single survivor lurking to try and ambush us on his own? Even you commented on how unlikely it would be for him to lay for us by himself, Arizona."

"The first thing you learn when up against Indians," Lone told her, "is that you can never be exactly sure how they're gonna act."

"Especially a pack of het-up young renegades like we know are prowlin' hereabouts," Arizona added.

"Come on," Lone said, his expression turning grim. "Let's go have a look, see if we can get a better idea what this fool was up to."

Continuing to display caution, even though they knew they'd pumped a tight group of three slugs into the target, they picked their way into the pine bramble on the back side of the pointy boulder. They found the brave lying there, sprawled spread-eagle, dull eyes staring up at the gray clouds slowly churning in the sky. He looked to be a youth, not more than seventeen. Amazingly, with three leaking bullet holes in him, he was still alive.

"Jesus," Velda murmured.

The brave's blood-rimmed lips moved and he spoke in a labored, hoarse whisper. Lone dropped to one knee and leaned closer to listen. The brave continued to speak, haltingly but at some length.

"Do you understand what he's saying?" Velda asked Arizona softly.

"I'm gettin' most of it. Yeah, he's the one who

escaped our earlier fight. I'll be damned, he's also one of the two who fled a fracas me and Lone had a couple days with three others who jumped us. I'll have to tell you more about that later, but because of that, because of bein' involved in two fights where he got away when others died, he was ashamed in his own eyes and also worried about goin' back to Blunt Nose and the rest . . . for fear they'd think him a coward for always escapin'. So he vowed to himself that he'd make another fight all on his own, and avenge himself by either killin' Wide Shoulders—that's what he calls Lone—or die tryin'."

"Jesus," Velda said again.

The brave abruptly stopped talking and his head lolled to one side. Lone stayed kneeling there for a minute, then reached to gently thumb the boy's eyes closed before standing up. Looking around at Arizona and Velda, he said, "Reckon you heard?"

Arizona nodded. "We got the general idea."

Lone's eyes dropped once more to the brave. "Damnedest thing," he muttered.

They all stood there for another minute. Until Lone somewhat abruptly looked up and said, "I got a foldin' shovel in my possibles pack. Neither of you may understand this, but I'm feelin' the want to proper bury this boy."

It took a beat before Arizona nodded again and said, "Your call."

A baffled-looking Velda reacted differently. "You're right, I don't understand. We need to keep moving, that sky up there is getting uglier right along. And . . . and we killed five other braves only a short distance back with no compunction to bury them." She gave a choppy shake of her head. "I don't follow."

Lone's jaw tightened as he sought the right words. "All I can say is it's a matter of honor. Those other braves back there—and this one, too, at that particular time—was lookin' to kill just for the sake of killin'. To blindly kill anybody and everybody with white skin. This time around, this one was out for something different. Even though that something meant aimin' to kill me, it was to prove a point of personal pride and to show honor and bravery to Watchers from his Spirit World in the hope of appearin' worthy in their eyes.

"He sure as hell didn't have in mind to impress me. But he did all the same. Leaves me seein' him as a proud warrior who deserves better than to be left here, maybe never discovered or paid no never mind by the others, and endin' up as nothin' but pickin's for the coyotes and buzzards." Lone wagged his head. "No, he deserves better than that."

Velda continued to look at him in a perplexed manner.

Lone heaved a sigh and said, "But you're right about the need to keep on the move. You double up with Arizona for a while, and go on ahead. I'll catch up when I'm done."

Though still looking confused, Velda replied firmly, "No. I won't agree to splitting up. If this is that important to you, Arizona and I will wait with you."

"Gal's right, Lone," said Arizona. "Pick a spot to lay the boy out, I'll go fetch your shovel."

CHAPTER TWENTY-EIGHT

"Five, by my count," stated Colby Strauss.

"Same here," said Benton, reined up alongside him. "Five dead redskins the world is better off without."

"And nary a sign of McGantry or Burke," added Tucker Wald, sitting his saddle just behind them with Tomeeka tethered at his back. "Unless it was somebody else who tangled with these bucks, I guess it shows pretty clear what you keep sayin', boss—those two are a couple of rough old cobs."

"Of course it wasn't nobody else. Who the hell else would it be?" growled Benton. "And, yeah, them two are a handful and a half."

Steering his mount up on the other side of Strauss, Toledo Slim sneered, "Cutting down a pack of scrawny feather-heads armed with spears and spindly arrows don't seem like such of a much. Besides, for all we know those old cobs got their asses shot up too, and just managed to crawl off somewhere."

The four had their horses checked down on the front edge of the rocky flat where Lone and Arizona (and Velda, though Benton's bunch had no way of knowing that detail) had engaged the renegades earlier. A swarm of buzzards and crows were now busy picking at—and drawing attention to—the gory aftermath they were gazing out upon.

Scowling at the young gunslick's remarks, Benton cut a sidelong glance in his direction and said, "I'll remind you that a pack of arrow-flingin' feather-heads—along with that gun-totin' bounty hunter babe out for your hide—queered the hell out of things for us not so very long ago. And you was right in the thick of the hightailin', so don't waste your chest thumpin' routine on me, sonny. There's times when not even a fast gun is guaranteed to carry the day, and ain't no shame in needin' to step back and do some course-correctin'."

Toledo met his scowl but made no reply.

Swinging his gaze back to the flat, Benton said, "When we have a closer look, we'll find out if there's sign of anybody crawlin' off wounded. But I wouldn't get my hopes up. In fact, we *want* those two to stay healthy enough to keep leadin' us on, remember?"

"And I keep telling you there's another way to find out same as what they know. Remember that?" Toledo replied, bold as ever. "Take a look over your shoulder at our little squaw right now. The sight of those bloody, pecked-at bodies out there has got her real primed for a little question-and-answer session with me. Wouldn't be no better time. I could have her spillin' everything she knows in a matter of minutes. And you said you was inclined to give me a chance once we found about the shooting we heard."

"But that was when we thought those two old toughs might've got cut down by the Injuns," spoke up Wald. "Now that we know otherwise, they're still our best bet for gettin' led back to Cody."

"Says who?" argued Toledo, his voice turning almost shrill. "That squaw might know *more* than those old prairie scrapes. Dragging her around and not bothering to find out is just wasting time. The only one getting anything out of it is you having those little squaw titties rubbing against your back all the time, ain't that right, big man?"

Wald's face turned flaming red with rage, maybe a touch of embarrassment. "God damn it, Ford!" he bellowed. "I don't have to take that kind of talk from that little pissant. Can't you see he's just a sick, twisted piece of crud who wants at the girl for his own satisfaction and could care less what she might have to say?"

"I gotta go along with Tucker on that, Ford," interjected Strauss. "I think it's clear that Slim is way too anxious to get at the girl—and, he's made it known, not in a regular way. Bringin' her along and takin' turns with her in a bedroll in the middle of the night, that's one thing. But doin' . . . whatever it is he seems to be out for . . . that just don't feel right."

Toledo swung his horse out wide and wheeled

it to face the others. "You go to hell, you two nances! How many bosses has this outfit got, Benton? I thought I signed on with you, not some voting committee. And, while I'm at it, I also thought I was hitching up for the kind of work you earned a rep for down in Kansas—not this wild-ass kidnapping thing that involves ridin' smack in the middle of a passel of scalp-happy damn redskins!"

Benton went rigid in his saddle and his eyes turned into glowing coals. "You signed on for whatever jobs I lay out for this outfit, you young pup! And if you ain't got brains enough to see what a once-in-a-lifetime chance this is to nab Cody for maybe as much as a million dollars, then turn around and rattle your stupid hocks outta here. Go back to nickel and dime bodyguard work in Laramie and showin' off on the side by out-drawin' drunk cowboys. Oh yeah, and tryin' to dodge the Wanted posters they got out on you."

"I ain't used to be talked down to like that. Not by nobody." Toledo's words had a hard, warning rasp to them. But there was also a slight hint of uncertainty.

Benton replied, his voice iron steady, "Then don't give me call to. I'll allow most any man to get out of line once. Once. So I'm willin' to let—"

The gang boss never got the chance to say what

he was willing to let. Because all at once came an interruption—a loud curse and a flailing of bodies—from the back of Tucker Wald's horse. When the faces of the others snapped around to look they saw the big man toppling out of his saddle and falling heavily to the ground. What they didn't see, not right away, was the girl Tomeeka who was supposed to be tethered to him. She wasn't on the horse and neither was she on the ground. Make that, not fallen on the ground with Wald. Instead, she was on the ground running. Racing away in long, clean strides, hands still bound behind her, plunging back down the shallow gully that fed out to the flat, her long hair streaming as she ran along with the loose end of the tether rope still tied around her neck.

"Damn it all! What happened?" demanded a furious Benton.

Puffing and cursing as he scrambled back to his feet, Wald said, "The little shit caught me off guard. I was concentratin' too hard on what was goin' on between you and Slim. She all of a sudden swung a foot and kicked me upside the head, then peeled off the back and yanked the rope out of my hands—took off runnin' lickety-split."

"She's fast, but not that fast," said sharpshooter Strauss, reaching for the rifle in his saddle boot. "Want me to stop her, Ford?"

"No! I want that little bitch back."

"I'll get her," Toledo was quick to say.

Benton made a chopping motion with one hand. "No, not you. Tucker's the one who let her get away, it's his job to get her ass back!"

"You bet I will," declared Wald, swinging up into his saddle. "I'll drag her back by the hair of her head if I have to."

"If you do, you'd better keep better hold of that than you did the goddamned rope you had tied to her," snarled Benton. "I don't care how, just don't let her get away! You'll have to catch up, the rest of us ain't gonna wait. We've wasted too much time here already!"

"Go ahead then," Wald responded, spurring his horse into motion. "I'll be along before you know it."

Tomeeka heard the men shouting and cursing behind her and it was frightening. But the fear made her run all the faster. She was a very good runner, always had been. As a child, when her mother took her on visits to relatives on the reservation and she played with the other children there, she was always among the fastest at running games. Though she had outgrown such activities now that she'd blossomed into a young woman, she was still lithe and strong and never before was there more incentive to race any harder than at this moment.

Having her wrists tied behind her back made it awkward, took away the rhythm and balance of her pumping arms. But raw desperation created by the awareness she was running for her life was a powerful off-setting factor.

Never was the limited balance or assistance from being able to reach out with her hands more troublesome than when she darted off the floor of the gully and began ascending up one of its rocky, weather-seamed walls. She knew, though, the move was absolutely necessary if she was to have any chance of escaping pursuit. For a few minutes, the sound of the men behind her had faded, drowned out partly by the distance she'd covered and partly by the sounds of her pounding feet and thudding heart. But then Tomeeka could hear the unmistakable rumble of hoofbeats—someone giving chase on a horse. No way she could stay ahead of that on level ground.

So as soon as she spotted an upward-angling fissure on the gully wall that looked halfway negotiable, Tomeeka veered over and began making her way up. It wasn't easy, not being able to pull with her hands, having only the strength of her thrusting legs to propel her. For balance, she bumped and dragged her inner shoulder along the rugged sandstone wall.

The rim above was choked with brush and bramble. Tomeeka couldn't tell for sure what was beyond that, but if she could make it at least that far it would be a start. Even if there wasn't higher terrain suitable for continuing to flee, she could try to hide. The man or men coming on horseback would have to dismount and climb too. If nothing else, she could buy time. She didn't think they would simply shoot her; if they'd wanted to do that, they would have fired when she was only a short ways into the gully. Besides, if it came to taking a bullet that would be preferable to letting the one called Slim get his hands on her and do the dreadful things he'd hinted at doing.

"Hey you! Stop! Get down from there before you break your fool neck!"

Tomeeka recognized the gruff voice calling up to her as that of Tucker, the man she had been tethered to. Glancing around and down she saw that, sure enough, he had just reined up in a swirl of dust on the gully floor below. He was alone, glaring up at her and looking very agitated.

"You can't get away. Come down before you fall and hurt yourself," he called.

"What difference if I harm myself or return and be hurt by you and your friends?" Tomeeka challenged.

"Nobody's hurt you, have they? Ain't I always stuck up for you against Slim?" Wald argued.

"But you would not do so against the mean-faced one, the one you call Ford," Tomeeka insisted. "If he told you to give me to the evil Slim, you would do so."

"But that ain't gonna happen. You heard Ford arguin' with Slim, didn't you? If you come back peaceful with me, I'll tell that to Ford and he'll see you get treated okay."

"I do not trust him," Tomeeka said, baring her teeth. "If you really want to help me, then let me go. Tell the others you could not catch me."

Wald set his jaw. "You know I can't do that."

"Then I will have to *make* it so!" Tomeeka declared, turning back and renewing her ascent with hard, frantic leg thrusts. She was less than ten feet from the rim and there appeared to be two or three more decent foot holds between where she was and the top. If she could make it up and over and through the bramble she might still have a chance.

Seeing her renewed efforts to keep climbing, Wald swung down from his saddle with a curse and started after her. "Damn stubborn brat," he muttered.

Being a thick-bodied man in cowboy boots quickly worked to Wald's disadvantage as he began clambering up the tight seam with its scant toe holds and wall bulges that pushed out against his bulk considerably harder than the lithe form of Tomeeka. Trying to hurry, he slipped and banged his knees and shins repeatedly, turning the air a steady stream of blue. When his hat fell off he cussed the loudest. And when Tomeeka kicked loose some good-sized chunks of rock and sent them raining down on him, he wailed, "Ow! Damn it, that hurt! That ain't fair . . . You wait 'til I get my hands on you!"

Finally reaching the rim—gasping for breath, her shoulder scraped and bleeding, and Wald continuing to climb in pursuit despite his agonies—Tomeeka folded her stomach over the lip and then kicked and squirmed her way through the bramble. Once free of it, she found herself on the edge of a sloping, grassy strip with high, impenetrable escarpments to the left and ahead and a spine of lower, jagged rocks about eighty yards to the right. Pushing determinedly to her feet, she broke immediately for the jagged rocks, viewing them to hold the promise of numerous hiding places.

She'd made it halfway there when, behind her, a sweating, panting, thoroughly disheveled-looking Tucker Wald came crashing out of the bramble. He stood for a moment, dripping sweat, leaning forward with his hands resting on his knees, and swung his gaze in search of his quarry. When he saw her, he groaned "Aw, shit!" but then, with the same determination Tomeeka had shown, he straightened up and went lumbering after her.

Just before reaching the rocks she hoped would provide refuge, Tomeeka was brought to a sudden, startling halt by the sight of a man emerging out of them directly in front of her. She checked her forward momentum so abruptly that it nearly made her stumble and fall. Her heart leaped into her throat and the impossible thought screamed through her mind that one of the other members of Ford's gang had somehow gotten ahead of her!

But then a single spoken word jarred her back to reality and a great flood of relief poured over her.

"Tomeeka."

The familiar voice, the darkly handsome, equally familiar face of the speaker, all still impossible seeming yet real and undeniable and wonderful. It was her bother Trace standing there with a Winchester rifle held angled across his chest!

"Get behind me," he said in a soft though commanding tone. His eyes touched her warmly for a moment, then shifted past and turned narrow and flinty. His gaze locked on the approaching Tucker Wald and held unwavering until the big man had slowed and drawn to within a dozen feet. Tomeeka stood close behind Trace, one hand resting on his shoulder.

"That's far enough," Trace told Wald, voice clear and steady.

The big man stopped, still breathing hard and dripping sweat, but he held himself erect and met Trace's flinty gaze with one of his own, at the same time twisting his mouth into a menacing grimace. "I don't know who the hell you are, mister. But you're makin' the serious mistake of stickin' your nose into something that's gonna turn out real bad for you unless you hand that girl over to me and clear your half-breed ass out of here pronto."

"It is not surprising you have the poor memory of a pig, since you are one," Trace said through gritted teeth. "To help you recall, my half-breed ass belongs to the brother of this girl you have on a leash like a dog—and also the son of the old man you savagely beat with your fists only two days ago."

Wald's eyes didn't change but now his mouth took on a sneer. "Oh, yeah. Now I remember. The snivelin' little coward who stood by and watched it all happen. Now trying to be the big, brave man out for revenge, eh?"

Icily, Trace said, "All I could do was watch because I had no weapon then—now I do."

"The question is, are you man enough to use it? You ever shot a man, sonny?"

"You're going to find out, one way or the other," Trace promised. "So the question to you is: Are you going to hold still for it like the swine past due for slaughter you truly are, or are you going to try and stop me with that gun on your hip?"

Wald's answer was to go for the gun. But he was a brawler, a slugger, his fists conditioned for pounding against faces not for pulling a hogleg.

And Trace had too much hate coiled up in him to be slowed the slightest by never having shot a man before. With a round already chambered, his rifle's muzzle dropped level and the slug it discharged hit Wald square in the chest before his handgun lifted more than an inch in its leather.

The big man staggered backward a step and a half, dropped to his knees, then tipped onto one side before rolling onto his back. Trace and Tomeeka walked up and stood over him. His eyes were open and he had an oddly baffled look on his face. When his eyes found Tomeeka, he whispered in a weak, almost childlike voice, "I . . . I was nice to you . . . I don't deserve this." Then he died.

CHAPTER TWENTY-NINE

Lone, Velda, and Arizona were on the move again. Having buried their most recent attacker to Lone's satisfaction, they were pushing hard to reach the cave where Velda had left Cody and Pony Bob ahead of the rain. They'd passed between the buttes and through the snaky canyon by now and were starting across a stretch of high, rocky ground, mostly open except for a staggered pattern of weather-worn upthrusts. The wind was picking up slightly, turning the air colder and damper.

As they covered ground, they remained constantly vigilant for further sign of any more renegades. This didn't stop them from talking as they went, though, filling in details for one another that had previously been left hanging fire.

For one thing, Arizona backtracked and finished telling Velda about the first encounter he and Lone had had with the brave they'd just buried—him and two companions, one of whom didn't make it out alive. This involved also mentioning the numerous wounds Lone was packing around, especially the most serious one to his thigh. Velda's expressed concern over him was naturally met by Lone down-playing it and in the process throwing some stern scowls Arizona's way for ever bringing it up.

The most eyebrow-raising account, however, came from Velda herself when she picked up where she'd been interrupted by the arrow skimming in and so narrowly missing Lone. She at the time had just revealed how the kidnap-minded Benton gang actually succeeded in getting the drop on Buffalo Bill and Pony Bob. "That was the scene I rode up on, practically stumbled onto," she explained from the saddle behind Lone. "Bill and Bob had stopped on the edge of a small clearing to rest their horses and make a noon meal. Benton's bunch showed up, friendly-like at first, and then caught them by surprise when they pulled guns on them. When I first saw it from a distance, I thought they had all joined together. It was only after I worked my way around on one side of the clearing and snuck in close that I figured out the difference."

"Wait a minute," said Arizona, frowning. "You sayin' you saw a total of six what you thought was all owlhoots and you slipped in closer anyway, meanin' to somehow still make your play on Toledo? Gal, you got more sand than one of them A-rab deserts."

"You only saw a piece of this girl in action," Lone told him. "No too many better you'd want sidin' you in a scrape."

"Hey, now. Don't lay the flattery on too thick.

I'm also the gal who got herself pinned down behind that boulder back there on the flat, don't forget," said Velda. "But getting back to those would-be kidnappers having the bulge on Buffalo Bill, it's not like I was ever figuring to just spring out and challenge the whole bunch. I was merely looking for an opening, some idea I could build a better plan around. When I got in closer, though, first I recognized Buffalo Bill—and then I heard Benton laying out his notion to take him hostage and hold him for ransom. Obviously, at that point I knew my interest in Bevins had to take second place to trying to help Bill."

"Lackin' just a minor detail like a small army to back your play," quipped Lone.

"Funny you should say that," Velda replied, arching a brow even though Lone couldn't see it. "Because a small army is just what I got. Only trouble, it was a pack of renegades, close to twenty I judged, swooping down on the whole lot of us. But it was enough of a distraction for me to rush out and go to the aid of Bill and Bob. I covered them so they could regain their guns and then we fought to make a getaway while Benton and his men were too busy fighting off the attack to stop us. That little weasel Bevins recognized me and he and I exchanged a couple shots, but we both had any other things to focus on."

"Bill, Bob, and I, foregoing any chance at making it to our horses, ducked into the fringe of trees and underbrush surrounding the clearing. Five or six braves followed us, the rest stayed fighting Benton and his men. They were trying to get re-mounted the last I saw, but I quickly lost sight. From there, I've got to give all the credit to Bill Cody—and Pony Bob, too—for making good our escape and keeping us alive. They knew every trick for masking our trail and dodging and outfoxing our pursuers. We shot and killed two, the rest we were able to elude but not before Bob took an arrow. Bill's injury, thankfully, didn't occur until just as we were gaining access to the cave he spotted for us to hide in. Some rocks gave way under his foot and he took a bad fall."

"Sounds like you had your share of good *and* bad luck," Lone commented.

"At least we got clear of Benton and his men. Until you said you recently ran into them, I didn't know how they fared." Velda shook her head as if in wonder. "Frankly, I'm surprised they all made it out alive."

Arizona spat. "Sad to say they did. Cockroaches are hard to kill."

"Not only did they make it out and did we have the misfortune of runnin' into 'em," said Lone, "but for a while after we parted ways we had reason to suspect they was keepin' tabs on us. We couldn't quite feature why, but now I got a hunch I know. I'm thinkin' they believed we was out here on a hunt for the colonel—which we was—

and sniffin' after us might help lead 'em back to him."

"So they were following you?"

"Appeared like. Leastways up 'til we made it as far as Robideaux's tradin' post. When we left there, it was in kind of a hurry and to be honest I wasn't thinkin' on 'em anymore. Ain't seen no further sign of 'em, though, but ain't really been lookin' neither."

"Same here," said Arizona sourly.

"So there's a chance they might have continued following you even here, that what you're saying?" prodded Velda.

"Ain't impossible," allowed Lone. "Be tricky to spot 'em in all these hills and rocks, especially was they workin' not to be seen while we wasn't particularly on the lookout."

"Damn," muttered Arizona. "This time we might be the ones headin' up a parade. And if those skunks *are* foggin' us, the last thing we want is to be leadin' 'em where they're hopin' we will."

Lone reined Ironsides to an easy halt and Arizona followed suit. The big former scout sat very still in his saddle for a minute, running the knuckles of his right hand back and forth along his jawline, pondering in silence.

Until Velda asked, "What are you thinking?"

"For starters," Lone grated in response, "I'm thinkin' how much I hate to admit I might not have spotted them polecats if they've been on our back trail since we left Robideaux's."

"I hear that," grunted Arizona.

"But at the same time," Lone continued, "I gotta face the fact that, all things considered, it maybe could be. If they hung back just far enough and used the rocks and pines for cover, they might manage it. I never counted Colby Strauss for bein' able to track more than muddy boot prints across a bed sheet, but I suppose the pompous ass would have a chance to keep tight pace with us since we made no effort to mask our passage." He paused to heave a ragged, frustrated sigh. "Thing is, it scalds out to there bein' no two ways about it. We're gonna have to make sure one way or the other before we go any closer to where the colonel and Pony Bob are waitin'."

"What you got in mind?" Arizona said.

Lone swung his arm, indicating their surroundings. "This high tableland works in our favor for doin' some reconnoiterin' and makin' some fixes if we need to. If they're behind us, then they're below us and that means they can't be glassin' us right now. So this time we *are* gonna split up for a bit. I'm gonna peel off and drop back on foot, skulk down and see what I can see on our back trail. Meanwhile, you two keep on the horses and do some ridin' around on these high rocks.

"Stick to the hardest, rockiest footin' you can,

where you'll leave the least amount of tracks possible. And ride in a pointless, zig-zag pattern so if anybody should come along and pick up pieces of sign here and there, it won't make a lick of sense. While you're doin' that, I'll try to determine for sure if we got owlhoots behind us or not. If we do, I'll mask our trail best I can between them and here before rejoinin' you."

"What about your wounded leg?" Velda asked.

"What about it?"

"You're talking about covering some pretty rugged ground on foot. Will your leg hold up to that?"

"I'll *make* it hold up," Lone told her.

"Something else," Arizona spoke up.

"What's that?"

The old frontiersman poked a finger skyward. "Before when I said rain can sometimes be a useful thing? Well, this might be one of those times. That sky goes ahead and opens up, it'd go a long way toward smudgin' any tracks we make from here on out."

"That it would," Lone agreed. "We'll take all the help we can get. But we'll still take our own measures, too."

CHAPTER THIRTY

Ford Benton's jaw sagged in disbelief. "How can that be? It don't seem possible. You tellin' me that squaw killed Tucker and then got clean away?"

"All I know is that Tucker's layin' back there dead and the girl is gone. And what else I know is that it was a hell of a thing to come upon." Colby Strauss fairly groaned these words, expression and tone conveying equal amounts of deep anguish. "Yeah, him and me snarled all the time at each other like a couple hounds over the same bone, but I knew damn well I could always count on that clubber in a tight and he knew likewise about me. Jesus, how long did we ride together behind you, Ford?"

"Long time. Long damn time," Benton answered, his voice a little hoarse and his eyes seeming to gaze at something far away for a long beat.

"How was it he got killed?" asked Toledo.

The four men sat their horses on the far side of the boulder-strewn flat, the spot also strewn with the bodies of the five slain Sioux renegades. The latter continued to be gouged and pecked at by a swarm of crows and vultures. The swarm was only now settling back to its grisly work after being scattered minutes earlier by Strauss's return from being sent to find out what was keeping the absent Wald. Strauss had ridden in at a frantic gallop, leading Wald's riderless horse and beginning to blurt the report of his findings even before he got fully reined up.

Responding to Toledo's question, Strauss said now, "Shot dead center to the chest. Only took one hit but it must've blew up his poor ol' heart."

"So the girl had to have got untied somehow and grabbed his gun."

Strauss shook his head. "His handgun was still in its holster and, as you can see"—jabbing a thumb to indicate the horse he'd led in—"his rifle is still in its saddle boot."

"They must've run into Injuns then," Toledo decided. "Killed Wald, took the girl."

"No," Benton countered, his eyes swinging back from their far-off gaze. "Injuns would've never left his gun. Sure as hell not his horse and rifle."

"And there was no sign of a struggle or no footprints except those of the girl leadin' off to some jagged rocks," said Strauss. Then his brow puckered with renewed anguish. "But I don't know what else that leaves. I—I don't know how to explain . . ."

"Where did you find him?" Benton asked sharply. "Somewhere still in the gully that girl ran into?"

"No, how I put it together was that the squaw found a way to climb up out of the gully and Tucker went after her," Strauss said. "I found his horse where he left it ground-reined and could see scrapin's on the side of the gully wall where they went up. I clumb up too. Over the rim, through some brush and weeds, a grassy strip ran for a ways. That's where I spotted Tucker, about forty or fifty yards out."

"Why didn't you bring his body back?"

Strauss winced. "I tried, I wanted to. But I only lasted draggin' him for a short ways, him bein' dead weight and all. He wasn't no small man, you know that. Woulda took me forever just to get him to the rim of the gully, and then . . . I figured too much time had already passed, it would be best to get back and tell you what I found and we could all return and bury him there. That grassy ground ain't likely as rocky as—"

"No. Tucker stays where he is, as he is," Ford stated bluntly. "Like you just got done sayin', we lost too much time already. I told Tucker when he went after that squaw—the one he let get away to begin with—we wasn't gonna wait for him. Well, I already broke my word on that by holdin' off and sendin' you to go find his slow ass. So now you did. That's enough. *Too much* as far as time lost. Wasted. Ain't gonna waste no more, not on no burial detail or nothing else." Benton paused, his eyes boring into Strauss's. "Everybody who rides with me knows the rule. If you can't keep up, you get left behind. Tucker's been part of leavin' others behind when they caught a bad break, now it came his turn. That's all there is to it."

"But what about how he died? Who killed him?"

"I can't worry about that right now." Thrusting an arm, pointing into the pine growth, Benton said, "What I'm concerned about is through there, on up ahead. All the way to wherever that mossy-horned damn Cody is. Once we get our hands on him again, then all our other worries will be over with. Crushed by the weight of the million dollars he's gonna bring our way."

Strauss looked down, unable to meet Benton's eyes.

"In that case, instead of just talking about not wasting any more time, let's get a move on," urged Toledo.

"I've got to hand it to you, son. The first time we met, even though you were upset and understandably a little hot under the collar, you still made level-headed sense in some of the things you said and I complimented you on it. Now—even though I was highly disapproving just a little while ago when your father told me what you'd undertaken on your own—I have to compliment you again on your bravery and the successful recovery of your sister."

So spoke Lt. Reeves, addressing Trace Robideaux shortly after encountering the young man and his sister a short ways within the western reaches of the Wildcat Hills' central mass. Reeves and his patrol, guided by scout Abe Timkin, had only recently reached the spot beside the tall, flat-faced butte where Lone and Arizona had camped the previous night. The lieutenant, Timkin, and Sgt. Skinner were dismounted, standing over and more closely examining the scene, when Trace and Tomeeka, riding double on Trace's pony, came around the side of the butte and out of the brush.

Responding now to Reeves's words, Trace said somewhat coolly, "I only did what I felt was necessary because no other action was taking place."

The lieutenant's mouth pulled tight for a moment before he said, "I can appreciate how you might have felt that way, even though I tried to explain about the protocols it was necessary for me to follow. I hope you, in turn, can appreciate that my men and I are here now, as promised. This man"—gesturing to Timkin—"rode all night from Fort Robinson in order to arrive and be of assistance."

Trace's eyes went from Reeves to Timkin and then back again, his expression remaining impassive.

"But the main thing," Reeves went on, "is that

your sister has been safely recovered, though no doubt having suffered a dreadful ordeal." His gaze shifted to Tomeeka and his eyes and his tone took on a sincerely compassionate warmth. "Can I or my men do anything to make you more comfortable, miss . . . Tomeeka, is it? Would you like to get down and rest for a moment? Can we get you a drink of water, a blanket perhaps? Have you had anything to eat recently?"

"A—a drink would be good," Tomeeka said somewhat hesitantly. Then, a bit less so, she added, "A blanket, too, if it's not too much trouble. The air is turning chill."

Reeves snapped his fingers at the nearest of the still-mounted troopers strung out in a column behind him. The man quickly dismounted and came forward with a canteen of water and a blanket. Trace and Tomeeka slipped from their pony to meet him. Tomeeka took the canteen and drank from it, Trace took the blanket and draped it over her shoulders.

Turning to Reeves, the young man said, "I guess I did not plan very well for her comfort in the event I found her. Thank you for that."

"Think nothing of it. You did the most important thing," Reeves told him. "She never really answered about something to eat. A biscuit or some canned fruit from our rations maybe?"

When Tomeeka silently but obviously showed an interest at the mention of canned fruit, Reeves smiled and said to the trooper who'd brought the other items, "Go fetch an airtight of peaches for the young lady." Pausing, he asked of Trace, "Anything for you?"

"I'm okay. I just want to get my sister and myself home before the rain comes."

The lieutenant nodded. "Understandable. Just give her a couple more minutes to rest and have a bite to eat. Then, if you'll allow, I'll send a detail to accompany you. In the meantime, please excuse me and my officers for a brief side bar."

With that, Reeves motioned to Timkin and Skinner and they moved a few yards away. When they were out of earshot of the others, Reeves said in a lowered voice, "Gentlemen, the situation has obviously taken an unexpected turn from the way things stood when we started out this morning. I could—and, frankly, *should*—call the mission complete and order the column returned to our post. But I am not so inclined. And by not doing so, I am likely jeopardizing my rank and possibly setting myself up for a court martial."

The lieutenant paused, letting the words sink in and regarding the reaction of the two men he was addressing. Then he continued. "You both know full well that the purpose of the temporary post I was assigned to establish down here was under strict orders to merely observe and report on any escalation in the area's Indian activity that might be considered hostile. Under no circumstances was I to take troops into the Wildcat Hills, where renegades under the influence of the Ghost Dance movement are believed to be gathered, due to the risk of such an act being seen as possible incitement to hostility. Even coming here today in pursuit of the kidnappers was tenuous.

"But even though we now have the kidnap victim, I mean to press further, regardless. We know that at least eight white men, including the kidnappers as well as Buffalo Bill Cody if he remains alive, are still somewhere in the interior. Every indication is that the kidnappers mean Cody harm if they can get to him. I propose to do everything I can to prevent that."

Timkin and Skinner looked back at him with uncertain expressions.

Until Timkin said, "That's all real interestin', Lieutenant. But why the long-winded explanation? What are you gettin' at?"

Frowning, Reeves replied, "I thought I made clear at the outset that I'm taking this action without sanction and most likely setting myself for serious repercussions. I accept that. The other men have no choice but to follow my command with no risk except what the mission might entail. But you two have a standing and a rank to consider if you go along with what you know to be in violation of a higher order. So I'm giving you the chance to stand down and return with the Robideauxs before I proceed."

Timkin's weathered face suddenly split with a wide grin.

"What's so funny?" demanded Reeves.

"The thought of me worryin' about my *standing* if I don't stick exactly to some high-handed instruction, that's what," Timkin replied. "How long you knowed me, sir? I'm a civilian scout. You ever seen any of us who are worth beans—and that'd include Lone McGantry and Arizona Burke, who I understand are also in that rock pile up ahead of us—give two shits about rules and regulations? I didn't rattle my hocks all night to get here just so's I could turn back a-fore the fun starts."

Reeves cut his eyes to Skinner. "And you, Sergeant? Your record shows plainly enough that you have your share of trouble hanging on to those stripes without the likes of me adding to it."

"If you're sayin' I got a choice, sir," said a scowling Skinner, "then my answer is this: Stripes or no stripes, I figure my job in this man's army is to fight if there's trouble, not serve as babysitter to a couple of . . . er, make that not perform escort duty. Again, that's if I got a choice, sir."

Now it was Reeves's turn to grin. "You do. And I had a hunch you'd feel that way. Glad of it. Now, pick two men to escort the Robideauxs when they're ready. Tell the rest to break out their foul weather gear. We leave in five minutes."

CHAPTER THIRTY-ONE

Lone had descended down off the tableland and worked three-quarters of the way back through the snaky canyon that led up to it. By that point he'd neither seen nor heard any indication of Benton or his men. Considering the distance covered and time involved, he decided he needed to return to Velda and Arizona. If Benton's bunch *was* on their tail—and, having accepted such as a possibility, Lone wasn't quite ready to dismiss it completely—then they had for some reason lagged too far back to be of immediate concern.

So, with that determined and some additional precautions now being taken (including the pending rainfall that was sure to help wash away any sign they currently were leaving), Lone was more anxious than ever to reach the reportedly injured Col. Cody. As he worked his way out of the canyon for the second time, he nevertheless took the extra measure of dragging a leaf-heavy cedar limb behind him to ensure more blurring of his passing.

He would later blame his concentration on this task as being partly responsible for not spotting the three renegades sooner. He had reached the pinch-point end of the canyon and was started up the slope that would give way to the higher tableland. It was as he was looking around for a good spot to ditch the cedar branch that his eyes fell on the braves emerging from a stand of pine and white birch twenty-five feet up the grade and thirty or so degrees off to his right. The trio spotted him at the same time and for a startled moment everybody froze, just gawking at one another in surprise.

But that changed in a hurry.

Lone had time to take note that one of the three carried a rifle, the other two brandished bows. A hunting party, he reckoned. And whatever they'd been hunting before, guess who they would be all too eager to switch to now?

Spitting a curse, Lone dropped the cedar branch and spun sharply to his left. The incline leading up to the tableland was gouged with an irregular pattern of furrows made by previous rain run-off, as if a giant hand had reached down and raked its fingers down the slope. It was into the nearest of these that Lone flung himself in order to seek cover. He'd barely made it, snugging tight into the depression and wishing it was deeper, before both a rifle bullet and an arrow cut the air close above him and buried themselves in the far shoulder of the furrow.

Shifting onto his left side, Lone palmed the Colt from its holster on his right hip and held it ready. He hadn't brought his Winchester Yellowboy with him, wanting to travel light for what was meant to be only a brief reconnoiter. Part of him wished he had it with him now, for the added punch and extra rounds it would provide; though at the same time it would have been unwieldy to try and use stuffed down in the furrow like he currently was. Given that and the relatively short distance between him and his targets, the freedom of being able to swing a six-shooter in one hand was more suitable. It was up to the user to make it pay off.

Lone got his chance to try a handful of seconds later when, as soon as the Sioux rifleman fired again, Lone thrust up and triggered a quick response. Expecting the braves to have scattered from where he'd originally seen them, the former scout was counting on some smoke haze left by the rifleman's shot to provide him a target. It did, and he rapid-fired two rounds at the bluish smudge before ducking back down. Unfortunately, though he'd seen some leaves and twigs splatter from his bullets plowing through, he didn't hear an outcry or see any indication he'd hit anything more meaningful. And the blink of time he'd exposed himself had drawn two more arrows from the rifleman's companions, each zinging in uncomfortably close.

This fracas had the makings to turn a heap more uncomfortable if Lone didn't figure out a way to turn the tide, and do it in a hurry.

The biggest problem was that the furrow he'd

dropped into offered pretty good cover initially but it gave him no maneuverability, except to go up or down within the depression itself. Otherwise it was open ground for several feet to either side if he tried to make a dash out of it. In the meantime, the Indians had the cover of trees and brush extending nearly to the lip of the tableland above and all the way down to the pinch point where the canyon ended below. If they had any tactical smarts, they could fan out and really put Lone in a bind. One of them, most logically the rifleman, could hold where he was, continuing to keep Lone pinned down, while the archers split with one working his way up higher and the other down lower until they'd formed what amounted to a reverse crescent giving them vantage points at each tip from which they could pour it on Lone.

It wasn't a pretty picture to envision. The only restraint might be how many arrows the archers were carrying or, for that matter, how many cartridges the rifleman had. Out on the frontier, getting one's hands on a firearm—for outlaws on the run, say, or for men like these breakout renegades—was sometimes easier than maintaining an adequate supply of ammunition for it.

Even as these thoughts tumbled through Lone's mind, two more rifle shots and two more arrows pounded and thunked into the shoulders of the furrow mere inches above him. Either the braves were too reckless or too damn dumb to care about conserving their ammunition—or they had plenty to spare. In any event, it came down to Lone not being able to count on the other side's ineptitude or bad luck to get him out of this fix. He damn well had to do something himself to make it happen.

And that's when it began to rain.

It came all at once, no initial patter of early sprinkles, no smaller drops building into larger ones, nothing like that. Just a single gust of cold wind and then a downpour of fat, equally cold drops pouring down as if a giant bucket had been upended in the churning gray sky. The effect was startling, like a slap in the face.

In addition to an immediate drenching, visibility turned to a milky blur for anything more than a couple feet away. The clump of trees and brush harboring the Indians was nothing but a smear of pale green in the seeming distance.

The rain came down so hard, so fast that the furrow Lone was in quickly became a trough filled with swirling, sluicing, foamy water. And that was before any run-off from above started being added in. What was more, the bottom and sides of the trough began turning slick with a loosening layer of muddy silt.

Lone's mind raced even as he was spitting and sputtering under the deluge. Maybe he didn't need to depend strictly on himself to get out of this fix after all. He wasn't ready to go so far as calling it anything close to divine intervention but, if played right, it certainly might count as help from on high.

Once the idea leaped into his head, he barely hesitated. Hell, the way the water was swirling stronger and stronger around him, maybe he couldn't have held back anyway. So he didn't even try. He simply rolled onto his back, lifted his feet, and let the torrent take him like a log released from a lumber camp and sent down a water chute to the river.

As his wet, muddy slide began picking up momentum, just for the hell of it Lone raised his Colt and triggered shots over at the approximate spot he figured the three renegades to be. He emptied the remaining rounds in the cylinder and, unless his ears deceived him through the hissing rain, damned if he didn't hear a painful outcry that sounded like he'd scored a hit.

Half a minute later he was the one barely able to hold back an outcry when his ride was over and he got dumped down into the pinch point where the canyon ended. Luckily the three or four other furrows gouged into the face of the slope were also pouring in spouts of water so the accumulated pool they made at the bottom was deep enough to provide sufficient cushioning to keep him from hitting the bottom too hard. The tumble and the flailing to get over to where he could pull himself up out of the catch pool still strained his wounded leg enough to send some pain knifing up through his hip, however. But it mostly passed once he was clear and was able to roll into some bushes and stretch out for a minute to catch his breath.

Lone was now at the lower end of the line of trees and underbrush that stretched up nearly to the lip of the tableland, the same string of growth the renegades had been shooting at him from, at a higher point. Plenty of the downpour still made it through the branches and leaves, though was diminished somewhat. And visibility was better, except for what the foliage itself blocked.

Lone's thoughts quickly turned to wondering how aggressively—if at all, especially if his wild volley had actually succeeded in cutting down one of them—the renegades would pursue him. On one hand they might be fired up to the point of feeling bound to finish the job on him. On the other, they might see the freakishly sudden downpour as an omen to leave well enough alone. Hell, there was even the chance they'd believe he'd been washed away totally against his will and was drowned or smashed down at the pinch point. Like Lone had told Velda, you could never be exactly sure how an Indian would act about anything.

So the only thing he could do was assume the

worst and be prepared. The first thing that meant was re-loading his Colt, which he'd managed to fiercely hang on to all during his slide and dunking. There was now the chance some of its cartridges might misfire due to getting wet but there was nothing he could do about that except hope all or most of them were sealed tightly enough for that not to be a problem. As a backup, he had his Bowie knife sheathed securely on his left hip. Wet or dry, hot or cold, night or day, it maintained its deadly efficiency in all conditions.

With the Colt re-loaded and the Bowie at the ready, Lone started up the incline once more, this time through the trees and underbrush. He needed to get back to Velda and Arizona regardless, and if the renegades got in his way again and he had to finish wading through them first, then might as well get it over with.

Outside the trees, the rain began to let up some. Not stop, just cut back to about half of its original strength. It still came down straight and steady, only softer. But the currents gushing down the ancient run-off furrows didn't slack off any, not yet. And the tap-tap, drip-drip of the raindrops working their way down through the branches and leaves didn't slow any either.

For just a second, when Lone first heard the distant-sounding pops he thought it was the trees groaning and creaking from the weight of all that sudden rainwater. But then, no, even filtered through the continuing hiss of the softened downpour and the splatter-patter of the drops trickling through the leaves, the sound was too familiar and had been heard too many times by the former scout for it to be anything else. Gunfire. Coming through the trees from somewhere higher up ahead.

Lone stopped moving and lowered himself instinctively into a partial crouch. Now that he'd identified what the popping sounds were, they seemed to come clearer and louder. Two more in rapid succession. A slight pause, then another. One more pause and then what seemed to be a final report. Lone stayed still and listened hard. Now there was only the murmur of the rain and the dripping leaves again.

He pondered what the shooting might have been and there was only one reasonable explanation. Cautiously, he moved out to the edge of the trees and looked up the slope. The rain seemed to have softened a bit more, or maybe he was just getting used to it. Visibility had improved enough so that he could make out the lip of the tableland above. Sure enough, as he swept his gaze across, two murky figures appeared.

One of them shouted. "Lone! Lone McGantry! Can you hear me?"

Lone grinned through the rivulets of rainwater running down his face. He eased further out of the trees and called back. "I hear you, Arizona! I'm down here!"

"Are you okay?"

"I am now. I was fixin' to take me a bath when some redskins showed up to try and steal my soap!"

Arizona barked out a laugh. "Well their soap-stealin' days are over, permanent-like! Me and Velda took care of that. So are you ready to come up, or do you expect somebody to come down and scrub your back?"

"If it was Velda makin' the offer, I might consider it," Lone responded. "But no, I reckon I'm out of the mood now. Wait there, I'm on my way."

"You sure it wasn't just thunder?" said Toledo Slim.

Benton pushed a palmful of rain off his scowling face and snapped back, "No, it wasn't no goddamn thunder. You see any lightning flashes? It's too stinkin' cold for thunder and lightning. It was the sound of gunfire again, meanin' McGantry and Burke must've got into another scrape with some Injuns."

"No longer than it lasted," pointed out Strauss, "it didn't sound like much of a scrape. Maybe they fell to an ambush."

The three men had reined up at the sound of distant gunfire and now sat very still in their saddles, continuing to listen hard even though the shooting seemed to have stopped.

Benton spat an exasperated curse. "I keep tryin' to get it through the thick skulls of you stubborn cusses that those two are too savvy and too tough to fall to a pack of rez jumpin' hot-bloods. Especially not when they're hell bent on makin' it to Cody. That's why I'm countin' on 'em to lead the way for us." He paused long enough to brand Strauss with a hard glare. "And I'm countin' on you not to lose track of *them*."

Strauss's rain-beaded brow puckered anxiously. "Jesus, Ford, that's layin' a lot on me. What with all the time we lost on account of Tucker and now this rain comin' down so hard and washing away—"

"I don't want excuses," Benton cut him off. "What the hell, you shouldn't even have to worry about the rain washin' away ground sign. The way they keep stoppin' and shootin' it out with another batch of Injuns every half hour or so, all we gotta do is keep followin' the noise. Now come on, we can't afford to stand here just jawin' about it."

CHAPTER THIRTY-TWO

When Lone ducked through the narrow entrance to the hideout cave and got his first look at Bill Cody, it came as something of a shock. It shouldn't have, really, not considering everything the old colonel recently endured. The betrayal and tragedy that prolonged his trip from the east, escaping a subsequent kidnapping attempt, the running battle with the renegades, the broken leg, having been holed up for days under tomblike conditions with limited supplies—it had all rightfully taken a toll.

Looking up from where he sat hunched in obvious pain, wrapped in a blanket, long hair trailing limp and tangled around his gaunt face, Cody appeared like he'd aged far more than the two-plus years since Lone had last seen him. But then, hell, Lone quickly and somewhat bitterly reflected, those years had contained a few personal rough spots that no doubt left some added wear and tear showing on him as well. Especially in his current bedraggled condition.

Almost as if reading the former scout's mind, Cody gazed back at him and a corner of his mouth twisted wryly. "You look like hell, Lone-boy," he rasped. "If you're here to rescue us, you don't appear very far from needing some rescuing yourself."

Lone grinned. Despite appearances and conditions, it was the same Bill Cody, as brash and outspoken as ever. Lone's momentary dismay lifted and he felt a rush of renewed conviction this was going to turn out okay after all.

He, Velda, and Arizona had reached the cave only a handful of minutes earlier. Velda had ascended to the well concealed opening first, announcing her return, that she had brought some help, and then naming said help as men both Cody and Pony Bob were well acquainted with. Inasmuch as they'd had to leave the horses tied in the shelter of some trees down at the base of the higher rocks where the cave was, Lone and Arizona came loaded with saddlebags and possibles packs that included welcome and much needed provisions for the holed-up pair.

Lone's quick appraisal of the cave upon entering showed a sandy-floored room, oval in shape, about a dozen feet at its narrowest with irregular rocky walls and a domed ceiling that extended up into murky shadows making its exact height indeterminable. There was a meager campfire burning in the center with Cody and Pony Bob hitched up close on either side.

Responding to Cody's wry remark as he unshouldered his burden, Lone said, "Matter of fact, Colonel, just a little while back I *was* in a spot where I needed a touch of rescuin'. And Velda and Arizona was right there to provide it.

I think you'll find we make a pretty good team plenty capable of gettin' you and Pony—hell, all of us—out of here in one piece."

The wry twist left Cody's mouth and was replaced by a grin of his own. "I never doubted it, son. I just wanted to hear you say so—and say it like you meant it." Then, after a moment's hesitation, he added, "With the understanding, of course, that the 'one piece' some of us are in happens to already be a bit dented and nicked around the edges."

"Yeah, Velda filled us in about that," said Arizona, unloading his own bundle of gear. "Means we got some patchin' up to do before we can get started out of here. The goal then will be to make it the rest of the way clear without any more patchin' bein' necessary."

"Sounds like a right fine goal to me," allowed Pony Bob Hallam from where he sat, also wrapped in a blanket. He was a man of average size and build, middle forties, with a dark-complected, strong-featured face that indicated some Indian blood running through him. This was enhanced by a headful of coal black hair worn in two long braids. Like Cody, there was a tightness in his mouth and around his eyes that indicated a man in pain but fighting not to show it. "But no matter how successful we are at reaching it," he continued, "just the sight of you two scoundrels showing up is powerful comforting."

"Amen to that," agreed Cody. "But, not to look a gift horse in the mouth, I've got to ask—how is it you crossed paths with our lovely Velda?"

"My path first got tangled up with a pack of angry renegades," Velda explained. "These gentlemen came along and encouraged them, in a permanent sort of way, to leave me be. From there we discovered we had a mutual interest in the wellbeing of you two. It helped that McGantry and I were already acquainted via a prior crossing of paths a number of months ago."

Cody's brows pinched together. "My faith in you just took a sudden dip, Lone-boy, hearing you encountered such a rare and spirited beauty in the past but somehow let her slip away?"

"Maybe you've got it backwards, Colonel. Maybe it was McGantry who slipped away from me," teased Velda.

"Apparently you need reminding that I neither require nor allow pretty ladies to call me Colonel. It's just Bill, remember?" said Cody. "And the notion of any red-blooded male purposely eluding your formidable charms, my dear, seems more unlikely than even some of the fiction dreamed up by Buntline and others of his ilk."

"Gettin' back to something else that ain't none of Buntline's fiction," interjected Lone, "and that's the injuries to you and Pony. Velda tells us you been sufferin' with 'em for some time now so I suggest we not waste any longer havin' a look to see what we can do."

Cody grunted. "You always were one to cut right to a thing, Lone-boy. And in this instance that might be a literal statement. Unpleasant as the prospect might be, though, I don't think Pony will disagree that both he and I do have some miseries needing attention."

"If you don't mind me asking," spoke up Pony, "does any of that gear you dragged in happen to have any coffee makings in it? Speaking for myself, a big cup of hot coffee would go a long way as a start toward healing my misery."

"You bet we got coffee. And plenty of it," Arizona assured him.

"I'll get the fire built up bigger and get to work on some," said Velda. "Luckily, not knowing how long I might be gone, I stocked a good supply of dry fuel before I left. For the sake of masking any escaping smoke that might be spotted in the day, we've been building our fires mostly only at night. But we also discovered the high ceiling in here seems to be porous enough or have some kind of venting that absorbs most of it anyway."

"If nothing else, the rain'll help smother it if any should escape," judged Arizona as he was digging out the coffee makings. "I keep tellin' everybody how rain can sometimes be a good thing."

• • •

The next couple of hours in the hideaway cave saw little but intense activity. Outside, the rain continued to come down in a straight, steady, cold drizzle. Under the overcast sky, the gray dimness of evening lasted a shorter amount of time than usual before giving way to the inkiness of full night.

At Cody's insistence, fearing that Pony's arrow wound might be on the verge of becoming infected, he was the first one to be treated. After allowing him his longed for cup of fresh, hot coffee (liberally laced with some pain duller whiskey), Lone and Arizona worked on him together. They re-opened the wound, bled it to drain any infection that might have begun, then sluiced it good with more whiskey before cauterizing it closed again. The patient clenched a leather strap in his teeth to bite off any outcries during this, and Velda stood over him mopping the beads of sweat from his forehead with a cool, wet cloth. Once an application of Shining Water's salve and a clean dressing had been applied, Arizona completed treatment with a cup of the healing woman's grog made from the fixings Tomeeka had also sent along to further aid Lone for his wounded leg, if needed.

"You fellas are a regular traveling medicine show," Cody commented to Lone as he observed all of this while sipping from his own cup of whiskey-laced coffee. "When we made our escape from that Benton polecat and his gang—thanks to the timely attack from those young hot-bloods and the even timelier appearance of your gun-blazin' gal Velda—we managed to grab our saddlebags and bedrolls on the way out. That got us some jerky, a sack of hardtack, a handful of coffee beans, and a single bottle of whiskey to get by on once we were forced to go to ground here. Making do with the jerky and hardtack wasn't so bad, even after the coffee was gone, but having to use up the last of the whiskey to keep treating Pony's wound . . . if you ever want to stand a real test of friendship, try that one on for size."

In recent years—though it was a closely guarded secret to the general public and especially hero-worshipping young boys who all wanted to grow up to be Buffalo Bill—behind the scenes, Bill Cody the man had developed something of a drinking problem. It was another of the many battles he'd fought in his life, an ongoing one. Not a lot of people knew and those who did tended to avoid discussing it.

"Well it appears you stood the test okay," Lone replied to the colonel's remark. "Since Pony's infection seems to have been kept at bay, I'd say he got his share. And now, I can say from personal experience, he's gettin' a dose of something that has even more potent healin' power."

"Good. You can give him all of that you want.

Just save some of the plain old whiskey you seem to have plenty of for me. I'm quite familiar and well satisfied with its benefits."

"If you say so," Lone allowed. "I won't argue you on that one. I will, though, on the matter of callin' Velda my 'gal.' Was she to overhear, she might take exception to the point of shootin' us both."

Cody eyed him shrewdly. "I'm not so sure, my young friend. I think you're the one taking exception . . . and foolishly so. I've seen the way she looks at you." He shrugged. "But, in your words, I won't argue you on it. Now's not the time."

But what it was time for, just a few minutes later, was tending to the matter of Cody's broken leg. Previously, neither Velda nor Pony had had the skill to re-set the fracture to his right fibula. It was a clean break, with the lower half of the bone jutting up out of line from the top, pressing visibly against the skin (though not puncturing through) to make a bluish lump. To stabilize it for the sake of preventing further injury, Velda had splinted it with sticks of wood. This helped but had left the colonel very limited in his mobility.

Once again working in concert, Lone and Arizona now removed the splint and positioned Cody for the task of putting the two halves back in line. Lone got a firm though initially gentle grip on the colonel's foot while Arizona held the flat, solid bottom of a skillet over the lump that marked the misaligned lower bone. The colonel lay flat on his back with Velda pressing down on his shoulders to help steady him. In a show of equal parts bravado and grit befitting his image, the patient eschewed a leather strap to bite on.

"This is only gonna take a second, Colonel, but for that short time it's gonna hurt like blazes," Arizona told him. "So say when you're ready."

"With a sales pitch like that, who would ever claim to be ready?" Cody grumbled. "But go ahead—get it over with."

At that, Lone yanked hard on the foot in order to fully extend the leg as Arizona simultaneously pressed down with the skillet and gave it a hard punch with the edge of his fist. The bones snapped back in alignment, making an audible pop that was mostly drowned out by the loud "Eeeyahoodamn!" issue by the colonel.

And then it was over. Cody settled back, breathing hard, gazing up at Velda as she applied a freshly wetted cloth to his forehead suddenly dotted with beads of sweat.

"Lovely lady," he said, "were it not for your presence, it is a certainty I would be turning the air blue with language apt to make Ol' Scratch himself blush."

Velda gave a little laugh. "Don't hold back on my account. If it will make you feel better, go ahead and cut loose. I doubt you could come up with too much I haven't heard already anyway."

"Don't tempt me with the challenge. But best we accept our individual convictions and leave it at that." He cut his eyes down to where Lone and Arizona were beginning to re-splint his leg. "Speaking of temptation, though, Lone-boy—and don't take this as meaning I'm ready to swear off your 'pain duller' whiskey altogether—it may be I've changed my mind about trying some of Shining Water's wonder grog after all. If you or your partner in torture can find time to brew me a cup . . ."

CHAPTER THIRTY-THREE

When Lone returned from graining the horses and stripping them of their saddles, he found Velda sitting on a ledge just outside the cave entrance, waiting for him. The rain had finally stopped and the dark clouds in the sky overhead were starting to break apart, allowing soft silver glimmers of moon- and starlight to peek through here and there.

Velda had a cup of coffee in one hand and another resting on a rock beside her. "I was coming out for a breath of fresh air and some coffee," she said. Then, gesturing to the second cup, "I heard you coming, thought you might like to join me."

"Best offer I've had all day," Lone replied, lifting the cup and settling down beside her.

"All day," she echoed. "Lord, it's hard to believe that's all it has been, isn't it? Not even a full day since you and Arizona showed up on that flat when the Indians were chasing me."

"Been a busy few hours," Lone allowed.

"You say that so nonchalantly, like it's a common thing with you."

He gave her a sidelong glance. "From what I recall, based on the last time you and me spent some time together, busy days of the sort we just had—minus the Indians maybe—ain't exactly uncommon for you neither."

Velda smiled as she lowered her cup after taking a sip. "I walked into that, didn't I? But when you get right down to it, who are we kidding—would either of us really want it any other way?"

Lone paused with his own cup raised partway to his mouth. "Don't know that I ever quite thought of it like that. Other than my younger years when I was filled with a bone deep hate and wanted to take vengeance out on every redskin there was. Once past that time, I ain't ever saw myself as bein' on the prod for trouble. Yet I can't deny I sure fire seem to have a knack for runnin' afoul of plenty."

"I guess I have to admit there is that difference in us," Velda said after some consideration. "Work I do, hunting wanted men sort of goes hand in hand with hunting trouble. With you, it's more a matter of seeing a wrong that needs to be righted and not being able to hold back from trying to do something about it, trouble be damned."

Lone's brows pinched together. "Sayin' it that way makes me sound like . . . like some kind of do-gooder goin' around *lookin'* for a spot of trouble to poke his nose into."

Velda's smile turned impish. "Isn't that what a White Knight does? Gallops around the countryside slaying dragons and rescuing fair maidens and what not? I already compared you to my White Knight once earlier today. Remember?"

"Yeah, I remember. And, if you remember, I wasn't crazy about it then neither," Lone said with a scowl. But after a beat, one side of his mouth curved up slyly. "Although I gotta admit as to how the hug that went with it wasn't all bad."

"Oh?" Velda said with sudden sharpness. "If the hug wasn't so bad then why, just a few minutes ago when Bill Cody referred to me as your 'gal,' did you seem to find it so offensive?"

Lone was caught off guard by the question and even more by the accusatory glare that went with it. "Whoa now," he said. "First off, you shouldn't be eavesdroppin' on other folks' conversations. Second, my reaction was only to set the colonel straight, tell him he was jumpin' to a wrong conclusion. I wasn't *offended* by the notion. If it was true, what fella wouldn't be proud to lay claim to you as his gal?"

Velda's glare softened almost as quickly as it had formed. She regarded Lone closely. "Do you really mean that?"

"Well, I said it, didn't I?" Lone could feel his ears burning. "Jeez, Vel, you gotta know what an attractive woman you are. You think you don't turn men's heads wherever you go?"

"Sure," Velda said wryly. "But usually it's because of the gun on my hip and the chance I might be carrying a Wanted poster on them."

"Aw, knock it off. You can bet men are noticin' your hips, but it's for more reasons than just the fact there's a six-gun strapped to one of 'em."

"Including you, Lone?"

"I'm a man, ain't I? And I ain't blind."

They drank their coffee in silence for a minute.

Until Velda said, "That time in Wyoming, when we finished our business with the Gun Wolves, I will shamelessly admit that, after spending those days with you, I badly wanted to believe you were attracted to me as much as I was to you. I'd have ridden away with you, you know, if you'd asked. But there was another girl. You were never very clear except to say it was an obligation you had to go take care of. May I ask what became of that?"

"Turned out," Lone replied, "she had an obligation of her own. One that didn't include me."

"Sorry."

"For the best."

They went quiet again for a while.

Before either said any more, Arizona poked his head out from the cave entrance. "I got the litter all ready," he announced. "Both the colonel and Pony are in a deep sleep from the grog I fixed for 'em. Think I'll go ahead and turn in, too. First light's gonna come awful early."

"Sounds like a good idea," Lone told him. "We'll be in shortly."

When the old frontiersman ducked back out of sight again, Velda said, "You really think it's a good idea to move those men so soon? When they wake up in the morning, even after whatever potion Arizona poured in them, they're still going to be in a great deal of pain."

"Maybe not as much as you think," Lone quipped. Then, more seriously, he added, "But no matter, they're gonna have to tough it out. And trust me, they're the kind who can. Besides, even if we waited another day, or two or three, they're still gonna be in pain. Probably almost as much. So the quicker we get on the move and make it clear of here, the better."

"I suppose," Velda said, albeit not without some doubt in her tone.

"The reason I'm pushin' so hard to get on the move," Lone explained further, "is that I figure the renegades are bound to be prowlin' serious-like come tomorrow. You three were able to succeed in holin' up here as long as you did largely on account of you stayed put, the Sioux had no idea you were anywhere around. After that skirmish you and the Benton gang had with some of 'em, Benton's crew got clean out. The renegades might've thought the same was true for you, the colonel, and Pony.

"But after the busy time we had today, leavin' a couple different bunches of 'em dead and missin'—like we just got done talkin' about—the rest have got to know there's *somebody* out here cuttin' down their bucks. And I can't see anything but for 'em to come lookin' for whoever it is with blood in their eyes."

"When you put it that way, I guess it makes sense," Velda allowed. "The sooner we get shed of this place, the better."

"Uh-huh. And another thing that makes sense is gettin' inside and grabbin' some shuteye while we can."

When Lone drained the last of his coffee and lowered the emptied cup, Velda reached out and rested her hand on his arm. "I know that now isn't the time to go into it more," she said. "But the other thing we were discussing a minute ago . . . When this is over, I don't want to leave that just hanging fire yet again."

Lone put his hand over hers and looked deep into her eyes. "We won't. You got my word on it."

CHAPTER THIRTY-FOUR

"Something must have spooked her in the middle of the night. A coyote, a cougar maybe. Could be all the rain had her nerves up. All I know is that she pulled loose and is gone. Your big gray is still there, solid as a rock, but my dun mare ain't nowhere to be seen."

Hearing this, Lone spat a curse.

The report from Arizona could hardly have come at a worse time. Outside the sky was graying with pre-dawn and in the cave preparations for departure were just finishing up. Both Cody and Pony Bob had awoken in good spirits and reasonably bearable discomfort after the care they'd gotten the prior evening. A hot breakfast including cups of whiskey-laced coffee braced them even more for what lie ahead.

Pony's wound received a fresh application of salve and a fresh dressing before starting out. Col. Cody was positioned on the crude but sturdy stretcher—two blankets layered together and slotted at the corners for wrist-thick tree limbs to be inserted to create a frame and holding handles—that Arizona had fashioned. Recognizing that carrying him down from the high rocks in this manner would be a bit precarious, he'd been secured in place by added strips of blanket wrapped and tied snugly about him.

Additionally, all gear was packed up and ready. Following their wetting from the rain, each gun had been cleaned and lightly oiled and individual cartridges had been carefully wiped dry. While the others were seeing to the last of these details, Arizona had gone down with the first load of gear to saddle the horses and get them ready. Now he'd just returned with the news his dun mare had run off during the night.

When all eyes swung expectantly his way, Lone gritted his teeth and said, "Well it ain't gonna stop us. We can't let it. We'll have to adapt, make some changes. But we still need to go ahead and move out. I got a hunch Blunt Nose is gonna have his hot-bloods out in full force this mornin', worked into a bush-beatin' frenzy to try and turn up whoever's been cuttin' down so many of their number in the past day. That means us."

"And if he knows, or even suspects, that I'm somewhere still in the mix, then his frenzy will be even greater," added Cody. "Unlike a lot of the other old chiefs, Blunt Nose's hatred for Whites has never cooled, not even a little bit. And the grudge he has for me burns hotter than all the rest."

"We should have turned and left this place as soon as we heard Blunt Nose, not Kicking Bear, was the one gathering the young renegades here," said Pony Bob.

Cody responded with a soft chuff and a faraway look in his eye. "Body gets as far down the road as I am and starts thinking about all the things he *should* have done different, old friend, it could make for a mighty long list."

"So let's not add to that list by hangin' around here any longer than we have to," said Lone. "The more we tarry, the unhealthier it's gonna be."

"When you say we'll need to adapt and make some changes, what have you got in mind?" asked Velda.

"Mainly, when we get to the bottom we'll put some longer poles on the colonel's stretcher and turn it into a travois, a drag litter," Lone said, gesturing. "We'll attach that to Ironsides so he can pull it along. Pony will go up in the saddle, maybe you, too, part of the time. Arizona and I can walk."

"That will be quite a load on your horse," Cody pointed out.

"You ain't seen Ironsides. He'll hold up," Lone assured him.

"What about your leg?" Arizona wanted to know. "You gave it quite a workout yesterday and we didn't even take time to re-dress it last night."

Lone grinned crookedly, appreciating the concern. "It'll hold up, too, Grammaw. We get to Robideaux's, I will gladly let Shining Water go to work on it some more. But for right now, let's get a move on."

The slope leading down from the cave was relatively short and not that steeply inclined, though with enough staggered foot holds to make it particularly tricky in a couple spots to keep Cody's litter level. But the strength and agility of Lone and Arizona were up to the task. Pony Bob, steadied some by Velda, descended behind them.

At the bottom, they lay Cody's stretcher on a patch of grass near the stand of trees where a saddled Ironsides stood waiting. Pony, breathing a bit heavy, sat down cross-legged beside the colonel. Overhead, the last of the night's lingering stars had faded altogether and the clear sky was steadily changing from pale gray to a murky bluish white.

Addressing Cody, Pony, and Velda, Lone said, "Okay, just sit tight while Arizona an' me go cut a couple longer poles for the travois. Won't take long, then we can get on with headin' out. Keep an eye peeled while we're gone."

With that, he and Arizona fanned out and moved into the trees in search of some saplings suitable for cutting and trimming to make the needed litter poles. Lone moved at an angle off to his left, pushing through a line of pines and then past some older cedars with boles too thick to be of use. A ways past the aged cedars he came to a scattering of newer growth that included some tall saplings of the type he was looking for.

Selecting one, Lone dropped to a knee beside it, drew his Bowie knife and began chopping at a spot near the base. Though heavy and sharp, the Bowie was nevertheless not the ideal tool for chopping down even a small tree. This was going to take a few minutes. Through the trees off to his right, Lone could hear Arizona also beginning to chop on a candidate he'd found. A thin smile curved the former scout's mouth and he felt an unexpected and uncharacteristic competitive nudge that made him want to be sure he was the first one to get his pole cut, trimmed, and dragged back. He began hacking faster and more aggressively.

So intent was he on this that his usually keen ears never heard even a whisper of faintly rustling leaves or the soft footfalls coming up behind him. What he couldn't help becoming aware of, however, was the metal gun barrel that whistled through the air in a hard swing and crashed against the side of his head just above his right ear. Then he pitched into a black pool of unconsciousness and was aware of nothing for a while.

"Hey now. Looky here. Appears ol' skillethead is startin' to come 'round."

The voice and the words sounded far away yet

at the same time very close. *That's odd, how can that be?* Lone thought. But what was definitely close—way too much so—was the fierce pain stabbing into his skull above and slightly behind his right ear. *Jesus, it feels like a tree fell on me. But why a tree? What would make me think of that? Of all the . . .*

And then it all came rushing in. What he'd been doing when his head exploded. Why thoughts of a tree falling on him might enter his mind. Lone knew when he opened his eyes it was going to make the stabbing pain worse. But he had to do it, had to see what was going on around him. So he went ahead and, yeah, the pain knifed deeper and sharper, causing him to suck a ragged intake of breath through gritted teeth.

Once his eyes quit burning and watering, he was able to make out he was lying on his back in some grass just outside a fringe of trees and there was a tall, rawboned man with a gun in his hand looming over him.

Lone's own hand, as if by its own volition, brushed up over his right hip and found nothing in the holster belted there. Neither did his left hand, automatically making a similar move, find anything in the knife sheath on that side.

Looking down on him, Ford Benton sneered and said, "Nothing but empty leather all the way around, McGantry."

When Lone pushed up on his elbows, Benton

took a half step back and aimed the gun at him. "Take it easy, tough nut. I held off pluggin' you while you was out cold, but that don't mean I ain't still got a bullet with your name on it. Had me a low grade itch for a long time, waitin' for the right chance to use it."

"Uh-huh. Like when I was laid out weaponless or had my back turned," Lone grated.

"Talk like that and givin' me the stinkeye the way you are is only gonna hurry it gettin' done."

Lone checked himself from saying anything more, at least not right away. Instead, he cut his eyes away from Benton and swept them over the rest of the scene about him. It wasn't good. It took the knifing pain from his head and twisted it into his gut.

He saw that he was once again in front of the trees at the base of the rocky slope leading up to the former hideout cave. Dragged there, apparently, after getting cold-cocked deeper in. Everybody else was present, too—Col. Cody still on his stretcher, with Pony Bob sitting beside him; Velda and Arizona, also seated on the grass—all stripped of their weapons and held frozen under the drawn guns of Colby Strauss and the rat-faced gunslick who called himself Toledo Slim.

After giving Lone the chance to take a good look, Benton said, his sneer stretching wider than ever, "Guess you see it plain, don't you, tough nut? Me and my boys are in complete charge here. All thanks to a little dun mare who came ploddin' up to our camp just before sunup. Poor thing was all frazzled from the rainy night. But we gentled her down and you know what she did by way of sayin' thanks?" Benton paused to chuckle nastily. "On the freshly wetted, muddy ground she left us a real nice set of tracks leadin' straight back here, that's what. We moved in spyglass close and by more good fortune was just in time to see you rude folks gettin' ready to leave without sayin' so much as a good-bye."

Lone's eyes cut back to him. "Okay. I'll speak for the whole group and apologize for our rudeness. And also say good-bye. That take care of it? If so, we'll take our dun back and be on our way."

"Oh, he's a real funny man, ain't he?" said Toledo from over where he stood. "I'll still leave you be the one to kill him, but in the meantime can I plunk a slug in his funny bone just for the hell of it?"

"Naw, you got your fun comin' up with the girl," Benton told him. "No need to be greedy."

"You're all a bunch of yellow curs!" exclaimed Cody. "The lot of you deserve to be hung up and flayed and left for the crows to tear away your shredded flesh!"

"My, my," said Strauss. "Sounds like somebody has been reading too many of those wild and wooly stories about himself."

"For certain you never read any of them, you illiterate lout," Cody scoffed.

Benton stepped over and gave the colonel a hard nudge with the toe of his boot. "Best keep your mouth shut if you know what's good for you, old man," he snarled. "You're worth a lot of money to me alive. Only that don't mean you have to be in prime condition, if you get my gist."

Cody glared at him. "Do your worst, you scum. But *to me!* If I'm your prize, then leave these others be. They gain you nothing."

Benton's sneer returned. "You think I'm that stupid? Or are you the stupid one? What I gain by leavin' McGantry dead—same for Pony and Burke, far as that goes—is not havin' to spend the rest of my days lookin' over my shoulder expectin' 'em to come for revenge."

"At least spare the girl," Cody urged.

"The girl?" Toledo echoed. "She's the worst of the bunch. She hunts down men for a livin'. I know—I'm one of 'em! But I'm gonna be the one to end her man-huntin' days permanent-like."

"Only not before you allow me a turn at her, right?" Strauss wailed plaintively. "A looker like her ought not fall to what you got in mind without first—"

Strauss's words ended abruptly in a short, wet-sounding gurgle accompanied by a meaty thud. When all eyes swung in his direction, they saw him standing with his upper body bowed back in an odd way, teetering unsteadily, with wide eyes staring skyward as his gun hand sagged at his side—and a Sioux war arrow impaled through his throat!

CHAPTER THIRTY-FIVE

Everything seemed to freeze for a startled moment. All eyes remained locked on Strauss. Until the gun slipped from his lifeless hand and then the rest of him, equally lifeless, finished toppling back and hit the ground flat on his shoulders.

In that same instant a wave of ululating voices rolled over the scene and with them came a dozen more arrows and half that many feathered spears arcing high through the air and curving down toward those gathered around the fallen Strauss. The missiles arrived with a dull buzzing sound, like a swarm of angry insects, and their menacing tips began sinking into the ground and slashing through leaves and bushes, amazingly striking no human targets in this initial volley. Following immediately came sight of the attacking renegades, at least three dozen in number, hurling more arrows and spears as they raced forward.

The high rocks where the cave was located extended in a ragged line eastward for fifty or sixty yards before curving south like a dog's tail and then falling away into a shapeless scatter of various-sized boulders choked with brush and high grass. It was from these bushes and boulders that the renegades came charging. A handful were mounted, but the majority were on foot, running with fierce determination as they voiced their *ki-yip-yip!* war cries. The horsemen, as well as a few runners, brandished rifles. The rest had spears and bows—and tomahawks and knives if they got close enough.

"Jesus Christ, where did they come from?" shouted a wild-eyed Toledo.

"Don't matter where they came from—where we'll send 'em is straight to Hell!" responded Benton as he wheeled to face the horde and extended his gun arm to begin triggering round after round into the charging mass. Toledo didn't hesitate to draw both of his Remingtons and join in.

Lone shoved to his feet. "Don't stand there burnin' powder out in the open, you fools," he barked. "Fall back! Take cover in the trees!"

As he said this he was reaching to take hold of the handles at one end of Cody's stretcher, meaning to move him. Arizona, sizing up things the same as Lone, stood up and started for the stretcher's opposite end.

Benton spun back on them, aiming his six-gun. "Hold it, you two! I give the orders around here!"

"Then give 'em, you jackass!" Lone barked. "Get everybody back in those trees or you ain't gonna have nobody left to give orders to!" As he was saying this, Ironsides, standing a few feet away, suddenly wheeled and bolted into the foliage, giving Lone reason to add, "See? Even my horse is smart enough to know!"

The renegades had faltered slightly in their charge when Benton and Toledo first started pouring lead back at them. But they were surging forward again now, whooping and howling with renewed vigor. Some of the riflemen began adding some lead of their own to the mix of barbed missiles gouging into the ground and hammering against trees ever closer to their intended targets.

Toledo interrupted his two-fisted shooting long enough to call over to Benton, "I think he's right, boss. We can't mow down those red devils fast enough standing out here in the open! We gotta take cover."

"Alright, alright," Benton replied. Then, waving his arms frantically, he shouted, "Everybody into the trees! Grab those shucked gun belts and the rest of that gear and drag it in too—hurry up!"

From there it was a mad scramble to fall back and seek refuge from the continuing incoming barrage. Lone and Arizona finished taking hold of the colonel's stretcher and went crashing into the pine growth. Velda and Pony Bob snatched up the gear indicated by Benton and followed suit, with Benton and Toledo right on their heels but continuing to return fire as they did so. As soon as they were within the tree line, Benton holstered his spent revolver, grabbed Lone's

Yellowboy from the pile of gear, and went to work with it instead. Toledo stuck with his brace of six-guns, given the chance to reload while Benton was laying down cover fire.

With their intended targets now finding refuge and retaliating with a burst of renewed intensity, the renegade attack again faltered. Several of the braves sought their own cover by dropping down in high grass or behind some of the scattered boulders. For a handful of minutes only the riflemen kept firing, pouring rounds blindly into the trees where their prey had disappeared.

Within these trees, Lone and the others hunkered low with bullets smacking sporadically into cedar trunks and slashing through pine branches above and to the sides.

"We got the sonsabitches backed up now," crowed Toledo, excitedly brandishing his freshly reloaded Remys. "Lookit, I count at least four of 'em layin' out there that we dropped already. We cut down a few more, they'll turn and run like scalded dogs."

"Don't count on it, sonny," grated Lone. "They didn't mount this big of an attack to turn tail quite so easy. I wouldn't even count on all those layin' out there as bein' really dead. It's an old Indian trick to play like that just so's they can jump up and attack again when you least expect it."

"In that case," Toledo said, "how about I pump a little extra lead into each of those lumps just to make sure they won't be jumpin' up to try no tricks?"

"Go ahead, if you want to spend good bullets on guesswork," Lone told him. "You might wish you still had those rounds a little later on, though, for a surer thing."

"Hold your damn fire, Slim," said Benton. "Don't be spendin' bullets unless it's on a certain target."

"No need to be stingy about it," argued Toledo. "Appears we got plenty of cartridges here in this gear. And there's even more in the saddlebags of our horses where we left 'em tied back down the line."

"You don't have any horses tied anywhere," chuffed Cody from his stretcher.

Toledo glared down at him. "The hell we don't. What do you know about it? We left 'em tied down this tree line just before—"

"You might have left them there," Cody cut him off, "but unless you left somebody to guard them, I guarantee they're not there now. There were braves laying claim to them half a minute after you moved off. You think that arrow striking your friend marked the first time the Sioux had you in their sights this morning? I judge they were on to you before you ever broke camp."

"What makes you think that?" Benton wanted to know.

"Because he knows Indians," answered Lone.

"Same as me and Arizona. We all three fought 'em a big chunk of our lives."

"And still got our hair and are here to tell about it," added Arizona. "And if you two polecats want to be able to make the same claim, then you'd better smarten up fast and start by listenin' to those of us who know our toe from a tomahawk!"

"If you're so smart," sneered Toledo, "then why are *you* the ones under *our* guns?"

"That right there is a good place to begin wisin' up," said Lone. "Give us our guns back so we can make this stand with you. We get done dealin' with the renegades, we can finish sortin' out our other business after."

"Give you your guns back—you think I'm crazy?" blurted Benton.

"You're crazy if you don't, you fool," insisted Velda. "Look out there, the renegades are massing up again, getting ready for another attack. Just the two of you can't possibly fight them off. And if some of them took your horses from farther down this tree line, what's to stop them from circling around and coming in through the trees behind us? How are you going to guard against that?"

"Don't listen to them, Ford," wailed Toledo. "No way I'm going to let that bitch get her hands on a gun—you know she has it in for me!"

"To hell with it. If I'm going to get killed anyway, it's not going to be without putting up a fight!" declared Velda, pushing away from Pony Bob and making a lunge for the pile of gear that included her gun belt.

"I'm warning you!" shrieked Toledo, spinning toward her with both of his Remingtons thrust out at waist level.

"Watch out!" shouted Arizona.

With amazing speed, Pony Bob uncoiled from his sitting position and leaped after Velda, flinging himself partly on top of her and in the path of the slugs exploding from Toledo's guns. As his body jerked and shuddered from each impact, Velda twisted around underneath him with her Colt now filling her hand. She extended her gun arm across Pony's riddled body and triggered a single shot square to the center of Toledo's forehead.

CHAPTER THIRTY-SIX

A burst of fresh and renewed activity immediately followed Toledo getting his brains blown out. The renewed burst came from the renegades suddenly rising up out of the high grass and from behind boulders and surging forward in another charge, howling for blood as they came. The fresh action happened amidst those within the trees, kicked off by Lone instantly twisting at the waist and swinging a powerful backhanded blow to the side of Benton's head before the gang leader recovered from being momentarily stunned by what had befallen Toledo.

Benton was knocked sprawling, the Yellowboy jarred from his grip. Lone immediately pounced on him and clamped his throat in an iron grip with both hands. Leaning close over the man's startled, wild-eyed expression, Lone bared his teeth in a snarl and hissed, "Choose fast! Agree to fight at our side or I throttle you right here and now!"

"Do it, Lone," Arizona urged as he rummaged through the pile of gear to find and seize his Henry repeater. "We can't trust him."

"We need his gun and he needs us to have any chance to live," Lone argued over his shoulder.

The first volley of bullets and arrows from the

charging renegades was starting to crash and slice through the trees all around them. Velda had picked up one of Toledo's dropped Remys and was using it along with her own retrieved Colt to trigger alternating rounds at the oncoming wave of hostiles. "A little less talk and a lot more help throwing lead would be nice!" she called tartly.

"I can shoot, damn it, if somebody will free me from these blasted bindings!" hollered Cody.

Arizona paused long enough to toss the colonel a knife and Toledo's remaining pistol before gliding up to the edge of the tree line alongside Velda and immediately opening fire with his Henry.

Struggling to find his voice through the pressure from Lone's hands, Benton grunted, "I'll do it. I'll fight with you. No tricks, I swear it. Th-the last thing I want is to fall to those redskins."

Lone stared for a long beat into the eyes staring desperately back at him, then made his decision. "You swerve me, damn you, I'll kill you, gut you, and feed your black heart to the crows! Come on, get up. We got fightin' to do!"

In less than a minute, five gun hands were aimed and pulling triggers on the attackers. Even Cody, who'd cut away the strips of blanket securing him to his stretcher for the ascent from the cave, had dragged himself to the front edge of the trees where, propped on one hip and an elbow, he was using a dead man's gun with punishing effect. In fact, the barrage of gunfire now pouring out of the trees—more than double what the renegades had faced on either of their previous charges—was pounding them savagely. Like running into a wall of lead. And while many of the braves showed the courage to live up to that which they were called, too many were falling and dying for it to last. Once again their ranks broke and they were forced to retreat and scramble for cover.

A sudden silence fell over the scene, like a switch had been turned off. The bluish gray haze of powder smoke hanging in the air mostly in front of the tree line took on hints of brighter blue as it was touched by the first rays of the sun poking up above the eastern horizon.

"That broke their back good," Benton said in a hoarse voice. Then, a hopeful tone creeping in, he asked, "You think it was enough for them to call off any more tries?"

"Not likely," Lone responded. "We cost 'em too dear, they're gonna want payback. Thing is, now they're apt to try and get it not by any more straight on charges, but by playin' the long game to wear us down."

"How so?" Benton wanted to know.

"For starters, they know they got us pinned down. We got no place to slip away and no horses to try makin' a run for it," Lone explained grimly. "They got no way of knowin' exactly what we got in the way of provisions, but they can figure it's limited. Hell, they could starve us out if they want to stretch it far enough."

"More like they'll try to hurry it along, though, by pecking at us and looking to take us out one at a time," suggested Cody. "Even though we trimmed their ranks by as much as a third, I judge, they've still got us outnumbered three or four to one. Means they've got plenty of men to keep the front door shut on us while they send others out to harass us in different ways."

"Like what?" asked Velda.

Cody gestured. "Those high rocks we recently came down from make a good spot for some of their riflemen to climb and take up positions from which to shoot down on us through the trees. Might not hit much, but it would sure keep us rattled. And speaking of the trees, as you were astute enough to observe earlier, the growth spread out behind us surely presents an opportunity for circling around and slipping up on our rear."

"And if they hold off until dark," Arizona noted sourly, "coming in through those trees then would be a big problem."

"Jesus! What a cheerful picture that paints," Velda exclaimed. "I refuse to accept that Pony Bob sacrificing his life for me amounted to nothing."

"It damn well didn't," Lone growled. "It got us

our guns back and it gave us a fightin' chance! And if it comes to holdin' off 'til dark, then maybe we start thinkin' about how to make the night work for *us*. But what we *don't* do, by God, is start believin' we're out of options."

"Well spoken," declared Cody. "As a matter of fact, I believe we have one option we should explore with all haste." He paused, somewhat dramatically, as was his wont, waiting for all attention to be focused on him before continuing, "That option, I suggest, is to exploit the rift that has so long existed between Blunt Nose and myself."

Lone frowned. "Exploit it how?"

"By giving him the opportunity to claim the blood rite for my slaying of his brother. In other words," Cody explained, "I'll challenge him to a duel such as Yellow Hand and I fought all those years ago. Once it is settled, no matter who wins, the condition will be that the members of our two sides will then part without further bloodshed."

"No," Velda was quick to object. "We can't agree to that. You're injured and in a weakened condition. You're in no shape to—to fight a duel!"

"Blast it, if somebody helps me into the saddle I can sit a horse, can't I?" Cody insisted. "That's how Yellow Hand and I did it. Mounted and armed with carbines, we rode straight at each other until my shot took him down. The only difference will be that on this day I have no desire—nor the agility—to dismount and take a scalp. All I seek is to end this and end any more suffering or killing."

"I still say no," declared Velda. Her gaze swept over Lone and Arizona. "Surely you're not willing to go along with this. There's got to be some other way."

Lone held her eyes, feeling a storm of conflicting feelings roil inside himself. Then he dropped his gaze down to Cody. "You sure about this, sir? I mean, no offense, but . . . well, this wouldn't be play-actin' no more."

The colonel's eyes turned flinty. "You think I don't know that? That's maybe the biggest part. You think I don't also know how that's the first thought that comes to mind when anybody hears the name 'Buffalo Bill Cody'? Oh yeah, Buffalo Bill—the showman, the stage actor, the character from all those wildly exaggerated adventure books and newspaper and magazine articles, the promoter of the Wild West extravaganza that has thrilled the crowned heads of Europe! All pretend, all play-acting strictly for entertainment.

"And yes, I've willingly gone along with all of that. It's brought me fame and fortune. But behind all the hoopla, what everybody seems to have forgot—all except for a handful who are left, men like you and Arizona, and Pony Bob before he went over, who were there for part of it—is that at the core of everything was true hardship and adventure and danger that it took a rare kind of grit and toughness to endure. I often regret how so much of that has been lost behind the glitz. Even the mission I was initially sent on, to come out here and meet with Sitting Bull allegedly for the sake of trying to help quell the Ghost Dance trouble was, I think now, just a sham on the part of some who wanted to trade on my name. They fooled me and they fooled Sitting Bull too, causing him to lower his guard and end up getting killed. That grieves me more than I can say and drives me to want to find a way to set the record straight."

"I think I have some understanding how you feel," Lone said softly. "That's what brought me and Arizona, at the request of your friends Powell and Major North, out here to check on you and help you stay safe. There are ways to address your grievances about what happened with Sitting Bull and the rest when you get back east. But I doubt anybody would see us agreein' for you to ride out and face Blunt Nose in a duel as us holdin' up our end of keepin' you safe."

Now Cody's eyes blazed. "Does that include you two *fighting me* to prevent it? Because that's what it's going to take. I'll by damn crawl out there and issue the challenge myself if I have to!"

Lone McGantry withered under the gaze of few men. But he did this time.

Averting his eyes, he cut a sidelong glance over to Arizona but saw no sign of hope there for a winning rebuttal to the colonel's stubborn stance. Even Velda appeared less resolute than she had only moments earlier.

Bringing his eyes back, Lone heaved a reluctant sigh and said, "Okay. How do you want to go about it?"

CHAPTER THIRTY-SEVEN

"He's willin' to fight you. But not with rifles. He says you're too good, that would give you an unfair advantage and that was how you bested his brother."

"What does he propose then?"

Lone hesitated slightly before answering, "Tomahawks. Tomahawks and war shields, mounted close quarter combat. I had no choice but to tell him about your leg and make the stipulation that the fight had to be on horseback."

Cody's mouth pulled into a tight, straight line as he considered.

This proposal was being presented after Lone, carrying a white flag of truce tied to one of the spears thrown earlier by a renegade, had walked out onto the grassy, boulder-strewn plain in front of the trees and signaled for a palaver. Blunt Nose had agreed to meet, but only after an allowance was made for his fallen men to be safely carried away. That done, the embittered chief came forward halfway and they spoke. It was brief. Blunt Nose listened, gave some partial agreements, made his demands.

Cody was chewing on these now. The others stood back, watching him, waiting for his reaction. While the renegades were carrying off their dead, Velda and Arizona had also been tending to some similar business in their group, arranging the bodies of Pony Bob, Strauss, and Toledo over to one side and wrapping them in blankets. They'd also taken care of another matter, that being to once again disarm Ford Benton; he didn't much like it, but they insisted that with no Indian fighting currently taking place everybody felt a lot safer with him having no gun to aim at their backs.

At length, Cody's reaction came, first in the form of a question. "Blunt Nose agrees that the noncombatants from each side will be left to take leave with no further conflict?"

"He repeated it plain, gave his word," Lone said. "Made sure that several around him heard and understood."

At which Cody gave a crisp nod. "Then I guess tomahawks it is. Can I borrow your big gray for my mount, Lone-boy?"

With the shooting now in a lull, Ironsides had come threading his way back out of the deeper growth a bit earlier. In answer to the colonel's request, Lone said, "Both Ironsides and me would be honored, sir."

"But how are we gonna get your splinted leg to stay in a stirrup?" asked Arizona.

Cody answered, "Once I'm mounted, you'll have to take part of the splint off, fit my foot into the stirrup, and then tie my leg to the saddle fender to keep it supported."

Arizona made a face. "Aw, Jeez, Colonel. We do that, what if you get knocked out of the saddle? You'll not only tear hell out of your leg all over again, you'll risk gettin' dragged to—"

Cody cut him off with, "Then I'll have to make sure I *don't* get knocked out of the saddle, won't I? Now, where's that 'hawk and shield Blunt Nose provided for me to use?"

Lone held out the items. The shield was an oval of tough, treated leather stretched and laced within a circular frame of intertwined willow branches. The tomahawk was well-crafted, steel headed with a flat hammer end and a flared, razor sharp blade opposite it. "I gave 'em a good lookin' over," Lone said. "The shield is sturdy, the 'hawk is well balanced. These weapons you've had much experience with, Colonel?"

Cody hefted the tomahawk. "Been awhile. Never was worth beans at throwing one of these, but I've used 'em to split a skull or three back in the day. Let's hope the reflexes kick back in when needed."

"I know it's no use, but I'm liking this less and less," Velda said, her brow puckered anxiously.

Cody smiled at her. "The die is cast as far as the event taking place, pretty lady. But don't look so dour about the outcome. Haven't you read any of those tales about my many miraculous escapes and heroic conquests over impossible odds? And certainly you've heard how, behind every legend, there exists a grain of truth, haven't you?"

Velda couldn't keep a smile of her own from being drawn out. "In that case, let's hope there's a grain that bursts into full blossom today."

"Give me my gun back," spoke up Benton, "and I can guarantee it. If the rest of you so-called 'Injun fighters' are too ignorant or too chicken, when ol' Blunt Beak comes sashayin' out, I'll happily blow his heathen red brisket clean back to the rez and this will be all over. Everybody knows Injuns won't fight when their chief gets killed and it makes a sign their medicine has turned bad. You don't need no fancy-ass duel or 'blood rite' or whatever you call it to set that up."

"Jesus Christ, how did you last so long bein' so dumb?" snarled Arizona. "You just spouted one more big reason for never bein' allowed to have a gun in my presence again. So stand over there and keep your mouth shut or I'll shut it permanent-like."

"Take it easy, Arizona," Lone advised. "Let's fight one fight at a time."

"Aw, I ain't gonna hurt him," Arizona growled in response. "I might kill the dumb sonofabitch, but I ain't gonna hurt him."

The next few minutes were spent getting Cody up into the saddle and suitably securing his injured leg. This wasn't accomplished without causing him a good bit of pain but he got through it with gritted teeth and no word of complaint.

When everything was ready, Lone handed his weapons up to him, saying, "Reckon this is it, Colonel."

Cody took the weapons without comment, fitted the shield to his left arm, once again hefted the tomahawk in his right hand. Lone stepped back and gazed up at him. Velda and Arizona moved in on either side and also stood looking up at the man, the myth known practically worldwide and envisioned much as he was poised in this very moment. The fringed buckskin jacket, the wide-brimmed hat cocked at a just-so angle, the goatee and the famous long, flowing hair (shot with streaks of gray in these later years, though no less distinct). And eyes as clear and steady and blue as chips of polished cobalt, gazing out across the stretch of plain where he was about to once again do battle.

Those eyes now swept down to meet the gazes aimed up at him. The old colonel smiled. "Take a good look, children. Remember it. I'm Buffalo by-God Bill Cody. No matter what happens here today, don't ever forget that. And don't let others, either, especially the nay-sayers and non-believers!"

With that, he wheeled Ironsides and gigged him at an easy trot out into the open area.

Continuing to hold her eyes locked on him, Velda said in a soft, slightly breathless voice,

"God. In that moment, he was . . . magnificent."

"Yeah," Arizona agreed, equally soft. "The colonel knows how to do that."

Lone said nothing. But he understood what they were feeling.

Out on the plain, Blunt Nose rode into sight, advancing to meet Cody. He sat very erect on his pony, an average-sized individual, bronzed, wiry, with coal black hair worn in two long braids, devoid of any headdress. He was clad in a fringed, bead-decorated vest, arms bare. Even at a distance, the facial feature that gave him his name was quite visible. The young hot-blooded braves who had become his followers formed a line back where he'd ridden out from and stood looking on silently, expressions grim.

The two combatants checked their horses about twenty yards apart and balefully eyed one another for several beats. Then, at some unseen yet simultaneous signal, each gigged his mount forward at a hard gallop and met in the initial clash. Shields were raised and tomahawks were swung and the sound of steel whacking against toughened leather rang through the air.

The horses brushed close, thundered past as the blows were traded. Then their riders wheeled them sharply and they charged at each other all over again. This resulted in another exchange of tomahawks hammering against shields, a brute strength attempt by each man to unbalance his opponent or maybe knock away his shield. Neither succeeded.

On their third clash, Blunt Nose attempted a change-up maneuver. As the collision neared, he leaned far forward, taking Cody's tomahawk strike early. But then, instead of reaching across and striking with his own 'hawk, the Sioux suddenly leaned back almost flat onto the rump of his pony and drove his foot in a piston-like kick that slipped in under Cody's shield and struck the colonel hard in his stomach. It was meant to dislodge the recipient or perhaps at least crack some ribs. It succeeded in neither but was nevertheless a telling blow that doubled Cody forward and knocked some wind out of him.

The onlooking braves cheered. Lone, Velda, and Arizona collectively sucked sharp intakes of breath.

"He's a tricky bastard," Arizona muttered. "Colonel's gonna have to stay sharp or better yet come up with some tricks of his own."

"He'll find a way," Lone grated.

Out on the plain, the riders clashed for a fourth time and it was once again another exchange of forceful blows hammered against each other's shields.

On the fifth collision, it was Cody who reached go-for-broke deep into his bag of tricks. As he and Blunt Nose closed, having secretly slipped his arm free of his shield's inner holding sleeve, the colonel suddenly and unexpectedly leaned forward and hurled the shield in a skimming, discus-like throw straight at Blunt Nose's face. This caused the Sioux to react by raising and swinging his own shield in a backhanded swatting-away motion that totally exposed his arm on the inner side of his own shield and momentarily checked him from swinging his tomahawk. But Cody didn't hesitate to swing his—in a vicious overhand chopping motion that nearly cut Blunt Nose's exposed forearm in two!

Blunt Nose screamed in agony and toppled from his pony. He immediately began thrashing about on the ground, clutching at his horribly severed arm as squirting blood filled the bowl-like inner curve of the shield. A dozen of the onlooking braves instantly broke into a run, rushing forward to aid their fallen chief.

The duel was over. Cody had won.

The colonel circled close for a moment, but then abruptly swung Ironsides away and came galloping back to the trees. Reining to a halt, he said breathlessly to those waiting, "Better get your guns ready. Now is where we find out if this paid off. Whether or not they honor Blunt Nose's word to withdraw and leave us go in peace."

CHAPTER THIRTY-EIGHT

As it turned out, the young hot-blood renegades did indeed honor Blunt Nose's word. After caring for their wounded leader as best they could at the scene (which in all likelihood was not good enough to save his arm or perhaps even keep him from bleeding to death), they lifted him back onto his pony and led him off with barely a look in the direction of Cody and the others.

Which left them in similar shape as how they had started out the day. Similar, though with a couple key differences. Gone, thankfully, was the concern over Indian threat. Also gone, not so thankfully, was Pony Bob. In his place they were now stuck with the dead Strauss and Toledo Slim, and a live Ford Benton. And still only one horse to transport everything.

They were in the midst of discussing this, whether to bury the dead here in this remote spot or find a way to load the bodies and take them back, when unexpected though most welcome salvation arrived in the form of Lt. Reeves and his cavalry patrol, drawn from a distance by the sound of the earlier gunfire.

After reining up at the head of his column and appraising the group with an impassive, though somewhat stern expression, the lieutenant's gaze came back to rest on Lone. "It appears, McGantry," he said, "that you and your people have run into a bit of trouble."

"That's a right accurate read of the situation, Lieutenant," Lone replied.

Reeves's mouth pursed. "Another 'read' I have recently made, is that you and Mr. Burke seemed to be taking purposeful measures to avoid me. Is that also accurate?"

Lone cocked a single eyebrow and looked deeply thoughtful. "Well now. Considerin' how me and everybody here was so plumb happy to see you and all them blue uniforms come ridin' into sight just a minute ago, I don't rightly see how that could be . . . sir."

Reeves's stern demeanor suddenly broke and his mouth spread in a wide grin. "Doggone it, Lone, it's good to see you too! And you as well, Burke." He swung down from his saddle and stepped forward to shake hands. "But, blast it, why *have* you two scoundrels been working so hard to steer clear of everybody?"

"It's a long story," said Lone, "but at the time it seemed important to keep on the move and not get bogged down tryin' to explain too much to too many folks."

"Much of the blame, Lieutenant, I fear lies with me," spoke up Cody from where he was seated once again on his stretcher. "I put myself in a predicament that required some very good friends—Lone, Arizona, the lovely Miss Beloit, and others—to not only bend certain protocols but to also risk their lives on my behalf."

Reeves walked over and stood looking down at the speaker, his face taking on an expression of high regard.

"Lieutenant, this is Col. William F. Cody," Lone introduced. "Colonel, Lt. Greg Reeves."

Cody extended a hand upward. "You'll have to excuse me for not standing. As you can see, I'm a bit stove in."

"Not at all. I'm deeply honored to meet you, Colonel," Reeves said, taking his hand in a firm grip. "I regret I have no medic in my patrol. But can we do anything to make you more comfortable? A drink of water? A touch of something stronger perhaps?"

Cody smiled. "I can see you'll go far as an officer, young Reeves. But I fear your civilian manners may need some polish." He tipped his head to indicate Velda standing nearby. "There is, after all, a young lady present who may also require some attention."

Reeves quickly straightened up and turned to Velda, sweeping off his hat. "Begging your pardon, ma'am! Is there anything I can—"

His words were cut short by the brief sounds of grunting, scuffling bodies and then the sharp report of a pistol.

When all faces snapped around, they saw Ford

Benton standing close behind Arizona with his left forearm hooked under Arizona's chin and Benton's right hand clutching the six-gun he had yanked from the old frontiersman's holster. But as everybody continued to stare, they saw Benton's forearm relaxing, easing up on its pressure even as the fingers of the hand holding the gun opened up and the weapon began to slip loose. At the same time, Benton, with a wide-eyed, surprised look on his face, was tipping back away from Arizona and the bullet hole high on the right side of his chest, just under the collar bone, became clearly visible a second before his knees buckled and he tipped out farther and collapsed.

A dozen feet away, where he sat his saddle at the head of the column, Sgt. Malachi Skinner was leaned slightly forward with his gun arm extended and a smoking pistol in his fist.

"Good God, Skinner! What have you done?" demanded Lt. Reeves.

Skinner gestured with his gun muzzle. "I saw that hombre put the throttle on Burke and snatch his gun. He had a wild, mean look on his face and it was plain he wasn't gonna be shy about doin' some killin'. I had a split second for a clear shot, so I took it."

"That man was an outlaw of considerable renown down Kansas way, no stranger to killin'. His purpose for bein' here, in fact, was an attempt to kidnap Col. Cody and hold him for ransom,"

Lone told Reeves. "Your sergeant did the world a favor."

The lieutenant looked past Skinner and motioned to the next two troopers mounted behind him. "You two. Go see to that man, make sure he's dead. If he is, get a blanket and wrap him up."

While that was being taken care of, Arizona picked up his gun and ambled over to where Skinner remained mounted, wiping the hogleg on his shirt as he walked. Holstering it again, he looked up at the sergeant and said, "That was a pretty good shot."

"I usually hit what I aim at."

"Not that I ain't obliged, mind you, but it was kind of a tight pinch what with him pressed up close to me like he was."

"Like I said, I had a clear shot for just a split second." Half of Skinner's mouth curved in a sly smile. "Don't worry. I wasn't about to hit you, Burke, not considerin' how we still got unfinished business when we both make it back to Fort Robinson."

Arizona's brows pinched together. "Yeah. Kinda puts me in, whatycall, a quandary, don't it?"

"What do you mean?"

"Well, based on what just happened—seein's how Benton was as likely to put a slug in me as anybody—when we're back at the fort do I owe you a drink for this piece of business, or still a rap in the jaw for the other?"

"See what you mean," said Skinner. "Me, I like to drink and I like to scrap about equal. We could do a little of both."

After thinking on it briefly, Arizona allowed, "Reckon it'd probably work out that way anyhow, wouldn't it? So okay, that's how we'll figure on it."

It was nearly noon before things were wrapped up and everything was ready for Lone's group, now joined and assisted by the cavalry patrol, to depart the rugged beauty of the Wildcat Hills. Lone and Reeves figured that with a steady push they could be back at Roubideaux's by dark. From there, many subsequent details still had to be seen to.

For starters, there were bodies to be buried. Benton, Strauss, and Toledo Slim went unceremoniously into a potter's field in Scotts Bluff. Pony Bob was buried in a different part of the same cemetery but with a full, well-attended service, including a eulogy by Col. Cody.

Reeves was reprimanded, though not seriously, for his unsanctioned foray into the Wildcat Hills. The information he was able to provide on the buildup of renegade activity in the area—with added input from both Lone and Cody—was considered highly valuable. Additionally, reports of a large number of the young hot-bloods who'd flocked there now starting to return to their reservations following the defeat of Blunt Nose was considered a welcome sign of easing tensions.

Finally, after having his leg treated and re-splinted in a new-fangled plaster of Paris cast, arrangements were made for Cody, accompanied by Arizona, to return to North Platte. From there, he vowed to all within earshot, he planned on raising plenty of hell about the "shenanigans"—calling out Major Laglen and others by name—he felt led to the untimely and unnecessary death of his old friend Sitting Bull. (An additional vow, one he shared with a closer circle of listeners, was that in the future he intended to perform any acts of conflict or derring-do strictly from the safety of a theater stage or in the arena of his Wild West show.)

And, lastly, there remained one other vow to be addressed—the one between Lone and Velda that they would stop letting their feelings for each other continue to hang fire but would instead make time to explore them fully and see where they led.

AUTHOR'S NOTE

Much of the preceding story is rooted in historical fact. The Ghost Dance movement did gain a good deal of popularity among many High Plains tribes in the 1880s. Kicking Bear's interpretation of Wovoka's original concept was much more aggressive and contained the notion of "Ghost Shirts" that could repel the White Man's bullets.

It is a fact that Buffalo Bill was solicited to go to North Dakota and meet with his old friend Sitting Bull in an attempt to encourage the old chief to use his influence to quell the movement before it got out of hand. In truth, Sitting Bull had very little involvement with the Ghost Dance and likely would have been of small help. But no one will ever know for sure because Cody's trip was canceled due to political wrangling and Sitting Bull was killed on the reservation, in a rather bizarre altercation, shortly after.

That much is fact. My fictional tale—freely mixing real and imaginary characters, sometimes as composites—picks up from there.

It is generally considered that the culmination of the Ghost Dance movement (though no part of my tale) came at the tragic Battle of Wounded Knee—or Wounded Knee Massacre, in the minds of many. The conflict resulted from a 500-man detachment of the 7th Cavalry arriving at a Lakota Sioux village of roughly 300 people (nearly half women and children) on Wounded Knee Creek to disarm the men of the village. Fighting broke out when some refused to give up their weapons and by the time it was done nearly 250 Lakota, many of them women and children, lay dead in the frozen snow.

Several of the Sioux dead were wearing "Ghost Shirts" that failed to stop the soldiers' bullets. So among the tragic toll of lives taken by the massacre, most of the promise and magic of the Ghost Dance also died.

—WD

ABOUT THE AUTHOR

Wayne D. Dundee is an American author of popular genre fiction. His writing has primarily been detective mysteries (the Joe Hannibal PI series) and Western adventures. To date, he has written four dozen novels and forty-plus short stories, also ranging into horror, fantasy, erotica, and several "house name" books under bylines other than his own.

Dundee was born March 24, 1948, in Freeport, Illinois. He graduated from high school in Clinton, Wisconsin, 1966. Later that same year he married Pamela Daum and they had one daughter, Michelle. For the first fifty years of his life, Dundee lived and worked in the state line area of northern Illinois and southern Wisconsin. During most of that time he was employed by Arnold Engineering/Group Arnold out of Marengo, Illinois, where he worked his way up from factory laborer through several managerial positions. In his spare time, starting in high school, he was always writing. He sold his first short story in 1982.

In 1998, Dundee relocated to Ogallala, Nebraska, where he assumed the general manager position for a small Arnold facility there. The setting and rich history of the area inspired him to turn his efforts more toward the Western genre. In 2009, following the passing of his wife a year earlier, Dundee retired from Arnold and began to concentrate full time on his writing.

Dundee was the founder and original editor of Hardboiled Magazine.

His work in the mystery field has been nominated for an Edgar, an Anthony, and six Shamus Awards from the Private Eye Writers of America.

Center Point Large Print
600 Brooks Road / PO Box 1
Thorndike, ME 04986-0001 USA

(207) 568-3717

US & Canada:
1 800 929-9108
www.centerpointlargeprint.com